Not According To Plan

Meg Doody

Nutmeg Media

This novel is a work of fiction. Names, characters, organizations, places and events portrayed are either products of the author's imagination or used fictitiously.

No part of this book was created using generative artificial intelligence. All em-dashes are the author's own. Okay, fine. Her editors also added a few.

Copyright © 2026 by Meg Doody

All rights reserved.

No part of this book may be reproduced in any form or by any electronic or mechanical means, including information storage and retrieval systems, without written permission from the author, except for the use of brief quotations in a book review. No part of this book may be used or reproduced in any manner for the purpose of training artificial intelligence technologies or systems.

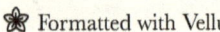 Formatted with Vellum

For Ben

Chapter 1

Brooke

The side door of the chapel catches as I push on the thick wood panel. Old churches—beautiful, but in desperate need of some love and a little elbow grease. With one gentle shove, I manage to get the door open and not-so-gracefully let myself out. Last-minute arrivals walk into the main doors as I make my way to the circular driveway in front of St. Thomas Catholic Church.

I check my watch, grab my favorite pen from my belt bag—it's about time the fanny packs I've worn for years got a rebrand—and check off *Bride and Bridesmaid Trolley Arrival* on my timeline as the vintage trolley pulls up.

Almost go time.

A group of guests chat away on the church steps as if the wedding will begin at their convenience and not at the precise moment my timeline indicates. "Excuse me, I hate to interrupt," I say with a sweet smile. *Please*, I love it. "The bride is arriving; I wouldn't want you to miss her big entrance inside."

In my six years of wedding planning, I've never once started a wedding late, and that is not about to change today. I keep my eye on the guests as they walk up the steps to the doors. An older gentleman in the group turns around, checking if I'm watching. I sure am, sir.

The trolley doors open behind me.

"How's my favorite wedding planner?"

"Good morning, Ernie!" I turn on my heel, counting the minutes until shoe-change number three of the day, and smile at my favorite driver. In addition to my meticulous planning, Ernie is one of the reasons for the wedding day punctuality. He has a magical ability to sweetly convince bridesmaids to, well, hurry the fuck up and get on the trolley. It's why I recommend him to every single client. That and his trolley is adorable with its red-paneled sides and large windows. The wooden seats inside are reminiscent of days gone by.

"It's a beautiful day for a wedding!" he shouts out the doors. Ernie always says this. It could be a Category 3 hurricane and it'd still be a beautiful day for a wedding, according to Ernie. He's right, though. Whenever two people in love commit to one another surrounded by the people they love and who love them, it's a beautiful day indeed. But it's too early in the day for me to get sappy. I'll save that for later.

"It sure is," I say, climbing onto the bus. "Good morning!" I project my voice over the trolley full of people. "Mom, Dad, ring bearer, and flower girl, why don't you all hop off while I get these beautiful ladies in order?"

They oblige and I take in the chaos of the trolley. All at once, the bride and bridesmaids acknowledge my presence with a chorus of questions, like songbirds on a spring morning.

"Can we leave our bags on the trolley?"

"You're sure the best man has the rings?"

"Did the cantor get the song change last night?"

"Why is it so damn hot in here?"

It's music to my ears. The nervous energy. The anticipation. That wedding day magic I love so much.

"Ernie will keep everything safe and secure. Best man has

the rings, I just checked. The cantor has the music and was rehearsing when I got here. She sounds beautiful. And it's hot because it's a Saturday in June and vintage trolleys don't have the best air conditioning," I say with a smile. "Let's do this, ladies. Bridesmaids, off the trolley please. Anna, you stay here until your dad comes back. Don't want anyone getting a sneak peek of you and your stunning dress!"

The bridesmaids exit the trolley, and I line them up in the order that they'll walk down the aisle. They look gorgeous. The dresses all match in style. A classic chiffon A-line with flutter sleeves. Anna selected a few shades of blue for them to choose from and they all found one that works perfectly with their complexions. Together they look like Nantucket hydrangeas in July.

"Now ladies, show me how you're holding your bouquets." They do as they're asked and look at me nervously. As they should—they're all elbows and awkward angles. "Let's fix this. Here's the trick, it's going to feel a little weird and unnatural, but it's going to look a hell of a lot better walking down the aisle and in pictures." I point to the maid of honor's bouquet. "May I borrow this?"

Bouquet in my hand, I look at the line of ladies and give them a grin.

"The secret is...bush to bush." I'm met with puzzled faces in full glam. "Like this." I grip the bouquet in both hands and point the stems down toward...well, my bush. It's been a while since any grooming was necessary. "Bush to bush," I repeat. When it clicks, they all laugh and visibly relax. Works pretty much every time.

"Keep the stems pointed toward your bush on an angle." I wink and hand the maid of honor her bouquet. "And don't forget to do that during pictures later."

I hop back on the trolley, leaving Maddie, my best friend and co-planner for the day, to finish instructing the bridesmaids. Did we go over everything last night at the rehearsal? Yes. Does every single group of bridesmaids forget what to do on the day? Also yes.

Anna's a picture of pure perfection sitting on the long wooden bench at the back of the trolley, her ivory gown pooling around her. It's all-over lace with a plunge neckline and sleeves she can remove for the reception. When we practiced removing the sleeves earlier, the lace reminded me of a different dress that I keep the memory of buried deep, but I put that out of my mind. It's Anna's day.

"You're up, Anna. Ready?"

"Ready!" She's positively glowing. Her hair is in a classically chic updo and her face is flawless, thanks in part to the talent of the hair and makeup team. But it's also because she's about to marry the love of her life and with that comes a glow not even the most talented makeup artist can manufacture.

Anna's been a dream client from the beginning. She contacted Spencer Soirees after I planned her brother's wedding last spring, asking specifically for me—much to Spencer Soirees owner Judy Spencer's chagrin.

Judy also happens to be my mom. You'd think she'd be proud of the success her only daughter, *her protégé*, is having, but even as she gets older, she's not eager to take a step back. More and more, brides want to hire someone in their own generation to plan their wedding. Someone who understands them. Not someone who reminds them of their mom and is likely to side with the mother of the bride during inevitable wedding planning disagreements.

There is a twinge of jealousy in Mom's tone every time she shares that we've received an inquiry requesting my availability, which has been happening a lot lately.

After ensuring the doors from the foyer to the chapel are closed, I escort Anna and her father into the church vestibule. Anna's dad is already tearing up.

I love an emotional dad, but it's going to be a long day if he doesn't pull it together. "You've got this." I give his shoulder a light squeeze. "I want you both to walk slower than feels natural, okay? Like you did last night. Deep breath in…and out."

They take a few breaths.

"Alright, Anna," I whisper in her ear so her dad can't hear. "Tits up!"

Anna laughs and straightens her posture. Another line that works every time.

The music changes. The congregation stands. Maddie and I open the doors and send them on their way.

"Done and done." I close the Spencer Soirees van door and look at my watch. It's been a fifteen-hour day and I'm starting to feel it. My legs ache, there's a dull throb in my head, and despite four shoe-changes, I can no longer feel my toes. Is it possible to be too old for this at twenty-nine?

"Nice work, boss," Maddie says, leaning on the back bumper. I roll my eyes in her direction. I hate when she calls me boss and she knows it. We're the same age, have the same years of experience under our belts, and are both lead planners at Spencer Soirees. Maddie started a year after I did and, technically, she reported to me for a short time. I'm pretty sure she bossed me around more than I ever did her, leading to a quick promotion and us being equals at work.

"Only fourteen more to go this season!" Maddie stifles a yawn. "Now, c'mon, tell me. What was your favorite part of this one?"

"One second," I say. I can't possibly debrief about the night until everything is checked off my timeline. "Load van: Check!"

"You're ridiculous. It's the end of the night, time to toss the timeline."

As if. I never toss a timeline. The first thing I'll do when I'm in the office on Tuesday is scan and upload a copy of the now-complete timeline to my computer. I'll save it within my FBI-level digital filing system to reference later as needed. The hard copy will go into my fireproof filing cabinet. Toss it? Absolutely not.

"Okay...favorite part." I sit next to Maddie on the bumper, giving my weary legs and feet a well-deserved break.

Moments of the evening run through my head like a highly curated TikTok edit. The groom's face when he saw Anna for the first time. The flower girl running to her mom, one of the bridesmaids, and refusing to sit with her dad in the church pews. The brother of the groom announcing the bridal party with quite possibly the best sports announcer voice I've ever heard, not that I watch a lot of sports. Fine, any sports. I love all the usual moments. The speeches, parent dances, even a garter toss can't make me cringe...that much. But it's those one-of-a-kind moments that happen at a wedding that always stay with me.

"Oh, when the bride's uncles sang that song...the rattling something and the flower girl started Irish step dancing." I'm a sucker for a choreographed dance or surprise musical performance.

"Rattling something?!" Maddie rolls her eyes. "It's The Rattlin' Bog. You haven't done enough Irish weddings."

"And yours?" Maddie's answer is always the first dance or the father of the bride's speech. Based on how tonight's speech went, it'll be the first dance. Anna's poor dad was blubbering through the entire thing, and no one could understand a word except apparently Anna, who nodded and cried along with him. "Let me guess."

"The first dance," Maddie blurts before I can get a word in.

"You're so predictable," I laugh, tapping her knee. "C'mon, let's get out of here."

My days off are so close I can taste it. But it's impossible for me to enjoy my precious Sunday and Monday if I don't complete my post-wedding routine. I've crafted it over the years to ensure my clients, the other vendors, and yours truly are all taken care of after a wedding.

With a slice of cake that I snuck from the venue next to me, I start with thank you emails to vendors. That cannot wait until I'm in the office on Tuesday. The vendors we work with are the best of the best and go above and beyond for our clients; they need to know how appreciated they are first thing tomorrow morning. Or, if they're like me and can't wind down as soon as they get home, they'll find out tonight.

I confirm that room service at the Four Seasons Lanai will deliver a bottle of champagne to the newlyweds' suite at the precise time I request to ensure the perfect chilled temperature when they arrive Monday. I love it when the time difference works in my favor.

I have to post some of the content I captured throughout the night to the Spencer Soirees Instagram stories. A grid post will have to wait until I get a sneak peek at the professional shots from the photographer. I wait for those sneak peeks with as much anticipation as the newlyweds. Maybe more, since I'm not busy consummating the marriage or tearing open cards to see how generous my guests were feeling. My favorite photographers, like me, are also still up working. Opening their laptops and quickly editing a few photos to share with their clients before they even wake up the next morning.

As I hit send on the last thank-you email, the sneak peeks arrive in my inbox. Perfect!

I always write myself an email with all my mental notes from the day to reference in the future. All the details need to go somewhere while they're still fresh in my head or I'll never remember them. What our team could do better or differently at future weddings. Favorite moments or details to recommend to future clients. If I don't get it down now, each wedding will end up like the novels I read during the offseason: Once they're over, the details are gone and I only remember the vibes.

With all that complete, I move on to my own post-wedding self-care routine, which includes foam rolling for fifteen minutes, a shower with my favorite eucalyptus shower steamer, evening skincare routine, two Aleve with a glass of water, brushing teeth, and a few pages of the romantasy novel that's been sitting on my nightstand for weeks. As usual, I only make it through two pages before falling asleep.

The buzzing of my phone rips me out of a luxuriously deep sleep. Ugh.

I have a wedding hangover. Not the fun kind that many of last night's guests are having this morning. And not the kind couples usually have after coming down from the high of the wedding and honeymoon. After they've spent months, sometimes years, planning and think *now what are we supposed to do with our time?* Beside screw each other until the newlywed bliss wears off, that is.

For a wedding planner, it's much closer to a real hangover. All that's missing is the nausea and the anxiety of remembering what you said or did the night before. And any of the fun that was had, too. The symptoms are an achy body (from being on your feet all day), a slight headache (from dehydration), brain fog (from using so much brain power), general fatigue (from working a near-16-hour day), and the need for a greasy brunch (from having no time to eat the day before).

My phone buzzes again. The clock on my nightstand reads 10:15 a.m., which means I got a solid eight hours of sleep. My book is strewn on the floor next to my bed, open to an unknown page that I don't remember reading. Well, I tried. Reading will have to wait until wedding season ends. I look at the phone and answer anyway.

"Hi, Mom," I say.

"Morning, my dear," she says in the bright tone of a person who went to bed at a reasonable hour.

"How did everything go last night?" She already knows how it went. Like every other wedding, I kept her updated throughout the night, sending photos and real-time feedback from the clients and guests. And I sent her a recap text when I got home.

"You know it went perfectly," I say.

"Never perfect, dear! It can always be better!" Here we go. "I'm sure there are a few things I would have done differently."

"You know what I mean." I'm not about to take that bait. "Why are you calling before noon on a Sunday anyway?"

"Can't I call my favorite daughter—"

"Only daughter." I remind her.

"Can't I call you to check in?"

"You can, but you and I both know that's not what you're doing," I say as lightheartedly as possible. Burying the twinge of pain in my chest that she never actually calls to check in.

"I know, I'm just the worst mother," she says.

That's exactly what I was trying to avoid. I can almost see the put-on pout she always makes when a guilt trip is coming. Should have kept my mouth shut.

"Sorry, Mom." It's easiest to apologize and move on. "I'm still pretty wiped from yesterday. I shouldn't take that out on you."

"That's my girl." Just like that, she's fine. "I'll let you enjoy today, but I need you to come into the office tomorrow at ten."

"Tomorrow? As in Monday?" She may not respect many boundaries, but one she's always adhered to is that time off after a wedding weekend is sacred. "What's going on that can't wait until Tuesday?"

"There's an important meeting and I need you there. That's all you need to know. Bye bye, love. Have fun tonight!"

"Wh—"

Click.

Tonight? The brain fog is real this morning. I open my calendar app. The Warehouse Party. How could I forget?

The Warehouse Party is the unofficial kickoff to the Charter Oaks wedding planning season. It's a night to see and be seen by everyone in the wedding industry in Fairfield County. Mingle with seasoned industry professionals, network with friends and colleagues, and honestly, get wasted and party like we're the guests for a change.

Warehouse Rentals, the top luxury rental and production company in the county, has held the party every year for as long as I can remember. Well before I joined the agency. They clear out the main floor of their warehouse and turn it into an epic event for wedding professionals only.

It's always been my favorite night of the year. Except for the party five years ago. I'd like to erase that night from my memories

I drag myself out of my cushy bed and over to my closet to figure out a '90s theme outfit. How am I going to find the energy for this party? I'm looking forward to it, but I could've used another hour of sleep and the dull throb at my left temple is getting stronger. I grab my medication from the clear organizer on my dresser appropriately labeled *migraine meds*. I take my cocktail and promise myself I'll hydrate better at next weekend's wedding.

Chapter 2

Caleb

"Are you sure this is a good idea? I don't see them going for it."

I'm in Dad's office at Foley's Market & Fine Catering. The front of house and kitchens were renovated a few years ago, but Paul Foley has kept his office exactly the same since he and Mom moved the business to this location in the late '90s. It's dark, drab, and wood-paneled. If I didn't already feel suffocated to the point of near-death being back East, this room alone would do it. The large metal desk is covered with piles of papers and folders. I'd forgotten how messy Dad can be, and coming from the clean and organized kitchen I left in San Francisco, it's a bit jarring.

I only got in last night and Dad's already putting me to work. I can't blame him. It's only six weeks into the wedding season and the Market is busier than ever. Time to put the years of culinary school and professional experience to work.

I knew what I was getting into when I chose to follow in my father's footsteps and carry on the family legacy. I knew my parents would pay for culinary school and let me do my own thing for a few years. And I knew I'd have to come home eventually. But I wasn't ready to pack up my life when Mom called to tell me about Dad's heart attack a few weeks ago. I wasn't ready to restart my life back in Charter Oaks. And I certainly wasn't ready for him to drop this plot twist regarding our biggest wedding of the season.

"They'll go for it, Caleb," Dad answers confidently.

"And you're okay with going against your number one unwritten rule for this?"

"Son," he says with a sigh. This conversation is taking a toll on him. More than it usually would. The doctors gave him an almost clean bill of health, but he's supposed to make some lifestyle changes and it hasn't been easy. Enter me to take the burden of wedding season off his shoulders. "This will be great for us and set you up for the success you deserve when you take over. It'll be worth breaking our unwritten rule just once."

"Not *our* rule, Dad," I remind him. "Yours."

"I have my reasons for it. Which, unfortunately for you, may become clear this summer."

I love my dad, but he can be cryptic as fuck sometimes.

"Well, tomorrow will certainly be interesting." I get up from the chair. "I've got to meet Joey, but I'll pick you up in the morning and we'll head over?"

He nods and shuffles through the piles on his desk. I hang by the door for a moment, studying him. He's thinner than he was the last time I visited, thanks to his new heart-healthy diet. The lines on his face are a little deeper and his once-jet black hair is shot through with gray. It seems like an already-established fact that I'm expected to take over sooner rather than later. I couldn't avoid it forever—as much as I wanted to.

It doesn't look that bad.

I park my old Wrangler on the street in front of the brick duplex. Joey's one of my oldest friends. I'd trust him with my life, but I was hesitant to ask for help with a temporary living situation. The guy once dragged me to a concert at Jones Beach with the promise of a place to crash. That place was the beach. It was the worst night's sleep of my life, but he's my only lead right now.

One night at my parents' house was enough. I love them and they adore each other…too much. I may be a grown man, but I don't need to see them making googly eyes at each other across the dinner table. I sent a panicked text to Joey asking if he knew of anywhere else to stay while I figure things out. He's the kind of guy who always has a guy for something or some connection that can get whatever you need. Sketchy, sure, but it does come in handy.

"The prodigal son returns!" Joey calls from the steps.

"Oh, fuck off." I hop out of the Wrangler and make my way up the walkway, eyeing the outside of the house. I grew up in Charter Oaks but never knew these few streets of nearly identical brick duplexes and small townhouses existed. They're much closer to the Metro-North tracks and I-95 than my parents' house. And much farther from the grand homes and country clubs where I spent my early twenties picking up catering gigs. But close enough to the Market and downtown, perfect for a thirty-something-old single guy, if that guy plans to work his ass off with little hope for a social life…which is exactly how my summer is shaking out.

"Not too bad, right?" Joey gestures to the door behind him before grabbing my right hand and pulling me in for a hug, clapping me on the back. It hits me that I've missed him. We spent our high school summers together as dishwashers and cleanup crew at the Market and gigged our fair share of weddings.

I haven't been the best at keeping in touch while I've been away, but with Joey it's easy to slip right back into our uncomplicated friendship.

"I'm still a little skeptical," I say, raising a brow. "I haven't seen the inside yet."

"Caleb, this is my property. I promise you, it's nice."

"You own this place?" When did Joey grow up and buy property?

"Yeah, man. While you've been away charming the pants off California girls, Morgan and I bought a couple of places, fixed them up, and now I'm landlord."

"A landlord or a slumlord?"

"Now you fuck off." Joey huffs out a laugh. "We've got this duplex here and one of the townhouses down the street. They're cool. Built in the 1920s when the industries nearby were booming. Companies built them as housing for their employees…" He rambles on about the history of the area, opening the door and leading me inside. Joey's big and burly with a scruffy beard. His looks and his interest in town history are very much at odds.

I don't know what condition the place was in before, but I have to hand it to him, it's pretty nice. There's fresh paint and updated fixtures. And it comes mostly furnished, which is ideal —I won't have much time to shop for furniture.

"How's your dad doing?" Joey asks as we wrap up the tour back in the kitchen. It's small, but has a decent amount of prep space and good appliances for a rental. I wouldn't expect anything less from a landlord-slash-chef.

"Something must still be wrong with him if he's still talking to you," I joke. Giving each other shit is one of our favorite pastimes.

While I dragged my feet, Joey moved up in the ranks at Foley's and eventually became one of the lead chefs under Dad. He stuck with it until last summer, when he was hired as a private chef up in the Hamptons. That's where he met his girlfriend, Morgan, who he convinced to move back so he could open his own small catering company—with Dad's blessing. Must be nice.

I didn't take the news so great. If I was going to have to take over Foley's one day, I wanted to do it with Joey by my side. We work great together and he makes everything fun. That might be why Dad gave him his blessing: We'd probably have too much fun and run the business to the ground. The truth is that I'm envious of Joey, starting something of his own from scratch. Like how my dad started Foley's.

"Aw, c'mon," he says with a laugh. "Your old man knows I only do smaller gigs. I can't do those two-, three-hundred-person weddings on my own. I won't lie, I sort of miss Foley's. But the crazy guests with questions like 'how many macros are in this?'—I don't miss that."

"Is that what I'm in for now that I'm back East?"

"If you thought California was bad, you've been away from Connecticut for too long. Is this it? You're back for good?"

I hadn't given it much thought. When Mom called, she assured me Dad was going to be fine, but it was time to come home. I found someone to sublet my room in the apartment I shared with another chef, sold a bunch of my stuff, packed up the rest, and now I'm here. Home. But it doesn't quite feel like that yet.

"Yeah, man, I think so," I say.

"It'll be nice to have you back, but I can only let you have this place through September. I've got a lease signed already, a professor at the university."

"That's all I need." Whether or not Foley's and I make it through Dad's big plan will be determined by Labor Day. Joey hands me the keys and helps me unload my pitiful amount of luggage and boxes from the car.

Home sweet home...for now.

Joey helps me get settled and heads out—but not before I agree to go to The Warehouse Party with him tonight. It's been five years since my last appearance at the infamous industry party, and I'd rather not be reminded of that night. I need to stay focused on the summer ahead of me.

Chapter 3

Brooke

We can hear the bass thumping from our Uber as our driver turns into the industrial park where the party rages. There's a reason Warehouse Rentals chose Sunday night for their annual kickoff: Nearby businesses are closed, ensuring nobody's around to call the police and complain about noise. Last year's party went long into the early hours of the morning, but I left promptly at 11:30 p.m. I only stay out after midnight for weddings. Much like Cinderella's carriage turns back into a pumpkin, I turn into a tired grumpy shell of myself that no one deserves to interact with.

"Always Be My Baby" blasts as Maddie and I get out of the Uber and head inside. I gasp as we enter the dark warehouse. The space has been turned into something right out of MTV, a combination of the ultimate house party and an episode of *Total Request Live*. If Carson Daly jumped on stage right now, I wouldn't be surprised. I'd probably also faint.

The Warehouse Rentals team always kills it with the theme. It helps that everyone in the industry loves the party, offering their services at no cost, and this year is no different.

"Holy shit," Maddie shrieks. She's dressed as Baby Spice

even though her red hair and fiery personality are perfect for Ginger. "This is amazing!"

First order of business: drinks. We head to one of the four bars occupying each corner of the space. If you've got a room full of wedding professionals, at a party for wedding professionals, I can assure you no one will have to wait more than two minutes for a drink.

"Stop!" I squeeze Maddie's arm. "I can't even!" The bar in the corner we've chosen is designed to look like *90210*'s The Peach Pit. I turn to see if I can spot the themes of the other three bars while Maddie orders us peach martinis. It's hard to tell, but diagonally across from us looks like The Max from *Saved by the Bell*. This is what dreams are made of.

We take our drinks to one of the high tops and people-watch. Everyone's gone all out with their themed outfits. Boy bands, girl groups, Fresh Prince, Run DMC, and some grunge bands I never listened to are enjoying themselves all around us. The cover band finishes their set and a DJ I've worked with before takes over the turntables. He's known for his epic mashups. Maddie and I make eye contact and smile. We down our martinis and skip over to the dance floor.

"Jordan!" I shout when I spot my favorite photographer and our third in the trio that is me, Maddie, and Jordan. She dances over and wraps one arm around each of us in a hug. God, I needed this night. So much has happened since last year's party, and I've got tomorrow's meeting with Mom looming over me.

Jordan's career has taken off, and she's made a name for herself beyond our seaside Connecticut town. She used to shoot nearly every wedding I worked. Now she can only squeeze in a few (specifically our highest budget weddings) between the destination weddings and elopements she has booked all across the country—some outside the country, too. It's hard to keep up with her schedule. I had no idea she was going to be here tonight, and I'm so glad she is, dressed as Daria with clothes she probably already had at home.

We join a group of photographers dancing to a mashup of Spice Girls hits. It's divine to be the one on the dance floor for a change. Watching from the wings at two dozen weddings a year is downright excruciating, and not just because I endure the same three Bruno Mars songs performed by a different band every weekend. Sometimes 24K magic isn't in the air. It gets harder and harder each week not to jump on the dance floor with my couples and their guests. Occasionally, a drunk groomsman will try to pull me into the crowd, and no matter how good the song is—or how handsome the groomsman is—I have to remain professional.

Everyone here is feeling the same. At this party, I—and every other vendor who wants to dance every weekend—can finally let loose. I can finally let my hair down. Figuratively. Literally, it's time to pull it into a high pony. The sweat from all the movement (my watch has started tracking a workout all on its own) and humidity is turning my waves to frizz. The high pony works better with my themed outfit anyway.

I lose myself in the next mashup until I notice Jordan and Maddie whisper-yelling to each other and looking at me, narrowed eyes of concern on both their faces.

"What?" I ask them.

"Nothing," Jordan says, but Maddie's eyes are glaring across the room. I follow her gaze. My stomach drops, does a summersault, then drops even more. I suddenly feel sweaty, and not from the dancing.

Fuck.

I look back at my friends. "It's fine."

"Are you sure?" Jordan asks.

Maddie brings her right hand into a fist and punches her open left palm. "Want me to go smack him in the throat?"

I'm not sure I'm fine, but I am sure I would like Maddie to

punch him in the throat. I can't let her do that, though. However, it is comforting to know she would if I wanted her to. Honestly, she'd do it even if I didn't want her to.

"Yes, I'm sure," I lie. "And no, Maddie. I appreciate it, but let's not get kicked out this early."

"Fine," Maddie says, resigning herself. She loves a fight. "Just say the word and you know I'll do it."

"Oh, I know you will. C'mon." I grab each of their hands and pull them deeper into the dance floor where no one can see us and, more importantly, I can't see *him*. "Let's keep dancing!"

We've been dancing for an hour, and I never want this night to end. The bass pumps through my chest, the drinks have me in that perfect balance of tipsy and happy, and I'm not thinking about to-do lists, timelines, or anything related to work. And I'm definitely not worrying about who we spotted earlier. It doesn't hurt that the DJ keeps playing throwback after throwback. I simply can't leave the dance floor in the middle of "MMMBop."

"Macarena" starts to play, and yup, I can absolutely leave the dance floor for this one. By the looks on their faces, Jordan and Maddie feel the same. We all raise our voices above the music at the same time.

"I need some water," I say.

"I'm going to use the bathroom," Jordan says.

"I see Baxter!" Maddie waves to her off-and-on, hot-and-cold situationship of a year. I turn and wave at him, too.

"You okay if I go?" she asks.

"Of course, I'm fine," I tell her.

"Okay, good," she squeals. "Because he owes me!"

"He owes you what?"

She winks. I roll my eyes, but she doesn't see as she runs off to Baxter and whatever sexual favor she expects. That's the last I'll see of Maddie tonight. Baxter's an account manager for Warehouse Rentals, so he knows all the good hiding spots. In fact, he's the Spencer Soirees account manager, which might be some kind of conflict of interest, but this industry is already so incestuous that no one would bat an eye. He's also one of the best-looking guys here. Warm, dark skin, short black hair, and a sweet playful smile. Who I am to take that away from Maddie?

The kickoff is as notorious for insane partying as it is for some pretty incredible hookups. Typically, it's the junior staffers and assistants getting entangled in one another. Assistants from competing florists making out in the back staircase. A junior photographer and an assistant catering manager heading home in an Uber together. Like I said, no one bats an eye. But every few years there is some scandal with more established industry leads, and everyone knows better than to gossip about those.

I wish I had Maddie's *no fucks left to give* attitude. I envy her ability to have fun and not let any awkwardness set in. Whatever they've had going on for the last year—since last year's party, actually—it's never weird between them. They could be in the middle of a huge fight and act like the best of friends for a client meeting. I pretend not to, but I still give lots of fucks about a lot of things.

I've had my share of fun, of course, but I know how awkward can creep up at the most inopportune time. And I have a lot to prove this season if I want to show Mom that I can take over the agency. Messing around at this party is a sure way to get on her bad side. Dancing my ass off is as wild as it's going to get this summer.

I need water. If I don't want a migraine tomorrow, I need to hydrate. I do a 360-degree turn to get my bearings. Where were Maddie and Jordan looking before? Right, over by the photo booth. Which means I'm going in the opposite direction.

The Max-themed bar area is packed. High-top tables with red diner stools are scattered around with bartenders sporting red t-shirts. It's all so wonderfully campy. For a moment, I wish I could work on some of the birthdays and mitzvahs the junior planners at the agency handle. I'd like to do something different every now and then, have some fun with a kitschy theme. Maybe I could convince some clients to do a '90s theme wedding. *Cringe.* Bad idea. Blame it on the peach martinis.

Mom would never allow it. And if I'm going to take over one day, it's strictly weddings for me. At the same time, she's increasingly annoyed every year as more and more new clients request to work with me. I can't win.

I nudge my way through the crowd, glancing at my phone to read a text.

> Jordan: Making an Irish exit. Have an early flight in the AM. xx

Classic Jordan move. As I type back an *xx* to Jordan, I bump my forehead right into the chest of a man at the bar.

"Shit, I'm so sorry." I fumble with my purse to put my phone away, lifting my head to find awkward looking right at me.

Fuck.

Chapter 4

Caleb

Well, if it isn't the very reason I was dreading coming back to town. And this party. My pulse races. I take a slow sip of my beer. I need a moment to compose myself.

Play the part, Caleb.

The ocean blue eyes with long lashes looking up at me hold me for a moment. I nearly get lost in them, until I realize who they belong to. Based on the shift in her gaze and how quickly she crosses her arms at her torso, it appears she just realized who she bumped into, too.

"Brooke Spencer," I say with a smile.

"Caleb Foley," she says, frowning. "What are you doing here?"

"I'm a wedding industry professional, aren't I?"

She rolls those eyes at me. The gorgeous, sparkling eyes I've been trying to forget for five years. Fuck if they don't still have me a little bit.

"Barely," she scoffs. "Picking up random shifts at the country club or helping your dad when they're understaffed doesn't count."

Ouch.

I lean my elbows back on the bar behind me. Her freckled cheeks turn pink and her brows furrow. She's *furious*.

"Excuse me, I need to get a drink," she snaps.

"What do you want?"

She ignores me and waves a hand trying to get the bartender's attention from where she stands and, not surprisingly, doesn't have any luck. On the one night a year the industry lets loose, the amateurs are handling service and, this late in the night, it's a complete shitshow.

She resigns, crossing her arms again, and finally looks at me. "Water."

I reach over the bar, grab her a bottled water, twist the cap, and hand it to her.

"Thank you," she says, begrudgingly. "I see you dressed on theme this year." She points a manicured finger at me, waving it up and down. I hardly planned to dress on theme; I barely have anything unpacked. I threw a light flannel on over my dark gray shirt on the way out the door. It might unofficially be summer, but the New England nights are still cool. I survey the room and, yeah, I guess I am a little on theme after all.

"What can I say, I love a theme party."

"You hate theme parties." She's not wrong.

"Maybe I've changed."

She scoffs again.

"And this." I point a finger at her, miming her motions from moments ago. "Is this on theme?"

It has to be, because the Brooke I know would never wear something like this unless it was for a theme party. *She* loves a theme party. She's wearing a black cropped tank top with thick straps, a leather skirt with some kind of odd-looking belt made of silver hoops, hot pink tights, and tall black boots. *Damn*. If I weren't so caught off guard bumping into her, or rather her literally bumping into me, I'd be into this. But it's a far cry from the polished and preppy, dress-and-heels-wearing wedding planner I know.

"It *is* on theme, Caleb." She puts her hands on her hips and spins in a circle. "You seriously don't recognize who I'm dressed as?"

I shake my head because I honestly don't—and to try to get the image of that skirt hugging her ass out of my head. It's going to be a long summer if that's on my mind every time I see her.

"I'll give you a hint." She stands on her tiptoes to get closer to my ear. "Naaa naaa na- nana," she sings, her breath warm on my neck. This is so much worse than I thought it would be when I agreed to come here with Joey.

I still have no fucking clue.

"Clarissa! From *Clarissa Explains It All*!"

I mouth an *oh* and laugh. I see it now, but it's fun to see her infuriated. It reminds me of when we worked the same weddings years ago, but I'm not about to let her know that.

"You're such an idiot," she says and turns on her heel, her tall black boot-wearing heel, and walks away, the long brown waves of her high ponytail swaying behind her.

I *am* an idiot. For so many reasons.

I've already been here much longer than I intended to be. I prefer to stay behind the scenes. I'm comfortable there. In the kitchen, focused on the task at hand. But if I'm going to be the new face of Foley's, I need to appear to enjoy an industry party. Mostly I'm enjoying that my colleagues are having a good time. This work is grueling; they all deserve a moment of fun.

My beer is empty, making it the perfect time to leave. I head to the loading dock so I can sneak out of this enormous place without having to cross the entire room and run into Brooke again. Turning the corner at a brisk pace, I nearly bump into a couple making out against the wall. I should have been prepared for that. The dark corner make outs are not a shock at this party, but what's with all the literal running into people?

I try to pass quickly when one of them calls my name.

I turn. "Hey Baxter."

"Caleb, get the fuck out of here," his female companion says. *Shit.* It was bad enough seeing Brooke. At least I know she doesn't have it in her to kill me, but Maddie Murphy is an entirely different story. It's been five years, but the daggers in her eyes tell me she's still holding a grudge.

"Maddie, always a pleasure," I say, taking a few steps back. Not because I'm scared of her. Fine, maybe a little. But I'd like to get the fuck out of here and go to bed so I feel ready for tomorrow.

"The only reason I'm not punching you in the throat right now, Foley, is because Brooke said I can't."

"Caleb, I can't let you go out that way." Baxter points to the loading dock doors. "I'll be in deep shit. The dock is shut down for the night, but there's a side door over there that will bring you to the front of the building."

"Thanks, man." I turn to the door. "As you were," I say with a wink at Maddie.

"He's such an asshole," I hear her tell Baxter as I walk away. Followed by the sounds of lips smacking. Good for them.

There's barely a crowd in front of the building. Only a few people waiting for their rides. It's 11:30 and the party will last at least a few more hours. I pull my old Hartford Whalers hat out of my back pocket and put it on so no one spots me walking to my car. I'm not so cocky to think everyone wants to talk to me, but it's already been a lot being back in town after so much time away. I don't have it in me to talk to anyone else tonight.

Until I hear a familiar voice. "I was not chatting up Caleb Foley."

I raise my eyes under my hat and catch Brooke muttering

to herself and frantically typing on her phone. I know I should keep walking, but I can't help myself. Not when it comes to Brooke.

"Twice in one night. How lucky am I?" I step in front of her. "And you were indeed chatting me up. Singing in my ear even."

She looks up at me with her big blue eyes open wide.

"I was not." She smacks my chest. "Ouch!"

Ha. She's given me a smack like that before, and it wasn't met with the same muscle. See, I have changed. Impossible hours in the kitchen can force a man to shape up in order to build stamina. I had to keep up with the younger chefs. The ones who went straight to culinary school instead of fucking around for years like me.

She looks me up and down. Taking me in for the first time tonight. "Hmm," she says.

I raise my brows and tilt my head. "Hmm?"

"Ugh." She shakes her head then looks at her phone. "My Uber will be here in two minutes. Can you please get out of here?"

I peek at her screen. "Looks more like ten minutes." She pulls her phone to her chest. "Let me give you a ride home."

Now that I've seen her and know that I'll be seeing a lot of her this summer, the need to get her home safely is resurfacing in a way I'm not quite ready to address.

"I'm not going home with you, Caleb."

My turn to roll my eyes. I didn't mean it like that. "C'mon, I just want to be sure you get home in one piece."

She steps back. Like she hasn't forgotten how it used to be.

"I've been getting home for the last five years without your help, Caleb," she bites at me. "I'll be fine."

Noted.

"Okay," I resign. "Goodnight, Brooke. See you soon." I walk away backward, smirking.

"I hope not!" If she's pissed now, tomorrow morning is going to be interesting.

There isn't enough coffee in the state to prepare me for today. Sleep evaded me for most of the night after seeing Brooke and knowing I'd have to face her again today. I knew I'd be seeing her, and as much as I want things to feel like they used to, they can't. I need to play the part of the unaffected jerk. The part I played the last time I saw her.

Today, I need to stay professional and keep our history buried, like I have for years. Maybe it'll be easy, seeing as she wants nothing to do with me. Ugh. Who am I kidding.

"Dad," I say, turning to where he sits in the passenger seat. "Are you absolutely sure about this?"

Driving down Post Road with him, I realize how much I missed New England. Downtown Charter Oaks is picturesque with the shops along Post Road. Banners hang near the town green promoting local events. Historical homes fill the side streets.

Some might argue that this small southwestern corner of Connecticut isn't New England enough, that it's too close to New York City. Anyone with that take is usually passing through and doesn't stop to see what it has to offer.

"Trust me, son," he says. "It'll all work out."

I haven't had a chance to talk to my mom to see what she thinks of this, but Dad must have her blessing. Years ago, Dad wanted to expand the business to the city, but Mom convinced him to focus on growing here. It was the right move. Mom, as she tells it, is always right. Dad may have the culinary creativity, but Mom has the business acumen.

Together, they've grown Foley's into one of the best independent markets and caterers in the area. This summer, we have more weddings and events booked than ever before. So many that Joey is helping with a few, and we've hired so much new staff I can barely keep up. And we're about to secure the biggest event of the season.

I turn off Post Road and onto a side street. I blow out a breath as I park the car.

"If you say so."

Chapter 5

Brooke

I fumble with the smart lock on the office door. Entering the code incorrectly twice before I can get into the old colonial home-turned-office that Spencer Soirees occupies off the Post Road. The door makes its usual squeak.

I've been all out of sorts since I saw Caleb last night. He was so cool and collected, acting like we'd seen each other a few days ago and not several years. I tossed and turned all night replaying our encounter in my head.

Of course, he had to come back looking all California with a tan and sun streaks in his brown wavy hair. And the muscles —I bet he spent all his time going to the gym. Isn't that what assholes like him do?

Why didn't I leave as soon as I saw him across the room? Then maybe I'd never have to see him. If he's back to work for his dad, our paths won't have to cross at all.

I need to focus and be at my best for whatever Mom dragged me in here for, but I can't get that smirk out of my thoughts. The one he flashed before he finally left me to wait for my Uber in peace. It's probably that fucking dimple that I once thought was the sexiest thing I've ever seen. Well, not anymore, Caleb. I shake my head, trying to push out any and all thoughts of him.

I walk over to my desk near the large bay window that fills the office with light on sunny days. There's a lot to be desired when you're the boss's daughter, especially when the boss is Judy Spencer, but I got my pick of desks when we moved the offices here. I drop my bag on my chair—Mom doesn't like clutter on the desks.

All of the sleek white desks, each adorned with a large Mac computer display and identical desk blotters, are empty. It's officially wedding season, so every single planner and assistant worked this weekend. They're enjoying their day off. And for some reason, I'm here.

Time to find out why.

Mom's office is a small room in the back, in the opposite corner of my desk. (The beautiful bay window wasn't the only factor in my decision.) I can hear the *click clack* of her slow typing from here. Despite my attempts to teach her proper typing, she insists there's nothing wrong with using only her index fingers and how dare I try to correct her.

Catching a glimpse of myself in the large decorative mirror on the wall—I'm almost certain Mom had it put there so she can keep an eye on us from her office—I realize I need to put lipstick on or risk being chastised for not looking put together. *You need lips*, she's constantly telling me. Lips applied, I tuck my hair behind my ears and dust off my sundress. Here we go.

Before I even cross the threshold into her office, Mom, still staring at her computer, holds up one finger telling me to wait before speaking. As if she herself didn't train me not to speak unless spoken to as a child. I sit in one of the matching pink chairs across from her. Finished with whatever she was typing, she finally looks at me.

"Good morning, my dear," she says with a tight smile.

"Hi, Mom."

She frowns. "Brooke…"

"Mom," I say, gesturing to her office door. "There isn't anyone here." Inside these physical walls—and the metaphorical ones when I'm working—she isn't Mom, she's Judy. It doesn't matter that everyone knows she's my mother. I'm to call her Judy. It's more professional, according to her. It's also ridiculous, but like many things when it comes to my mom, I pick my battles.

"There isn't anyone here…yet," she says.

I narrow my eyes. "What do you mean?"

"Tell me about last night, any drama I need to be made aware of?"

Dodging the question.

"Nope, no drama."

"Oh?" She purses her lips as her dark brown eyes peer into the depths of my soul, and I swear she can tell I'm thinking about Caleb and the waves of his hair peeking out from under that stupid old Whalers hat. Get it together, Brooke. This has been Mom's tactic since I was little: Stare me down until the guilt of whatever secret I'm trying to keep takes over and I spill it. If that doesn't work, she finds the right words to guilt me. It's why there are rarely secrets between us. Not for lack of trying on my part, but because she can guilt me into a confession every single time.

"Well…" I give in. She'll find out soon or later. "I did see Caleb Foley."

"Oh, is that so?" she says without the hint of surprise I was expecting.

"Yes, that *is* so." I sit up in my seat. "What do you know, Mother?

"Oh, don't you *mother* me." She shoos a hand in my direction. "I did indeed hear that Caleb was coming back. He's working for his dad again."

It takes every fiber of my being not to ask why she didn't

tell me. But why would she think to tell me? It's the one secret I've managed to keep from Mom: the friendship Caleb and I once had. Only because she'd never suspect it. We may not be friends anymore, but she can't know about our history.

"So, he's freeloading off his parents this summer?" I say, rolling my eyes.

"I take it you haven't been keeping up with him on all those app things on your phone?"

Nope. I blocked Caleb Foley and never looked back. Fine, Maddie blocked him for me. And whenever I even consider looking, I think of how disappointed she'd be. And that she might physically harm me if she found out.

"Have *you*?" She barely knows how to text. I can't imagine she's figured out social media.

"Of course not, Brooke," she says, clasping her hands together on her desk. Unlike the simple modern white desks for the staff, her desk is a small vintage dining room table. "But I do know that Caleb finally finished culinary school and was the head chef at a notable wedding venue outside San Francisco. And now he's back, I imagine to eventually take over Foley's like his father always wanted him to."

That can't be true. And how would she even know? Caleb always said he didn't want to take over Foley's. He wanted to do something on his own, he just hadn't figured out what that was yet. I told him he'd be amazing at whatever he decided to do. I once told him a lot of things.

But she knows everyone around here and they know the best way to spread information is to share it with Judy. Even without having social media, she's the influencer many strive to be.

"Wow," I say. It's all I can manage.

"You seem awfully surprised, dear. Caleb was always going to take over Foley's."

No, he wasn't. But she doesn't know that.

"Right, of course." I say. "I guess I thought he'd stay in California longer, that's all."

Something occurs to me. If Caleb was head chef at a wedding venue, he has actual experience now. This should genuinely concern Mom. It concerns me, that's for sure. Foley's Market & Fine Catering has been our biggest obstacle for years. They have a hard rule of never working with outside wedding planners. Ever. Zero exceptions. Not since the falling out Mom had with Paul Foley two decades ago. The details of which Mom refuses to share. It keeps us from booking several weddings a year, but I'm happy for it now.

"Mom..." I need to tread carefully here. Questioning her isn't always the best idea. "Should we be worried about Foley's? Caleb probably thinks he knows every fucking thing about weddings now—"

"Language, Brooke!"

Oops, Judy hates cussing. Very unbecoming.

"Sorry, Mo–Judy! They refuse to work with planners and now they can use Caleb's experience to poach prospective clients. I thought you'd be a little more worried?"

"About that," she says.

"About what..." I stand up from the chair. Frantic energy coursing through my body. Something isn't right here. Caleb is back. Mom isn't acting like herself. None of this was part of my plan for this wedding season. My plan was to focus solely on work. Give all of my attention to my clients. Manage and mentor the newer planners. Prove to Mom that I can take over Spencer Soirees—and soon. Like, *the end of this season* soon. She's been dangling the prospect of her retirement in front of me for the last three years. My plan for this season is to get her to finally do it.

It's stifling in here. I open a window, hoping an early summer breeze will calm my nerves. "They hate working with planners. Mr. Foley may be one of the best caterers in the area, but he's a prick. You've said so yourself! And now Caleb probably is, too. He was acting pretty prickish last night."

He was acting exactly the way he did the last time I saw him.

"I don't disagree with you, Brooke, but—"

I turn from the window and raise my brows. *But?*

"It's about the Quincy wedding. We have a shot at it."

The Quincy wedding.

If we could land Hannah Quincy's wedding, who the hell cares what Caleb, his dad, and Foley's Fine Catering are up to?

New plan: Land the Quincy wedding. That would prove to Mom exactly how capable I am, and she'd finally feel comfortable passing the torch. This is the year she won't be able to say *just one more year* at the end of the season.

When news of Hannah Quincy and Preston Redbank's New Year's Eve engagement began to spread, the local industry was buzzing in a way it hadn't in years. Every Fairfield County vendor wants that wedding and the clout that will come with it. The Quincy wedding could be career-changing for the planner who lands it.

The Quincys are one of the wealthiest families in the county and Hannah has made a name for herself as a social media influencer. The kind followers and locals both genuinely love. And believe me, there are other influencers in town that can't say the same. Her fiancé Preston, a tech startup CEO, also comes from family money. If Instagram is to be believed, they're absolutely smitten with one another, and all signs point to a classic New England wedding next summer.

Landing this wedding could mean truly making a name for myself and proving to Mom that I'm ready to take over the business. That is, if she even assigns me as lead planner. There's a good chance she'll want to hold on to this one. But if she were to assign it to me, I'd prove to her that Spencer Soirees is in extremely capable hands. She's built an amazing agency, but it's becoming more and more obvious that a change is needed.

"Mom, you're kidding me!" I shriek. "I thought they might hire someone from the city?"

"Hannah wants to keep it authentic and use local vendors. Which brings us to the Foleys."

No, no, no.

Not the Foleys.

The only thing worse than not booking this wedding would be not booking it because we lost it to Paul and Caleb Foley.

"What about them?" I'm afraid to hear the answer.

"The Quincys have already hired them."

Fuck.

"Oh." I slouch against the windowsill. My mom has done some questionable things over the years, but sucker punching her own daughter? Ouch. "Well, then our chance is zero."

"Brooke, let me finish," she says, calmly. "They've hired Foley's, but they also want to hire us. Paul wasn't able to convince them that they don't need an outside planner. Hannah is set on having a *real* planner to manage the entire wedding weekend."

Mom's never considered the wedding coordinators at Foley's to be real planners. Glorified servers, she once called them. A few have applied for jobs here and she prints out their resumes only to tear them up.

"Okay…?"

"She's set on…" she says slowly, like the words are difficult to get out. "Hannah's set on having *you* as her wedding planner."

Hannah Quincy knows who I am? Knows my work? I try hard, but I fail to keep the corners of my mouth from curling into a smile. Hannah Quincy wants *me* to be her wedding planner.

"Paul called me himself to ensure you're available for a Labor Day wedding."

"He called *you*?" I may never know what happened between Mom and Paul Foley, but I do know that Paul Foley calling her is a big deal. I don't think they've even been in the same room in twenty years, let alone spoken to each other.

"He's afraid they'll lose the wedding unless we...well, *you* are on board. Foley's will finally have to work with a real planner."

My head is spinning. Hannah Quincy has personally requested me to plan her wedding. No, the full weekend of wedding events. Mom sure buried the lede. We don't just have a shot, we have it. *I* have it. As long as I agree to work with Foley's, with Caleb. A project of this scale will require a lot of collaboration. How the hell is this going to work?

I straighten my shoulders and take a centering breath. I can come up with a plan for this. A plan for getting through this unscathed. Paul might be a prick, but maybe I can work directly with him and avoid Caleb all together.

"Yes," I say. "They will!"

I can't help but move to stand behind Mom where she sits at her desk and hug her shoulders. She's not a hugger. Sometimes I don't know how I came out of her. She lets me have this one quick hug. After a moment, she pats the arms I have crossed around her chest, signaling to me that this display of affection must end immediately. I let her go.

"They've got about..." I count on my fingers, "sixteen months to get used to the idea."

"Oh no, dear. We have three months. The wedding is *this* Labor Day."

"*This* Labor Day?" How will I manage the scope of work for the Quincys on top of my other weddings?

"Don't fret, Brooke." She purses her lips. "You have a lot

more free time this summer than we originally thought you'd have, don't you?"

The dig lands exactly where she intended, but I don't let her see that. I don't have time to, because I hear the familiar squeak of the front door, followed by an equally familiar voice.

"Good morning, Brooke!"

I was wrong.

The only thing worse than not booking this wedding is booking this wedding and working this closely with Caleb Foley for the next three months.

Chapter 6

Caleb

Two things are clear when I see Brooke's face: She had no clue about any of this and she's not happy about it. Her jaw is dropped and her wide eyes dart between me, Dad, and Judy as we settle into Judy's small office.

She's absolutely furious. Again.

Judy looks at Dad and gives him a tight nod, which he returns. She turns to me and wraps her arms around me like I'm her favorite nephew she hasn't seen in years. It's unsettling. She lets me go, but rests her hands on my biceps. "Caleb," she says. "You've grown into such a handsome young man."

If I didn't know any better, I'd think she was being sincere. But sincere is one thing this woman is not. The smile on her face is forced and the rest of her features strain against whatever injections she gets in an attempt to appear younger than she is.

Leaning against the desk, Brooke clears her throat and Judy finally lets me go. I give Brooke a nod in thanks but she's avoiding my eyes. She moves to the window and leans on the windowsill. Putting as much distance between us as she can in this small space.

Dad takes one of the pink chairs across the desk, the one closer to the open window. Closer to Brooke.

Finally, her eyes meet mine. I gesture toward the other pink chair. "Brooke, would you like to—"

"I'm fine here," she says, crossing her arms at her chest. I take a seat. Judy is making some small talk with Dad and he's giving her one-word answers. Brooke watches them like it's a Wimbledon match, deliberately avoiding my eyes again. She's in a short-sleeve white dress with thin vertical stripes in shades of blue. This is the Brooke I remember, a classic Connecticut girl all put together in her preppy dresses. Though, this dress has buttons down the center that start at a deeper V-neck than Brooke from five years ago would have worn. She would have considered it too revealing, though it's arguably still modest. I'm glad she's wearing it now. It suits her.

A few moments of silence pass. "Caleb." Dad knocks his knee against mine. Ah, not silence. Me caught staring at Brooke. This is off to a fantastic start.

"Thanks for joining us, son," he laughs. "I thought you could share with Brooke and Judy how you'd like to approach the Quincy events."

"Mr. Foley." Brooke stands from the windowsill. Interrupting Paul Foley on day one. This is going to be fun. "Foley's is the top caterer in the county, and I've only recently learned of the new experience Caleb brings to the table, which will be a tremendous asset, but Hannah Quincy has specifically requested *me* as the planner for the wedding and the additional weekend events." She picks up a folder from Judy's desk. The furious woman from moments ago is gone, replaced with a confident professional. She flips through the papers in the folder. "Lobster bake rehearsal dinner and welcome drinks on Friday evening, four-hundred-person wedding on Saturday, and the farewell brunch on Sunday. Three events in three days. You might be the experts for food service, but *we're* the experts in planning. The approach, if you will. I'm happy to sit down with you and Caleb to discuss the catering requirements, workflow, etcetera, after we've created our planning timeline for the next three months."

Holy shit, she's good.

I don't want to take my eyes off of her, but I can't miss Dad's reaction to this raking. He may not be in fighting shape these days, but he doesn't take someone speaking to him like this lightly.

"You're right, Brooke," he says.

I'm sorry, what?

"My apologies. Though one correction: Caleb will be your main point of contact on our end. I won't be working on this one. I'm not keen to work with your mother again, and I'm sure as shit she doesn't want to work with me."

Judy coughs in shock.

"You'll be working exclusively with Caleb," Dad says.

Brooke looks at her mother. Hannah may have explicitly asked for Brooke, forcing us to work together, but there's no way Judy is going to stay out of this wedding—a wedding that'll be the talk of the local industry and beyond. No fucking way.

"And Brooke will be leading on our end," Judy says. "With my supervision, of course."

Yes, of course.

Dad and I survive our first—and his last, supposedly—meeting with the Spencer women. They run a tight ship. For someone who only learned she booked this wedding an hour ago, Brooke knows what she's doing. But so do I.

Dad gets into the passenger side of his car. I hate driving his car, but he insisted.

"Caleb Foley!" I hear Brooke call from the porch.

Oh, I'm in trouble.

"You knew about this," she says, pointing at me as she skips down the steps and onto the sidewalk. "Last night at the party."

"Is that a question?"

She tilts her head to the side, raising her brows at me. In her heels she comes up to my shoulder. Her hair is down today, loose waves falling around her shoulders.

"Yes, Brooke, I knew."

"Why didn't you tell me?"

"Didn't seem like you wanted to chat with little old me, sweetheart."

"Don't call me sweetheart, you…" She searches for the right word. "You…jerk."

"Whoa." I bring my fist to my chest, feigning injury. "What a burn, Brooke. What a burn."

"Shut up," she says, her nose scrunching her face into a look of disgust. "I hate those cutesy nicknames, especially if you're the one saying them."

"I thought you wedding planners lived for all the cheesy lovey-dovey shit. Sweetheart, honeybuns, babe, baby."

"Ew, Caleb. I hate *babe*. Baby is even worse," she says, hands on her hips. I bite my cheek to keep from smiling at her and her indignant pose. "Not all of us wedding planners are the same, you know? I don't know your problem with us, but you're going to have to suck it up for the next three months."

"I can do that," I say. It won't be easy, but not for the reasons she thinks. And because I can't help messing with her, I whisper, "babe."

The exasperated look on her face makes me want to call her babe all summer long. "I'm sorry, I had to."

"Are you going to be this much of a pain in my ass all summer?" She's pretty adorable when she's annoyed with me.

"Can we please just be civil for the sake of this wedding? I need everything to be absolutely perfect. Pulling this off could change everything for me. Not one single thing can go wrong."

"Change everything?" I ask.

She shifts on her feet. "Forget I said that. Civil, okay?"

"Okay, okay." I hold my hands up in defeat. "I'll be civil from here on out."

"Thank you." She pulls her phone from a mystery pocket of her dress. "Does Thursday at two work for you to meet Hannah and Preston at the venue?" she asks, eyes glued to the calendar app on her phone.

"Yup."

She looks up at me like I just told her who dies in the most recent season of *The White Lotus*. Absolutely shocked.

"You just know you're available then?

I look at her screen. "Is that color-coded?" All the colors of the rainbow are represented across each day of the week. "Are you ever not working? When do you breathe? Do you ever have fun?"

"Obviously my calendar is color-coded! And, yes, I have fun. During the off-season."

"Believe it or not, I don't use a calendar." I tap my forehead with my index finger. "It's all up here."

"Actually," she says, rolling her eyes. "I very much believe that. Caleb, if you fuck up this wedding because you forget to show up for a meeting, so help me god!"

She has absolutely no trust in me, does she? It's a good reminder that I made the right decision before I left for California.

"Brooke, this wedding means a lot to me, too. I have no plans to fuck anything up. In fact, the plan I have is to prove everything you're thinking about me is wrong."

"Fine," she says. "I'll see you on Thursday."

"I'll pick you up for the meeting," I say, walking around to the driver's side of Dad's car. "Wouldn't want you to forget and fuck everything up."

I get into the car before she can protest.

"Enjoying yourself?" Dad asks as I start the engine and pull out into the street.

"Maybe a little." I can see him smiling to himself from the corner of my eye. At a red light, I turn to him. "Are you going to tell me what exactly that was in there?"

"I don't know what you're talking about, son," he says, shrugging and gazing out the window.

"You're right, Brooke. My apologies," I say in the deep voice I put on whenever I mimic him.

"Oh, that?"

"Yes...*that*!"

"It's complicated. And a longer story than we have time for."

We're heading across town on Post Road back to the Market, hitting every single red light on the way thanks to midday traffic. We've got time. I wait for him to elaborate.

"The Quincys may have come to us first, but Brooke is the planner and she's in charge. She was right about that, but your role is just as important. It's been years since I worked with Judy, but if I remember anything, it's best to keep the peace with a Spencer. So that's what I did."

There's plenty he isn't telling me, so this nugget of information will have to do for now. Brooke never struck me as very similar to her mom. They don't look much alike. Judy's skin isn't as fair as her daughter's and her hair is lighter, so blonde it's almost white. Brooke must have inherited most of her features from her dad, but he was out of the picture a long time ago, so I'll never know. They don't act alike either, or they never used to. Judy was cold and curt. Brooke was always warm and kind. Even if she's giving me shit now, and I can't blame her for that, she isn't mean. I don't think she has it in her. The only thing they seem to have in common is their careers. Unless Judy has rubbed off on her more over the last few years.

"Do you think she's become a lot like her mom?" I ask.

Dad's quiet as we hit yet another red light. "I don't know," he finally says. "She wasn't when you both were younger, when Judy and I were dragging you two around as we worked. Or when your mother watched the both of you. I always noticed how sweet Brooke was and thought to myself, how could she possibly be Judy's daughter? But I haven't seen her in years, Caleb. She has a good reputation, though. I hear nothing but praise about her work. I'm sure it'll be smooth sailing as long as Judy doesn't get too involved."

I bark a laugh. "I don't think she's going to stay very far from this wedding."

"No, I don't think she will."

We drive the rest of the way to only the sound of the radio.

Brooke's words linger in my mind. *This could change everything.*

What could she possibly need to change? She's the most popular planner in town. Everyone loves her. I...I push the thought out of my head. I can't go there. Brooke and I were friends once, we could be friends again. But nothing more.

Chapter 7

Brooke

THE RARE WEEKNIGHT WEDDING HOLDS A SPECIAL PLACE IN MY heart. I love the pomp and circumstance of an over-the-top three-hundred-person Saturday night wedding, with a twelve-piece band, three outfit changes for the bride, and a sparkler sendoff as much as the next wedding planner. But these more relaxed, smaller weddings are something special—and a hell of a lot easier.

Plus, this one is keeping my mind off Caleb and our meeting with Hannah Quincy tomorrow. But mostly Caleb.

Tonight's wedding is a small and intimate ceremony on the beach with a beautiful view of the Long Island Sound, followed by cocktails and dinner at a small beach club. Only fifty guests. I could do this in my sleep.

The ceremony was lovely, short and sweet, and the weather is everything you dream of for an early summer night. Warm enough for a new summer dress with a gentle breeze coming in off the coast. Guests gather on the clubhouse porch for cocktails as a trio of musicians play pop covers on string instruments. After assessing the scene and checking off *Cocktail Hour*

Begins on my timeline, I move inside for one last check before the reception begins.

"Could you ask the waitstaff to begin lighting all of the votives?" I ask one of the servers.

Everything is in place, as it was an hour ago. Four long farmhouse tables fill one side of the room. There are sheer ivory table runners along each table, on top of them are mismatched vintage plates and glassware of various blues. Bright but soft late-spring florals weave across the tables in a way that looks perfectly haphazard, meticulously arranged by the florist.

On the opposite side of the room, the five-person band finishes setting up before moving into a quiet sound check. Small weddings make for some of the best dancing. Families are closer and more comfortable with one another, happy to dance and let loose without copious amounts of alcohol.

Flipping through my clipboard for the seating chart, I check the place cards for the third time. The grooms put so much care and consideration into the seating arrangements tonight. It's another thing I love about these smaller weddings. They've put together old friends who haven't seen each other in ages. There are two single guests who they've been trying to set up for years. Is it ridiculous that I'm checking these again, when I'm the one who arranged them originally and reviewed the chart with my clients half a dozen times? Yes, it is. But I wouldn't be this good at my job if I didn't ensure every detail was perfect.

My phone buzzes in my hand.

> Unknown number: Nice fanny pack.

There's only one person who would give me grief about my fanny pack.

Glancing around the room, I only see the waitstaff lighting

votes and the band tuning their instruments. Guests are still out on the patio.

No sign of Caleb. Where the hell is he and what is he doing here?

Hands land on my shoulders from behind. "Hey!"

"Jesus Christ!" I jump, dropping both my clipboard and phone on the floor. I turn around and swat Caleb's arm.

"Ow!" he fakes. I keep myself from actually saying *ow*. His arm is solid. Super solid. And now it's scooping up my clipboard and phone from the floor.

"I have guests coming in here in fifteen minutes! What are you doing here, Caleb?"

"Nice to see you too, Brooke," he says. "I've got a wedding here next weekend. Thought I'd come see the space. Didn't think it'd be occupied on a Wednesday night, but when Joey told me he was working and you were the planner, I had to come see you in action. Make sure you're up to my standards if I'm going to be working with you."

"If *I'm* up to *your* standards?" I blow out a breath. "You've got to be kidding. You know I'm good at my job, Caleb."

Caleb, now standing back up, still has my clipboard and phone.

"Gimme those!" I grab for them, but he takes a step back.

"Let me look over this timeline." He skims through the pages on my clipboard. I don't even let Maddie, my best friend and most trusted colleague, hold my clipboard, let alone other vendors. They each receive their own final copy via email the night before and printouts the day. He'll be reacquainted with my planning style and timelines soon enough.

I cross my arms and start tapping my foot. "Caleb, I'm serious, I need that!"

He smiles and it looks genuine. "Not too bad." He hands me my beloved clipboard.

I hold out my free hand to him. "And my phone?" I'd like

to tear it from his hands, but I can't do that in front of wedding guests.

"You promise not to block my new number?"

"I'll wait until after the Quincy wedding, since unfortunately I'll have to communicate with you regularly for the rest of the summer."

"Works for me." He hands me my phone, and I place it in my belt bag.

"Will you be on your way now?"

"Believe it or not, I didn't come here to bother you, Brooke," he says. "As much as I enjoy it. I need to see the kitchen and what I'm dealing with. I won't be long. No one will know I'm here." He winks and walks away.

I'm behind on my timeline now, but the only behind I'm concerned about in this moment is Caleb's as it walks away in snug dark wash jeans. It's not fair that he's somehow gotten more attractive over the last five years.

Get it together, Brooke.

Where was I? I shake my head, take a breath, and look down at the timeline. I'm not about to let Caleb or his behind let me get behind on this wedding. He cannot mess up any of my plans.

Chapter 8

Caleb

I'll never tell Brooke this, but hers is the most organized timeline I've ever seen, and I worked with a few celebrity planners in San Francisco who are supposed to be the best in the country. Not surprisingly, it was color-coded like her calendar. This time by vendor with key moments of the night in bold. The margins on her copy were full of notes, and everything up until 6:45 p.m. had been checked off. The small pout on her face as I was reading it was cuter than the angry face she made at me a couple of days ago.

Brooke Spencer. So practical in her crewneck sleeveless black dress, wearing her little fanny pack, tapping her foot with her arms crossed against her chest. The way she tilted her head up at me caused the brown waves of her high ponytail to sway against her shoulders.

I know I'm smiling to myself like an idiot as I head into the kitchen of the Seafarer Beach Club. No way I'm letting her see that. How the hell am I going to get through this summer?

When Dad told me Mrs. Quincy had hired us for Hannah's wedding, I was ecstatic. Three events, three menus, and a chance to level up Foley's in the eyes of the industry. For decades, Dad's been growing Foley's to be a full-service events company, but some people still see us as just the caterers. Good caterers—fucking great caterers, actually. But still, we're the help. Our in-house wedding coordinators do a damn good job, too. Though I'm beginning to realize maybe not as good as Brooke and Spencer Soirees.

Then Dad dropped the bomb that Mrs. Quincy, on behalf of Hannah, was also insisting on a *real* planner. And that infuriated me. People like Mrs. Quincy, the wealthy families who've lived here forever, are exactly the kind of people that look at us as the cooks. The people at the little market where they grab some prepared foods for dinner when their chef has a night off. I know them, and the feeling of being looked down on, all too well.

Part of the reason I stayed in California for so long was to nurture the craft of hospitality and event management specifically for weddings like Hannah Quincy's. It's what Dad always wanted me to do. Bring Foley's into its next chapter.

This client is huge for Foley's and, while it's not my dream, I'm doing it for Dad. He's worked so hard his entire life to get the business to this point, and now we have to share it with a planner.

Not just any planner—Brooke. Daughter of Judy Spencer, the reason Dad stopped working with wedding planners. He and Mom have been tightlipped about the falling out, but it was bad enough that I knew better than to keep asking about it. But now that we're working with them, I can't not know. Judy's been a looming presence in my life for long enough, ever since Brooke and I worked the same weddings at the country club. We had the best time together, but we both knew our parents wouldn't be thrilled about our friendship.

We worked hard and had fun. Okay, Brooke worked hard, but we both had fun. Brooke's always been organized and put together, focused on following in her mom's footsteps. While

I'd been—let's just say not so motivated. I was content to get by and push off the inevitable for as long as possible.

At the end of each wedding, I'd make sure Brooke got home safely. She'd tell her mom she was getting a ride from one of the other planning assistants, but it was always me. We'd go to the Duchess drive-thru for grilled cheeses and fries. I'd park a few houses down from theirs and we'd eat and laugh at whatever antics happened that night until we were too tired to talk anymore. She'd text me when she was in the house, and I'd count down the moments until our next wedding together.

It never went further than that. No matter how much I wanted it to. Or how much I sensed she wanted it to. I always held back.

Now, though, she wants nothing to do with me. Not after how we left things.

I can handle this. I'm used to working with planners. Though I'm not used to working with a planner *I've* had a falling out with. I'll have to keep playing the part I've resigned myself to in order to get through the summer.

I push open the double doors to the kitchen.

"Caleb!" Joey calls out to me from the prep table. He's the real reason I'm here. I was going to swing by tomorrow morning when the club manager said I could, then Joey mentioned he'd be here tonight working with Brooke. I couldn't resist.

"Hey man," I say, looking around the space. It's not too bad for a seasonal club that mostly serves snack bar fare. "I'll stay out of your way, going to take a look around." I know better than to interrupt him in the middle of plating.

"Go for it. But if you stick around too long, you're going to have to wash dishes for me."

I scoff and walk to the back of the kitchen. It has plenty of prep space, a few ovens, and easy access to the main room for the servers. I can prep here on Saturday without having to bring much in. The Market is absolute chaos on Saturdays. I'd rather be out of there if I can. It'll also be a welcome break from a full catering tent. Humid summer nights firing up surf and turf over a hot stove aren't ideal working conditions, but they're the conditions that come with the job.

From the back of the kitchen, I hear the doors swing open followed by the clacking sound of heels. How she does this in heels, I'll never know.

"Guests are seated and we're ready for salads," Brooke says to Joey.

Through the chandelier of pots and pans hanging in the middle of the kitchen, I watch her meticulously check off multiple items on her timeline. Behind her, servers are lined up to collect platters of salads to serve to the awaiting guests. Brooke stands by the door, inspecting each tray of plates with narrow eyes as they go out the doors. Come on. She's become one of those micromanaging planners. *Great.* Just as I think I'll be able to handle this, that it might be enjoyable.

Joey's an excellent chef and experienced caterer. He plated the salads himself. Brooke doesn't need to handle quality control. I'm tempted to emerge from my hiding spot and call her out for the excessive supervision, but I can't step on Joey's toes like that. This is his gig, and I wouldn't appreciate it if someone, even one of my oldest friends, stepped in on one of my jobs. Unless it's to help wash dishes.

Brooke doesn't find anything wrong with the salads—I'm not surprised—and follows the last server out.

"What was that about?" I walk back over to Joey. He's moved on to plating the entrees.

He doesn't look up from the assembly line in front of him. "What was what about?"

"That," I say, pointing to where Brooke stood moments ago. "Brooke inspecting all of the salads looking for mistakes."

Joey looks away from his work at my sharper-than-intended tone. "Eh, she always does that," he says. "It drove me nuts at first, but she caught a few mistakes. Nothing major, just inconsistencies, and it's been helpful."

Helpful? Since when is having a wedding planner nitpick your plating helpful?

"Listen," he says. "She's a bit of a perfectionist and concerned with everything being perfect. Like per-*fect*. But she's helped me step up my plating. I've landed some much fancier weddings since I started listening to her."

"Humph, interesting." I hadn't noticed before, but Joey does look more professional now than he ever did when he was employed by my dad. For one, his chef coat is immaculate. Not a single stain or speck of food. That was once his signature look. Seeing the care in how he plated the entrees, I don't doubt he's improved.

"Something you don't have to worry about with all that new experience and your dad never working with planners." Joey laughs.

"Not anymore," I mumble, running my fingers through my hair and looking away from Joey. I haven't had a chance to share the recent turn of events with him, and somehow the news hasn't spread. Judy must not be so eager to share this particular piece of industry gossip or it would have already made its way to him.

"What?" Joey turns his head to the spot where Brooke had been standing and back to me. "No way," he says, eyes wide, letting out a loud guffaw. "Spencer Soirees and Foley's Fine Catering, working together? I don't believe it."

He's loving this.

"Believe it. We're doing the Quincy wedding Labor Day weekend. Hannah wanted to hire us *and* Brooke."

"So, you," he says, pointing to me and back to the door, "and Brooke...working...together?"

I shrug and fist my hands into my pockets. "Yup."

"Wow." He shakes his head and goes back to plating. "I mean, you're both the best of the best. This could be good for you guys and your relationship."

"Our working relationship," I clarify. "Yes, it will be great for that."

"Sure, sure. You're not worried about your *feelings*?"

He knows right where to hit me. "No, I'm not worried about my *feelings*. I'm worried about pulling off the biggest wedding of my career so far and dealing with an overbearing perfectionist wedding planner who isn't all that thrilled to be working with me. Did you see her timeline? It's color-coded!"

Joey taps the corner of the long prep table. There's a copy of Brooke's timeline with Joey's chicken scratch in the margins and checkmarks of his own. I take a closer look. It's color-coded but it looks different from the version I paged through earlier. Like it's been personalized for each vendor.

I scoff. Of course it is.

"What? It's helpful!" Joey says. "Listen man, I've got to keep plating these, but working with Brooke isn't that bad. She might drive you crazy with her notes, checklists, and occasional snippy tone, and she's definitely going to drive you crazy because you still have—"

"Joseph, don't you dare finish that sentence."

He has the gall to laugh.

"Okay, okay," he says. "Get out of here before you get stuck with dishwashing duty."

"I'll see you later man," I say, pushing the doors into the main room.

The guests are finishing up their perfectly inspected salads. A few couples are dancing. I spot Brooke across the room looking out to the dance floor, hugging her beloved clipboard to her chest. She's wearing the first genuine smile I've seen since I saw her Sunday night. Her eyes are on one of the older couples dancing, her body swaying ever so slightly to the rhythm of the song. Thoughts of dancing with her, having that smile directly at me flood my head without my consent. I blame Joey. When I shake the images away, I see Brooke looking right back at me, smile gone.

Well, that settles that. I give her a wave and leave.

Chapter 9

Brooke

CALEB IS LATE.

Shocking.

I'm sitting on the front steps of the office and look at my watch. Again.

I should have never agreed to letting him drive. The more I can separate myself from him this summer, the better. We're going to have to attend several meetings together, communicate regularly, and spend all of Labor Day weekend together. That's more than enough. I dig through my bag for my car keys. If I leave now, I can make it a few minutes early.

The double honk of a horn sounds from the street.

Caleb pulls up in his navy Jeep Wrangler. The same car he would drive me home from the country club in. The roof and sides are off. That was fun in my early twenties, but now it's going to ruin my hair before an important meeting.

"You're late," I say, pushing off the steps.

"Late? The meeting starts at two and it's only ten minutes away." He looks at the clock on the dashboard. "It's 1:45!"

"I'm always early to meetings. Early is on time and on time

is late." I stand next to where the passenger door should be. How the hell does one get in and out of this thing in heels?

Caleb stares. "Are you getting in? It's going to be your fault we're late."

I place my foot on the step and attempt to grab the frame above me, which isn't easy with my purse, workbag, and a big-ass water bottle in my hands. Taking hold, I hoist myself up and into the car. I overshoot and tumble over the center console right into Caleb, my free hand landing high. *High* on his thigh.

He looks at me, eyes wide, before fixing his face into a neutral expression. "Graceful, Brooke," he says with a laugh.

When I realize my hand is still on his thigh, I pull away quickly, straightening myself in the passenger seat. I turn to look out the…well, to just look out, hoping Caleb can't see the fire I feel flushing my cheeks.

"Just drive," I say.

He shifts into drive and we're on our way. The landscape quickly changes from quaint downtown to the older beach neighborhood. It feels like you've been dropped in the middle of Nantucket or Martha's Vineyard. People who have the audacity to say Connecticut isn't part of New England have clearly never seen these picturesque views.

We pull into the circular driveway in front of a magnificent multi-million-dollar waterfront home, one I recognize from Hannah's many Instagram posts and stories. Not Hannah's current home, but the home where she spends holidays and summer weekends. Her family home.

"Welcome to the venue," Caleb says, cutting the engine.

The what? I assumed the wedding was going to be held at Charter Oaks Country Club down the road. I'm entirely too distracted lately. We're only a few days into this partnership and I've already let Caleb rattle me enough that I'm not focused.

"Excuse me?" My mouth hangs open a moment before I remember I need to be presentable. The wedding is here. A backyard wedding. Mom failed to include that bit of important information. We have three months to plan an at-home, backyard wedding. For four hundred people.

Shit.

Though there is something oh-so *Father of the Bride* about a backyard wedding that makes my little wedding planner heart sing. Especially when, like the Banks' family home in the film, the houses are gorgeous classic colonials like this one. Only, this one is a lot bigger. Thousands of square feet bigger. The Quincys live on the more historical side of the beach neighborhood where the houses are old and the money is older.

I do love a backyard wedding, but they're particularly labor-intensive. Often, I end up convincing couples not to do one unless they're going for an extremely causal vibe or have the means to do it right—like the Quincys do.

This venue means bringing in every single thing. Caleb will have to construct a full catering tent, bring in all the required appliances, and install a generator. Every single piece of furniture we need will have to be brought in. Everything from the tent to the butter knives will have to be rented. There's trash collection, traffic flow, and parking to think about. I'd better give my contact at the police station a call. What's the noise ordinance for this part of town? Eleven o'clock? For the right price, I'm sure we can arrange an extension to midnight. Have the Quincys spoken to their neighbors? Invited them? There is a good amount of land between them, but a wedding of this size will inconvenience the neighborhood during an already busy holiday weekend.

I'm so caught up in the mental checklist of our tasks for the next three months that I don't notice Caleb get out of the car until he's standing next to the doorless passenger side, holding his hand out for me.

"I can get out on my own," I scoff.

"Based on how gracefully you got into the car, I doubt it," he says. "Just take my hand, Brooke."

I collect my things and attempt to get out on my own. It's not going well. I can't manage holding on to the frame of the car and my belongings at the same time. "Fine," I sigh, taking his hand and hopping out with a tad more grace than I had getting in. When I let go, my hand tingles.

We stand side by side, taking in the beautiful house. It's a stone colonial-style mansion with exquisite landscaping. A stunning, one-of-a-kind wedding venue.

I wish I could control the weather. This wedding is going to be epic. The only thing that could ruin it, besides Caleb fucking something up, is the weather. To-dos continue to spiral through my head. Cocktail hour around dusk means they should spray for ticks and mosquitoes. I'll need to check what time sunset is on the wedding day so I can build in time for the photographer to get some golden hour photos. I need to call Jordan. I should have texted her the second I found out about this wedding. And I'll need to come up with a rain plan.

I have the urge to smack Caleb. So, I do. Right in his toned, muscular arm. *Ow.* I need to stop doing that. He's wearing a short-sleeve button-down linen shirt, sleeves tight over his biceps. The light blue color brings out his tan, which only makes his arms more appealing.

"Geez, Brooke," he groans. "Do you hit all of your caterers?!"

"Just you. When were you going to tell me this was a backyard wedding? No one mentioned that tiny little detail."

He smirks and that dimple has to make an appearance. "Afraid you can't hack it?"

"Of course not! I can plan a backyard wedding in three months, I've done it before. But the wedding of the year? Do you have any idea how much work I have ahead of me?"

"Believe it or not, I do."

The double front doors of the home swing open.

"They're here!" a beautiful blonde calls back into the house as she bounces down the front steps. It's not Hannah, but she looks familiar.

"Shit," Caleb says, under his breath.

"What?" I whisper.

Before he can answer, the blonde's made her way to us. To Caleb. She wraps him in a hug and I watch them with narrowed eyes. The way she's holding him is very...affectionate.

"Caleb," she says, pulling away from the hug but leaving her hands on his shoulders. "It's been too long. It's so good to see you."

Caleb's stiff as a board. Who is she and how does she know Caleb? And why does it look like he wants to speed away in the Wrangler, leaving a trail of dust in his wake? Seeing him this uncomfortable should bring me immense joy, but it doesn't.

"Hi!" I interrupt, extending my hand to her. "I'm Brooke from Spencer Soirees."

She finally lets go of her grip on Caleb, and I don't miss the quiet exhale of relief he lets out.

"Oh my god! Hannah and I are so excited to meet you! I told her there was no way you'd still be available on such short notice, but I was wrong! Normally I hate being wrong, but this time I'm so glad I was." Her hands are now on my shoulders and squeezing tightly. Too tightly. Before I know it, I'm engulfed in one of the tightest hugs I've ever experienced. I look at Caleb with pleading eyes that say *who the fuck is this, why is she hugging me,* and *we're in this together whether we like it or not, I recused you, now you have to rescue me!*

He seems to relax at the expense of my peril. "Brooke," he says, with a laugh that makes my stomach flip. I want to hear him say my name like that again. "This is Jennifer."

I'm released from Jennifer's arms as quickly as I was engulfed into them.

"Oh my god! I'm so rude. Please forgive me. There's just so much excitement today and I've completely forgotten my manners! Jennifer, maid of honor, reporting for duty!" She salutes me then turns, bounding up the steps. "Hannah and Preston are inside."

We follow a few paces behind her. "What was that all about?" I whisper to Caleb as we enter the grand foyer. If it's possible, the inside is more stunning than the outside. Classic transitional style with modern touches. Not stuffy and dated like I've come to expect from some of our clients with this kind of generational wealth.

"First, no one tells me it's a backyard wedding," I say through clenched teeth. "Now you've also forgotten to mention you know the maid of honor?"

"I barely know Jennifer," he says, but I don't believe him. "She's just a hugger."

"That was the most aggressive hug I've ever received. I think I'm going to have bruises on both of my shoulders."

Caleb places his hands on my shoulders, giving a gentle squeeze. It feels good. Better than I want it to. "You'll be fine," he says. This isn't going to work if Caleb keeps touching me. I shake my shoulders and he removes the loose grip.

"It might be time for shoulder pads to come back in style," I say.

"I'd pay good money to see you wearing some '80s blazers."

"You've seen me in shoulder pads, Caleb," I say. "The first Warehouse Party I went to was an '80s theme. I wore my mom's old pink cheetah blazer and teased my hair."

He laughs with his whole chest. "How could I forget that ensemble?"

I'm brought back to the summers I was home from college,

working and snickering with Caleb in the corner about how drunk the guests were and critiquing their dancing. I didn't realize how much I missed that laugh.

"C'mon, let's find out exactly how massive this to-do list is going to be," Caleb says, leading me behind Jennifer with his hand on the small of my back.

I gasp audibly when I step into the room and see the wall-to-wall built-in bookshelves filled to the brim. The room is painted a dark navy, but large windows let in plenty of light and the beige furniture provides a nice contrast.

Hannah's a picture of Instagram perfection sitting on a love seat next to her fiancé, Preston. Her dark brown hair, so dark it almost looks black, is pulled off her face with a simple thin headband. She's dressed in jeans, a white shirt, and a navy cardigan. It might be a simple outfit, but it screams money. Preston looks like he came in right off the golf course. He probably did. They're huddled close together, each holding one side of an iPad. Hannah is swiping across the screen repeatedly. In front of them, the coffee table is covered with swatches of fabric, catalogs of rentals, and papers with estimates. The mess of it all makes my eye twitch.

In the corner of the room, Mr. and Mrs. Quincy stand at the wet bar. I recognize them from the country club. Mr. Quincy holds a cocktail shaker and pours the golden contents into lowball glasses. Mrs. Quincy takes each glass and places it on a tray. A well-practiced ritual.

"The dream team is here, everyone!" Jennifer says, gesturing to Caleb and me.

All eyes in the room are on us at once. Or are they all focused on Caleb? Yes, they are definitely focused on Caleb.

Mr. Quincy puts the cocktail shaker down and walks over to us. "Caleb, long time no see, my boy."

"Hi, Mr. Quincy." Caleb extends his hand. "Mrs. Quincy." He nods in her direction as he shakes Mr. Quincy's hand.

Mrs. Quincy walks over to us with the tray of drinks. "Whiskey sour?" Preston, Hannah, and Jennifer each grab a glass from the tray. I shake my head. A drink might calm my nerves, but I'm too busy trying to figure out the dynamic here. Trying to put together the pieces. "And please, call us Susan and Doug. You don't have to follow the country club rules when you're in our home."

Hannah gets up from the love seat and gives Caleb a hug that's not nearly as aggressive as Jennifer's. "Caleb, it's so great to see you!"

"Nice to meet you, Caleb." Preston comes up behind his fiancée and shakes Caleb's hand. "When Jennifer told us she had an ex who's a chef, we weren't sure what to make of it, but then she told us it was someone at Foley's and, well, here we are!"

That explains a few things. But when did Caleb date Jennifer?

I rack my brain for any memory of their relationship and I come up empty. There's a twinge in my chest that I ignore. I'm here to work, not think about Caleb any more than I need to.

"You're good to do this, Caleb," Mr. Quincy says, taking a sip of his drink. "I wasn't sure you'd agree to it. It was quite the spectacle when Jennifer's father found out about you two."

"Mr. Q!" Jennifer groans playfully. "Let's not bring that up!"

Caleb's tense again. His hands fist at his side, and his jawline looks more defined, like he's clenching hard. Our clients don't seem to notice.

"Oh Jennifer, it was years ago," Mr. Quincy says with a laugh. "Caleb's over it by now, aren't you boy?"

I wish Doug would stop calling him *boy*. He's thirty-two for god's sake. This man is ribbing him over what sounds like a dramatic breakup. It's childish. Caleb isn't the one acting like a boy.

I need to take control of this situation—both the awkwardness of whatever is happening right now and the mess of all things wedding covering the coffee table. My eye's still twitching.

"Hi, everyone!" I put on my most gentle and soothing voice. The voice that calms the most nervous bride. That never swears. The voice that says *I have my shit together and everyone is going to shut up and listen to me*. I step forward to put space between the Quincys and Caleb. "I'm Brooke, it's so wonderful to meet all of you! What do you say we get started on planning this amazing wedding weekend? We have a lot to do this summer, don't we?"

I settle into one of the armchairs and look back at Caleb. His lips curl into a soft smile and his dimple shows again. He gives me a nod of thanks. I open my notebook to get started. We're in it together now.

Chapter 10

Caleb

Two hours and, for the Quincy family, three rounds of whiskey sours later, we're heading back to Spencer Soirees. Brooke did a much better job of getting into the car this time. It helped that I insisted on holding her bags.

Once Brooke took control of the meeting, it went better than I'd expected after those first few minutes. Despite the short amount of time to plan, and the chaos of the coffee table that made Brooke visibly anxious, Hannah and Preston have a beautiful vision. And Mr. Quincy—I can't bring myself to call him Doug, old habits and all—has the deep pockets to bring his daughter's dream wedding to life.

I knew there was a chance Jennifer would be there, but I didn't believe life was cruel enough to throw that into the mix. Jennifer and I ended things *mutually* the summer before I left for San Francisco, despite what Mr. Quincy seems to think. Our short relationship was such a textbook cliché: The rich country club girl sneaks around with a member of the staff for the summer to piss off her parents.

It wasn't the relationship that made me react the way I did. We had a fun summer. It's how it ended and the emotions that often come with remembering. Mr. Quincy wasn't wrong that Jennifer's dad wasn't thrilled to learn about us. I remember his words to Jennifer as if I heard them yesterday: "Fooling around with a line cook, Jennifer? You could've at least aimed for the tennis pro." It still stings. And it brings up other feelings about a different person that I don't want to think about.

Even without any further mention of my relationship with Jennifer, I couldn't relax. I was restless the entire meeting, shifting in my chair and struggling to focus.

I turn on the radio as soon as I start the car, hoping for a quiet ride back. It's a short enough ride that I might get away without divulging too much. But Brooke is her mother's daughter, and she might love the drama and gossip as much as Judy, though she never did before. Brooke writes feverishly in her notebook as I drive. At the rate she's writing, she must go through four or five notebooks a month.

We pull up to the building and I cut the engine. Brooke puts her notebook in the bag at her feet.

"So...." She clasps her hands in her lap and turns to me. "You barely know Jennifer, huh?" She cocks her head, raising a brow. She's wearing her hair down today and the short strands in front fall across her face. She's quite satisfied to witness me in this situation, but there's a kindness in her eyes. The same kindness that interrupted Jennifer's hug and kept today's meeting on track.

I loosen my grip on the steering wheel, blowing out a breath. "Here I thought you were letting me off the hook after that quiet drive back."

"Based on that meeting, she'll be involved with the planning," Brooke says. "I don't need the whole dramatic saga, but a little background might be helpful. I'm the last one to know about anything with this wedding. It's getting old. I need to know what I'm dealing with here. I can't create a plan without the details."

The pit in my stomach urges me to tell her everything. About Jennifer and what her dad said. How that's all connected to Brooke and why I did what I did before leaving for San Francisco. But I can't. It will make this whole situation even more complicated than it already is. So I go with the short answer.

"Jennifer's great, I mean that," I say. "And so are Hannah and Preston, as I'm sure you can tell. But Hannah's parents are…they mean well, but they're…"

"…affected…WASP-y…pretty fucking rude?" She says it all with a hint of indignation.

I love seeing her when she's not playing the part of perfect wedding planner. The side of her that isn't trying to be polished or polite and says *fuck* regularly. The side I used to see a lot more of.

"Sure, a little bit of all those things." I laugh. "Jennifer and I dated for a couple months the summer before I left for San Francisco. But it ran its course and we ended things."

Her blue eyes narrow. "The summer before you left?"

Shit.

I've been so caught up in my own feelings that I forgot about Brooke's. I may have been dating Jennifer, but Brooke and I were inseparable at the weddings we worked that summer. Just friends, but…

"Mr. Quincy made it sound pretty rough," Brooke says, moving on from things she may want to forget about, too.

"It's not that dramatic, I promise," I tell her. "There's no need to try to keep her away from me. This wedding is as big of a deal to me as it is to you and I'm going to treat it that way."

"You better, Caleb." She offers a smile. "But if anything changes, let me know. I don't need a heartsick caterer ruining this one, so I've got your back. Not for your sake, obviously. My mom wouldn't let me hear the end of it."

A heartsick caterer. She has no idea that's what she's already dealing with.

"Oh, I'm sure she wouldn't. Looking forward to unpacking that relationship with you."

She gives me a puzzled look. "What do you mean? There's nothing to unpack. My mom and I are great," she says, all too fast.

"If you say so."

"Goodbye, Caleb." She hops out of the car on her own and I hand her the ridiculously large water bottle she seems to drag everywhere. "I'll send you a meeting recap tonight."

"Will it be color-coded?"

She smiles. "What do you think?"

Of course it will. I turn the engine back on.

"See ya later…babe!" I call from the car.

As expected, she rolls her eyes but with a soft laugh. It feels good to be the one making her laugh again. It's been a draining afternoon, but that sound will carry me through the rest of the week.

Between moving back, getting reacquainted with Foley's, and the Quincy wedding, my first week home has been a complete whirlwind. On top of that, I've got a four-year-old corgi to take care of. If Brooke is my pseudo-rival this summer, then my parents' dog, Wendell, is my nemesis. He's never been a fan of me, but Mom's focused on taking care of Dad and Wendell's a little needy. I wasn't here to help right after Dad had his heart attack, the least I can do is take care of the dog now.

After scooping Wendell up from my parents' and struggling to get him buckled into the safety harness Mom insists I use, I'm running late for my meeting with the real estate agent. Thank god this meeting isn't with Brooke, she'd have my neck.

But it might be worth it to see the look she makes when she's mad. Does she know she bites the inside of her lip and her cheeks go pink when she's angry?

This isn't the look I envisioned if I ever had a dog in this car. It's a Jeep. I should have a *real* dog, a German shepherd or golden retriever, not a little corgi in a baby-blue harness. It's not doing great things for my brooding caterer-slash-chef persona. When he's finally settled in the passenger seat, I text the agent that I'm on my way.

The drive away from downtown and into the backcountry is beautiful. The smell of fresh cut grass in the air. I take the backroads so I can drive slower with Wendell in the car. He must smell a lot more than me because his nose leads his head in every direction as we drive, but he's content and not nipping at me (for once). Maybe the harness was a good idea after all.

It's nice to get away from downtown. It's stifling sometimes. It sounds ridiculous when I was in a bustling, crowded city for years, but at least there I could be anonymous. Just another guy in the city doing my job. Charter Oaks, as much as I love it and have missed it, is a place where everyone knows me and my business. They know I'm the one who gave my parents a hard time and fucked around with my career in my early twenties. They know I'm the catering guy's son. The help. In San Francisco I was still me, still that guy, but no one knew that, so they couldn't judge me for it.

Charter Oaks will always be home. Whether I want it to be or not, my future is taking over Foley's. Running the market and catering. It's what my parents—and everyone in town—expect of me.

I don't want to let them down, but I do want to see what I might be able to do for myself. Even if I never get to actually do it.

"The main house is move-in ready. The guest house and barn, which is what you seem more interested in, need renovations. The current owners sold most of the acreage to the nearby working farms, but you're still looking at about five acres," Melissa says. She's the real estate agent I impulsively messaged before setting my phone to airplane mode on my flight back.

For years, I've casually searched properties in the area to see if anything felt right. A few came up here and there, but I never did anything about it. Now the dream of my own farm-to-table restaurant is just that—a dream. Maintaining operations at Foley's will keep me busy enough. My path has been chosen for me.

I shouldn't have made this appointment, because now I know what's possible. Seeing the vision I've been curating in my mind stretched out before me makes it so much harder to *not* forge my own path.

The main house is set back further on the property, with a guest house between the main house and the barn. It must have been the main house originally. I bet Joey could help me find out some of the history. It's older, with a beautiful, wide wraparound porch. In need of renovations is perfect. I can work to keep the historical farmhouse charm but install a state-of-the-art kitchen. Nearby farms would be our vendors, and the menu could change seasonally.

Between the barn and the guest house are rows of overgrown garden beds. A small kitchen garden for seasonal vegetables and herbs would be a nice touch…if I knew how to garden. The barn—well, I don't know what I'd do with the barn, but it's got potential.

"So, a restaurant?" Melissa walks up the guest house porch stairs. The porch could fit half a dozen two- and four-tops. Calling this a guest house implies it's significantly smaller than the main house. It is, but not by much.

"That's the plan." We walk through the first floor. There's

an addition in the back that I'd gut for the kitchen. I'd update the rest to keep the charm of the space. In the corner built-ins of what was once the dining room, I'd display local artwork. The living room fireplace, if we can get it working, would help the restaurant feel much cozier in the winter.

"Let me know when you've made up your mind," Melissa says when we get back to my car.

If only it were that easy. I'm expected to carry on the family business as it exists today. Maybe if I hadn't lollygagged my way through my twenties, my parents would support an addition to the Foley's brand. But I did, and it's time to make it up to them.

Chapter 11

Brooke

The office is a flutter of activity after Caleb drops me off. Most businesses are closing their doors around five o'clock, but the staff here is in the middle of their day. Busy couples can't meet during the typical workday, so meetings and calls happen when it's convenient for them. Planners type away on their keyboards. There's a consultation in the conference room. Two assistants assemble guest gift bags to drop off at nearby hotels for this weekend's weddings.

Maddie's on the phone when I stop at my desk to drop my bags before heading to Judy's office. Judy's been texting me all afternoon, sending me questions to ask or reminders to mention certain items at the meeting. Like I haven't been doing this job for six years, working in the service industry long before that, and learning from her since I was five.

I don't mind keeping her in the loop—it's her company after all—but the constant micromanaging grates. All my experience isn't enough for her to trust me to do my job. I take a deep breath just outside her office where she can't see me, mentally preparing for the onslaught of questions and critiques.

"Hi Judy," I say, settling into a chair.

"Ah, there's my girl." Apparently, it's okay for her to acknowledge that I'm her daughter at the office, but not the other way around. "Too busy to answer my texts?"

"As a matter of fact, yes, it was a busy meeting." I straighten my shoulders. Confidence is crucial with Judy. "You forgot to mention this is an outdoor, backyard, at-home wedding. There was a lot to cover. And before you ask, we reviewed the full at-home wedding checklist and they have everything covered. Parking's arranged. They've spoken to, and invited, all of their neighbors. Landscapers are scheduled."

She purses her lips, and it occurs to me that this was all a test I didn't know I was taking.

"What about—"

"Trash? Handled. Mosquitoes? The yard will be sprayed four days before the wedding. Catering tent? Caleb's on it. Bathrooms? Confirmed the luxury package from Flush King while we were there. Anything else?"

"Well, you certainly seem to have it all covered," she says with a pinched frown, like it's a bad thing to be excellent at my job.

Shit. That look. My tone slipped. Sometimes confidence is interpreted as defiance and she does not like that. I have to tread carefully now.

She needs to know I can handle this, like I've handled every other wedding, to perfection. But I can't upset her to the point where we get into our usual fight. The one that starts with her accusing me of thinking she's a terrible mother. It turns to me being ungrateful for everything she's done for me. In the end, she's in tears and I'm apologizing. I'm never entirely sure what I'm apologizing for, but it's the only way to end the argument. I'm in no mood for it now. It's been a long afternoon, and a dull throb is beginning to pulse at my temple.

"I've got this," I say, smiling sincerely. "Just like you taught me."

She started Spencer Soirees at our kitchen table in the small garage-loft we rented. It was set behind a mansion on an estate in the country part of town where she moved us when I was barely two. That must have been when my dad left, but I'll never get that story. Mom was a waitress and occasionally helped our landlords with lavish parties at their home, of which there were many. She started with serving and cleaning before slowly starting to help with some of the planning—brainstorming themes, handling vendors, overseeing the event. Guests started asking for her number to help with their own parties.

And thus, Spencer Soirees was born. When I wasn't in school, she'd drag me all around town for meetings and site visits. I'd do my homework while she made vendor calls and wrote out timelines. She didn't have a village around to help her, so she taught me to sit quietly with my books and coloring pages while she took meetings at clients' homes or coffee shops. I remember clients and vendors alike commenting on how well-behaved I was. Mom telling them that I was her perfect little girl. I'd beam a toothy smile proudly. The praise trained me to be obedient and perfect. I wanted Mom to be proud of me so I could continue to tag along.

It's no surprise I fell in love with wedding planning. I was enamored with the beauty of it all. And I'm still striving to be her perfect little girl.

But as I've gotten better and better at my job, I feel less perfect in Mom's eyes. Lately, perfect isn't enough for her. Any little slip-up or possible mistake is caught and called out.

"I did teach you well," she says, smiling proudly. "Didn't I?"

Crisis averted, for now. I relax in my seat, but my head continues to ache.

"You did and you know it," I smile, and she glows. "Now let me show you their design inspiration! You're going to love it."

Event design always puts her in a good mood. Even when she loathes a couple's vision, she loves the game of taking it, reworking, and making it better. Playing with all the pieces until it's good enough to be a Spencer Soirees wedding. We spend the next hour gushing over Hannah and Preston's vision.

It's close to seven o'clock before we wrap up. I rub my temple discreetly before gathering my files and papers from the desk.

"Oh dear," she says, pursuing her lips again. "Not one of your little headaches, is it?" Not discreet enough.

If it wouldn't cause even more pain, I'd roll my eyes. Mom's been dismissing my attacks since I was diagnosed with episodic migraine as a teenager. When we left the doctor's office, she told me it didn't sound like a real issue but took me to CVS to fill my prescription anyway. I try to hide any indication that an attack is coming on, and I'm usually successful. She truly has no idea how often I have *one of my little headaches*. Especially after we had a blowout fight about it a few years ago. It ended with me apologizing for accusing her of being a bad mother who didn't care about her own flesh and blood. (Her words, not mine.) She never once apologized for being so dismissive of my legitimate diagnosis. Instead, she called me dramatic and attention-seeking.

"It's nothing," I say. "Just been a long day, I'm tired."

"If you say so, dear," she says, picking up her purse to leave for the day.

At my desk, after making sure Mom has left, I take my medication and say a silent prayer that I didn't miss the window that guarantees I won't have to go right to bed with an ice pack when I get home. If I don't catch an attack in time, it can mean worlds of pain and discomfort. The last thing I want to do tonight is prepare a meeting recap for Caleb and create a design presentation for the Quincys while battling a migraine. But that's exactly what I end up doing, because I always push myself for my clients.

For the next hour, I block out the noise in the office and focus on my work. The other planners and assistants begin heading out for the day. One of Maddie's sisters drops off dinner for the two of us. Taking a bite of the salad, I realize I've barely eaten today. No wonder I had an attack. The office gets quieter and the pain in my temple finally subsides. Brooke: one, migraine: zero.

With the recap complete, I move on to creating the planning timeline and checklists. This is where I shine. It's my superpower: Taking all the moving elements and all the to-dos and putting them in a digestible format that won't overwhelm. The color-coding helps it make sense for the vendors, but of course Caleb gave me grief about it. Yes, it's aesthetically pleasing thanks to the Spencer Soirees branding color palette, but it does serve a purpose. It highlights the most important details and gives vendors a quick way to find the information that pertains to them. It's a genius system, thank you very much.

By nine o'clock, it's just me and Maddie left in the office, and I've taken Hannah and Preston's inspiration and created a stunning proposal. Their weekend of wedding events is going to be the most beautiful thing I've ever worked on.

Unfortunately, before I can share the proposal with them, I have to run everything by Caleb. So much of this particular event design depends on service logistics, and that requires his cooperation.

I email Caleb the meeting recap, but there's no way I'm sending something as proprietary as a Spencer Soirees event design to anyone at Foley's. Even if it's only a draft. I shoot him a text asking if he has time to review it tomorrow.

I start typing another message. Then delete. Type. Delete. I want to proactively address any wrench Caleb is going to throw at me, but I have no idea what wrench he might throw. I believe him when he says he cares about this wedding as much as I do, but that doesn't mean he's going to make my job any easier.

My phone buzzes in my hand. Caleb. *Shit.*

"Did you mean to call me?"

"Hey babe," he says, and I don't respond. "I can practically hear you rolling your eyes."

Guilty.

"Why are you calling me? You're not supposed to use your phone for actual phone calls unless it's an emergency or work-related."

"Is this not work-related?"

He has me there. "I take back what I said about us being in this together. Now I keep hoping I'll wake up from the nightmare that is having to work with you."

"I'm just happy to be in your dreams."

My cheeks flush and I'm glad he can't see me. "To what do I owe the pleasure of this work call, Caleb?"

"I missed the sound of your voice."

"Oh, shut up," I say. I doubt Caleb has missed one thing about me. He made that crystal clear.

"Well, I'm trying to decode your seven-page meeting recap and accompanying documents—"

"I sent those five minutes ago," I say. "You couldn't possibly have reviewed them already."

"Of course I haven't, Brooke." The way he slowly says my name, making it two syllables instead of one, gives me goosebumps. "I knew you were Type A, but this is next level. The reason I'm calling is because I'm waiting with bated breath to see your event design proposal."

"I'm sure you are," I say, sarcastically.

"Fine. I called you because I got your text and I'm in the middle of cooking and I couldn't text back."

"It's called voice-to-text, you should try it sometime."

"I'm old school." He laughs. "I have to prep most of the day tomorrow. Do you want to come by the Market sometime in the afternoon?"

"Hold on, let me check my calendar," I say, putting him on speaker. He laughs and all that does is make me more nervous that he's going to screw up the time of an important meeting. "How's two-ish? I have a rehearsal at four."

"That works. My favorite color is blue."

"Huh?"

"For your calendar. Make me blue."

"You can't be blue," I say. "I have a system!"

"C'mon, what's the worst that could happen?"

The worst that could happen is forgetting something important, dropping the ball, messing something up, letting Mom down. The list goes on. But I'm not letting Caleb see that part of my crazy.

"I don't know, but I don't plan on finding out."

"Alright, fine. I'll see you at two tomorrow. Bye—"

"Don't even think about saying babe," I say.

"I think you kind of like it."

I'm afraid he might be right.

"Goodbye, Caleb."

Fridays are chaos in the office. Organized chaos, but chaos nonetheless. While everyone else is leaving work early to begin their weekend, we're just getting started. You'd think a dozen wedding planners would make the office look like a bomb of rose petals and tulle exploded, but nope. We move around each other gracefully, preparing supplies, making last-minute changes to timelines, and putting out pre-event fires. Planners buzzing around is a calming white noise to me.

There are six weddings this weekend. By the time I get to the office at eleven, half the staff is out and on site at their respective venues, including Maddie. We're doing tomorrow's wedding together, but she's working with Kelsey tonight, filling in for an assistant who claims she's sick. The thing is, I overheard her complaining about missing a girls' trip earlier this week. She's not going to last in this industry if she isn't willing to give up her weekends.

It leaves me handling tonight's rehearsal on my own. Fortunately, I have a few interns working on last-minute preparations, tying ribbons on ceremony programs, and ironing specialty tablecloths we had delivered to the office this morning. There are few things I hate more than fresh linens with creases on a wedding day.

Meanwhile, I'm failing miserably at making the groom's last-minute request a reality. Requests like this one always disrupt my final day of prep, but this is a disruption I'm happy to get behind. Unfortunately, I'm having zero luck making it happen. I've called most of the McDonald's in the county, asking if they can make a hundred Happy Meals for tomorrow night. The groom wants to surprise the guests by putting one on each seat of the coach buses driving them back to the hotel.

I've been at it for over an hour and haven't made much progress. One franchise can do a few dozen. Another said twenty. I can cobble together the rest and pay our interns overtime to drive around town to get them, but that'll add to the logistics *and* the stress.

I take a break to send final timelines to tomorrow's vendor

list, updating my own timeline as they inevitably change arrival times or day-of contacts. Then I head to meet with Caleb.

Foley's Market isn't what I remember at all. I haven't set foot in here since Mom and Paul were still on speaking terms. And even though the current working partnership has their blessing, walking through the doors feels like crossing enemy lines. I half expect Mom to jump out from behind a display and yell *gotcha, Brooke!* It's completely different from what I had in my head; there's something about being here that's oddly comforting. The smell of baked goods wafting through the air pulls me toward the back of the store.

I pass a display of flowers and several cases of prepared foods. Foley's is the go-to for party dips, show-stopping desserts, or a ready-made dinner when you don't feel like cooking. It might be the only takeout establishment in town that I don't frequent, enemy lines and all. I've been tempted to pop in on more than one occasion, but I'm always convinced that someone will recognize me and it'd get back to Mom. Not worth the risk. Until now.

The bakery case stops me in my tracks. It's an absolute dream for me and my sweet tooth. A dozen varieties of cookies and cupcakes. There's key lime pie, my favorite. It'd be okay to pick up a few things on the way out, just this once, right? In the name of research. I reach the counter and ask the teenage boy wearing a green Foley's apron where I can find Caleb.

He pauses and gives me an apologetic frown. If Caleb stands me up for a work meeting, he's in for it. The boy turns to the door behind him. "Caleb, the prissy, preppy wedding planner is here," he calls.

Excuse me?

He quickly leans forward over the case. "I'm so sorry," he

whispers. "One of the wedding coordinators said she'd give me ten bucks if I said that to you, and I want to buy some flowers for my girlfriend." He shrugs sheepishly. Sweet kid.

Two can play this game. "Ten bucks, huh? I'll give you twenty to tell me who it was?" Curiosity has gotten the better of me.

His eyes go wide, and he tells me the name I suspected. She applied for a job last season. I liked her, but Mom won't hire anyone who's worked here, and since Spencer Soirees isn't mine yet, my hands were tied.

"Thank you," I hand him a twenty and walk past the bakery case, eyeing the key lime pie again. Yeah, one of those is coming home with me.

I pause at the opening between the bakery and the kitchen. I expect there to be several kitchen staff chopping, dicing, mixing…whatever cooking entails. I wouldn't know. I've never been much of a cook.

Instead, I find Caleb alone at one of the long stainless steel tables, prepping some hors d'oeuvres. Looks like pigs in a blanket. Is it even a wedding if there aren't pigs in a blanket? He's wearing a black short-sleeve shirt that hugs his arms and the same green apron as the teenager at the counter. He's got his worn-out Hartford Whalers hat on, those brown waves peeking out.

And it's on backwards. The ovens must be on because it's hot in here.

Leaning against the wall, I watch him methodically roll each little cocktail frank in a blanket of pastry dough. Even from here I can tell they're perfectly uniform. His forearms flex with each roll.

I hate how much I'm enjoying this. A man who can cook, that is. Not Caleb specifically. Though seeing Caleb in action is definitely piquing my interest in his ability to cook well for our clients.

"Are you going to keep swooning over there or are you going to show me your top-secret proposal?" Caleb doesn't look up from cutting more strips of pastry, but there's a smirk on his face. I push myself off the wall, brushing my hands over the front of my navy shift dress.

"I wasn't swooning!"

I might have been swooning at little. At the idea of a man who can cook.

"Sure you weren't—"

"Don't you dare call me *babe*." I point my index finger as I walk over to stand across the table from him.

"I wasn't going to call you babe, Brooke," he says. "I was going to say 'sure you weren't checking out my wieners.'"

"Excuse me?"

Caleb points to the counter. "Wieners. Hot dogs. Cocktail franks."

I shake my head, but my lips betray me and form a smile. "I wasn't swooning over you or your wieners. Please tell me that you don't call them wieners in front of clients."

He laughs. "Nope, pigs in a blanket. I only call them wieners in front of my favorite wedding planner."

"Your favorite prissy, preppy wedding planner?" I raise my brows at him. "You know one of your wedding coordinators paid him to call me that?"

He looks up from his task, and I can't read the look on his face. It's a mix between anger and embarrassment. "Shit, I'm sorry—"

I've been called way worse. "It's okay, Caleb. I am a little bit prissy. And preppy." I am carrying a monogramed L.L. Bean Boat & Tote, after all.

"Let me wipe this down and we can review the proposal."

Standing in the middle of the kitchen, I take in more of the space. It's huge. And clean, almost spotless. I expected chaos and mess and, well, for Caleb to look out of place, not like he fits right in.

Two cooks come into the kitchen as Caleb finishes wiping down the prep table. I listen as he speaks to them. He's firm but kind as he lays out his instructions for the rest of prep and they listen attentively. For the first time, I see that Foley's will be in excellent hands whenever Paul decides to retire, and despite what he said years ago, Caleb's right where he belongs. Watching him is bringing me back to a place I cannot afford to be. It's getting harder and harder to shove that down deep, far away from my busy summer plans.

"Brooke?" Caleb's voice shakes me out of the trance I'm in.

"Yes, chef," I drawl. The words fly out of my mouth before I even realize what I'm saying. I clasp my hand over my mouth and freeze. Caleb looks at me with raised brows and nods to himself, his lips in a thin line trying to keep his composure and leave me with one shred of dignity. No chance. I can hear the two cooks giggling across the room. "Oh my god. Pretend I didn't say that. I've been binge-watching *The Bear*."

Caleb blows air out of his mouth. "Oh, it's too late for me to do that, Brooke."

My cheeks are on fire, and with this fair skin, I know my embarrassment is on full display for Caleb and the cooks. Did they turn more ovens on? I'd very much like to melt into a puddle right here, never to be seen or heard from again.

"Knock it off, you two," Caleb says to the chefs. "C'mon, Brooke. Office is in the back."

Chapter 12

Caleb

Yes, chef.

Brooke walks in silence behind me, where I hope she can't see me adjust myself as I lead us through the hall that runs behind the kitchen and market.

Christ.

We get to Dad's office at the end of the hall. The sign on the door reads *Paul Foley*, but I take the seat behind the large desk.

Brooke sits in the old chair across from me. Her cheeks aren't red anymore. Only a little pink, and it's not helping me forget those words.

"I'm sorry it's such a mess here. Dad isn't exactly known for his organizational skills."

"No, no, it's okay," she says, taking stock of the mess. She's lying.

I laugh. "I can tell you're getting all squirrely."

"Squirrely?"

"Yeah, like your brain is going all over the place. You're having trouble focusing, looking at all the different piles. You want to grab a trash can and start purging and organizing. But you're worried that I'll think you're crazy…is your eye twitching?"

Her jaw drops at my observation. "No," she says, touching the corner of her eye.

"I'm working to get it in better shape, but it's baby steps. It'll be a while before he can handle color-coding."

"I'm happy to help when he's ready." She clasps her hands together and sets them in her lap. "As much as I'd love to chat about the joys of organization, I need to be quick."

"Right down to business. I like it."

"*Har har.* I mean it, I've got a rehearsal at four and still need to figure out how to get a hundred Happy Meals for tomorrow night."

I shake my head. "Brooke, if you need a last-minute caterer that badly, just ask. Don't feed those poor guests fast food." I thought Spencer Soirees was a luxury wedding planning agency. Fast food for wedding guests? I hate this idea. Years of culinary school and work in a kitchen will ruin fast food for you pretty quickly.

"Don't you dare knock the Golden Arches, okay?" she says. "There is a time and place for it, and one of those times is at the end of a five-hour open bar. Not to mention, their fountain Diet Coke is superior to all other Diet Cokes."

Is there some kind of Diet Coke ranking system I don't know about?

"And I don't need a caterer tomorrow. If I did, you wouldn't be my first call."

I plunge an invisible knife into my chest. "Way harsh, babe."

She rolls those blue eyes a little dramatically and laughs. Something tugs at my chest. Her eyerolls are getting more playful.

"I need fast food because the groom wants to surprise everyone with Happy Meals on the buses back to the hotel.

Don't you think that's a great idea? Imagine how happy you'd be if you were drunk at the end of a wedding and the smell of burgers and fries welcomed you onto the bus! I need to cobble together more meals somehow." She's downright giddy about this, talking fast and moving her hands. Less polished than she usually is. Like it excites her in a way other things don't. It's adorable.

"Not a bad way to end the night." I think about the times I've been a wedding guest. How even after dozens of hors d'oeuvres and a three-course dinner, you're still starving at the end of the night. Might be all the alcohol and dancing. "No luck, huh?"

"I'm pretty sure I've called every location in a thirty-mile radius and none of them can handle the entire order. A few locations can do some, so I need to find a few more and figure out the logistics of picking them all up. Our staff is tapped this weekend, but I could pay the interns or maybe offer your guy out front another twenty bucks…"

Or I could help her. I rest my chin on my hand and watch her with amusement.

"Caleb." She looks at me skeptically. "What are you thinking?"

I'm thinking Dad's going to be pissed at what I'm about to do.

"Hear me out before you say no, okay?" She probably won't, but she nods anyway. "What if I made something—"

"I can't ask you to—"

"Uh-uh, you said you'd hear me out."

"Fine," she says, shaking her head with another playful eye roll, making me feel the things I'm trying so hard not to. She crosses her arms and leans back in the chair.

"We've got a light weekend and I'm already bored with the catering menu. I could do brown bag burgers and fries. All greasy and salty. Perfect late-night food." The wheels in my head are turning. "If it works, I can start offering the same kind of to-go items at weddings we're already catering."

She scoffs. "My mom will kill me if she finds out I'm helping you and your dad make more money." I believe her. Judy is ruthless. "And my clients have already gone way over budget."

"It'll only cost them whatever they were planning to pay." This is going to cost me at least triple that. Mom won't be thrilled when she does the books. But it's hard for me to say no to Brooke Spencer. Especially when her blue eyes are sparkling with excitement like they are right now.

"Are you sure? That's a lot to ask…though for the record I didn't ask. You offered."

Am I sure? I don't *need* to help her in order to put the idea on the menu. We have one wedding to work on together and that's it. We don't have to work together any more than that. But despite what my head says, something else is saying *I'm sure*.

"I'm sure. And the record will state that I offered"

She releases a breath and smiles. "Okay."

"Fantastic! Now we have plenty of time to go over the deck together."

Brooke pulls out her iPad and walks me through the presentation.

Chapter 13

Brooke

SATURDAY BRUNCHES WITH JORDAN AND MADDIE ARE RARE. They almost never happen during the summer, and they've been happening less frequently in the offseason too. Back when we were starting out and had lives outside of work, we brunched every weekend. Now, Maddie and I are swamped at the agency. I barely have to time to help my sweet neighbor, Mr. Edwards, with his kitchen garden. Maddie doesn't get to see her sisters as much as she used to. Jordan's booking clients all over the country and is rarely in town, no matter the time of year. I get to see Maddie almost every day, but I miss having Jordan at my side with her camera. She's so damn talented that it's almost annoying. She's always patient with her clients, amazing with children in the wedding party, and the queen of capturing candid moments throughout the night.

For the first time in over a year, the three of us are all working the same wedding. The combination of a full-service venue and second marriages for both the bride and groom means a little less work for us and a later start to the day. Therefore, brunch!

We fall into our usual chatter about work and life. It feels just like all of our other brunches, except for the lack of mimosas. We'll have to wait for drinks until our secret end-of-the-night toast.

"So," Jordan says, champagne-free orange juice in hand. "How are things at Spencer Soirees? Judy still digging in her claws and micromanaging the hell out of the two of you?"

Maddie raises her eyebrows and turns to me. Bless her heart for attempting to not answer that question honestly for my sake. Let's see how long she keeps her mouth shut.

"She hasn't been so bad lately," I say, my voice a pitch higher than normal. My cheeks warm and I bite my lip as Maddie and Jordan take in the lie.

"Actually," Maddie says, putting her fork down.

Fifteen seconds. She tried. I grab my coffee mug from the table. When Maddie's fired up, she talks with her hands, and when it comes to my mom, Maddie starts at a ten and only goes up.

"She's been just as bad, if not worse; lately she's unhinged. She agreed to work with the Foley's in order to get the Quincy wedding. And she's making Brooke work on it which, like, will be amazing for Brooke but now she has to work with Caleb Foley after he basically took her heart, ripped it out of her chest, stomped on it, and then left her there in front of everyone and moved away like a little bitch." Maddie's hands are still wide open in the air when she stops speaking.

"Take a breath, Maddie," Jordan says. "I was there, too."

"It wasn't *that* bad," I protest. "It's not even the most crushing thing that's happened to my love life in the last five years."

They both cast me a sidelong glance.

"You keep telling yourself that, Brooke," Jordan says. Oh, I will. It's my one and only coping mechanism.

"I'm sorry, she just, ugh," Maddie continues. "I can deal with a tough boss, a micromanaging boss. I thrive under that kind of pressure. You don't believe in me? You don't trust my judgment? Watch me prove you wrong. What I can't deal with is how she treats you, Brooke. She holds passing down the business over your head and treats you like you're not one of the most coveted wedding planners in the area."

I smile at my friend, my eyes stinging with the threat of tears. Maddie's always had my back, and it means the world to me that she comes to my defense again and again. Her words sound harsh, but what she always forgets is that I've been dealing with Mom my entire life. I know how she operates, and I know that she loves me and will eventually pass Spencer Soirees over to me. She has to. It's my job to carry on the legacy.

"It's not that bad. The Quincy wedding will be planned flawlessly by yours truly, and she'll finally realize she can take a step back and let me step up." I bite into my bacon, egg, and cheese (perfect pre-wedding fuel), and try to ignore the looks Maddie and Jordan give each other.

"Don't for one second think I didn't see that," I say. "Listen, it sucks that I have to see Caleb all the time now, but it's fine. I'm pretending that incident at the party never happened. And honestly, he seems to have completely forgotten about it. Maybe he was blackout drunk and doesn't remember what happened."

Another look between Maddie and Jordan.

"I hate both of you," I say and take another bite of my sandwich.

The Thompson wedding got off to an amazing start. Jordan nailed the awkward dynamics of photographing a blended family. She should add *good with angsty tweens who are super emo over having new stepparents* to the About Me section of her website. Maddie managed to find the missing best man just in time for his toast. And, with Caleb's help, I'm about to pull off the end-of-the-night-burger-and-fries surprise.

I look down at my clipboard for the upcoming action items.

10:30 p.m. - Caleb arrives with to-go burgers and fries.

It's 10:20 p.m. He'll be here any minute. The guests (and my stomach) are doing the Cha Cha Slide. I want to pull off this epic surprise for the guests and make my clients happy. I'm anxiously tapping my pen on my clipboard when Jordan appears next to me. "Excuse me," she says, looking across the room. "What exactly is Caleb doing here?"

"I forgot to tell you at brunch. You're going to want to get photos of this!" I so did not forget to tell her. In fact, as the photographer, this is something she should have known in advance, so I tell her now. By the time I finish, Caleb is next to us.

"Good evening, ladies," he says. His hair is wavier thanks to the humidity and lack of Whalers hat. "Brooke. Jordan." His smile grows as he looks at me and then at the clipboard I'm holding close to my chest. "Can I see that?"

I find myself handing it over to Caleb's waiting hand. I'm not one to let my clipboard out of my hands at any point during the night, but somehow this is the second time it's ended up in his hands. I look next to me, expecting Jordan to still be standing there, but she must have snuck back into the dancing crowd to snap more candids.

"You'll notice I'm even a few minutes early." Caleb pulls a pen from his white chef coat. The sleeves are rolled up just enough to have me staring at his toned forearms. Until he draws a line through *10:30 p.m. - Caleb arrives with to-go burgers and fries.*

A line! I press my lips together to hide my horror. I'm a checkmark person. Not a cross-a-line-through-it person.

"That's going to drive you crazy, isn't it?" Caleb teases, handing the clipboard back to me.

"Yes," I sigh. "It sure is. You're really good at that, you know?"

"At what?"

"Driving me crazy."

"Brooke." He lowers his mouth closer to my ear. "I don't hate the idea of driving you crazy."

My mouth opens and I suck in a breath.

"Brooke," Maddie interrupts. "Buses are here!"

"C'mon," Caleb pats my shoulder like an old pal, giving me whiplash. What was that about? "Let's make these guests' night!"

Outside the venue, Maddie grabs an armful of brown paper bags from the catering truck. They're crinkled and greasy. Perfect.

"God," Maddie groans. "These smell delicious."

Caleb smiles, all teeth and dimple. "Thanks, Maddie. I made extra for your team and the other vendors."

"You did not!" Maddie yells, hopping onto the first bus.

"I did!" he shouts back to her.

We work together to load bags on both buses. Caleb grabs two bags from the Foley's van and makes sure each bus driver has one of their own. He's still the kind and considerate guy he's always been, despite his ability to get under my skin.

"You didn't have to make extras," I say.

"I know, I wanted to." He hands a greasy bag to me and another to Maddie as she hops off the bus. She opens it, unwraps the burger and takes a giant bite. I'd give anyone else a good talking-to about eating while we're in the presence of wedding guests, but only a few are out here getting some air, and I know better than to give Maddie a talking-to about anything.

"He's making it hard to hate him," Maddie says with a fake whisper.

Caleb laughs. "I heard that."

"I know," she says, and pats his cheek with two quick taps. "I'll work on getting the guests out here." She skips to the venue entrance, stopping to talk to Jordan. I can't wait for her to get shots of the guests' reactions.

"She is..." Caleb says.

I laugh. Maddie is so many things. "...amusingly endearing?"

"Something like that, I don't think anyone has patted my cheek like that since I was a kid."

"You better get used to it," I say, nudging his shoulder with mine. "She's going to be working the Quincy wedding with us."

"Is that why she doesn't like me?" he asks.

Maybe he *was* blackout drunk five years ago. If that was the case, I should try to forget it ever happened.

"Oh...the whole Foley's planner thing. How you hate us and refuse to work with us."

"I don't hate you, Brooke" he says.

"Yeah, but you don't like us," I say. He opens his mouth to say something, but I speak before he can. I don't need him saying anything nice to me. "Thank you for doing this, Caleb. I mean it. The groom's ecstatic and these guests are *so* wasted. Those burgers are going to make their night and improve their morning."

"You're welcome," he says, his brown eyes fixed on mine. He opens his mouth like he wants to get out whatever he started to say before, but the double doors of the venue open and guests stumble out. Jordan is suddenly next to us, shooting me a mischievous grin before she turns to the guests and captures the final moments of the night.

Another successful wedding.

Only a few more tasks before I can dive under my fluffy white comforter and fall into that glorious sleep that only comes with the exhaustion of a wedding day.

I devoured Caleb's food on the drive home, and it was the most delicious burger I've ever had in my life. Way better than any drunk fast-food burger. He failed to mention he was making smash burgers on brioche buns with some kind of delectable sauce I can't quite describe. If he had, I might have snuck a few bags off the bus. Okay, I wouldn't have. But I would have wanted to.

He was tolerable tonight, nice even, but I can't understand why he'd helped me. Why he'd made extras for the vendors. Maybe it was a selfish favor. He's right about it being a great addition to the catering menu. Guests were practically salivating as the smell of greasy food hit them from across the parking lot. The best part of the night had been hearing the squeals and groans as they boarded the buses.

No. The best part had been the smile on Caleb's face. He stood by the doors, listening to all the delighted sounds coming from inside. I couldn't take my eyes off of his smile, dimple on full display. That is, until the flash of Jordan's camera nearby shook me from my daze.

I'm finishing the final step of my skincare routine when my phone buzzes from my bedroom.

> Jordan: Really sucks that you HAVE to see Caleb all the time, huh?

Above the message is a photo. The first thing I see is that amazing smile on Caleb's face. I don't need a photo to remember it, but I'm glad I have one. He's looking toward the door of the bus and I'm standing next to him, looking at him with...*oh god*...a big fat grin on my face like a pathetic, lovesick teenager. Ugh, I basically was one with him. And Jordan captured the mortifying moment. I throw my phone onto my bed and walk back to the bathroom. If I ignore it, maybe it will cease to exist. I don't even make it to the door, though, before I turn around and pick up my phone again.

I lay on my bed and look at the photo. I save it to my camera roll. Caleb has a glow I haven't seen from him before. He's proud of himself. And me, I look happy. Incredibly happy. Something I haven't felt in a while. The feeling starts to come back and I'm grinning that big fat stupid grin all over again.

> Brooke: I hate you

> Jordan: You're so fucked.

Chapter 14

Caleb

I can't get Brooke out of my head. Her voice saying *yes, chef* has been on repeat in my head, and that's dangerous. I've been thinking about those two words coming out of her mouth (among other things involving her mouth) ever since. The way her cheeks turned pink when she realized what she said, it was fucking adorable. This is going to get me and my feelings in trouble.

My parents aren't upset about the burger and fries surprise. It didn't bother Dad that it was for Spencer Soirees, making me wonder if he's softened since his heart attack. He liked the idea. Foley's has offered late-night bites at weddings ever since the trend took off years ago, but to-go bags at the end of the night is a new twist.

It's been over a week since that wedding, and I'll never forget the sound of all those happy drunk guests. It felt like a small something I created on my own. With a little help from Brooke.

We've only been in touch via email about the Quincy wedding. She shared the event design with Hannah and

Preston after a few minor tweaks, and they happily approved. Brooke's pretty fucking good at her job. Not that I'm surprised.

The last wedding we did together at the country club before I moved was a near-disaster. The Spencer Soirees lead planner showed up two hours late with no explanation. The bride had one too many mimosas getting ready and stumbled through photos before the ceremony. Brooke, an assistant planner at the time, turned the whole thing around. She led setup flawlessly and, with the help of coffee and french fries, helped the bride sober up. The lead planner, probably knowing her time at Spencer Soirees was up, left early without telling anyone. Brooke was on her own for breakdown until I realized and helped her. After, we sat in my car for hours eating our Duchess grilled cheeses and talking about everything except for the one thing I wanted to.

I need to forget all that. I need to get through this summer, through the Quincy wedding, and move on for good.

With the design plan officially approved, our to-do list grows by the day. Brooke already scheduled meetings with all of the vendors, and I was able to convince her it was essential that I attend the meeting with Warehouse Rentals. We're catering three meals in one weekend and I'll be serving the food on these rentals, so it's not a huge stretch. Even the most Type-A, micromanaging wedding planner can see that.

Her ears must be burning.

> Brooke: 5:30 p.m. tomorrow at the Warehouse Rentals downtown showroom.

> Brooke: Don't be late!

> Caleb: I'd never keep you waiting, babe!

Brooke is late.

It's shocking.

I stand outside the showroom obsessively checking my watch, looking up and down the street for the polished brunette who drives me crazy. The meeting starts in ten minutes. She should be here by now. I've been taking the Brooke Spencer approach recently, arriving at least fifteen minutes early to meetings.

I dig into my back pocket for my phone. No texts or calls from *Babe*, the name I've given her in my phone. She's going be so annoyed when she realizes.

"Caleb!" My heart skips and I look up.

It's Hannah.

I force a smile and give her a hug. Jennifer is by her side, and I hug her too, quickly. I'm not getting stuck in that death grip again.

"Where's Brooke?" Jennifer asks.

"She'll be here any minute. Probably hit some traffic," I say, looking up and down the street one more time. Normal rush hour congestion, nothing more. "Why don't we head inside? We can start with the catering rentals."

I usher them inside and glance at my watch. 5:30.

She's officially *very* late. I call her cell. No answer.

Baxter talks Hannah and Jennifer through several options for the table settings, walking around the oversized table in the showroom with half a dozen combinations of chargers, plates, napkins, glasses, and silverware.

Under normal circumstances, I can hold my own when it comes to table settings. I worked closely with our wedding coordinators in San Francisco, helping bring a couple's vision to life while also serving the food they wanted. I've already had meetings like this one with other Foley's clients.

But these are not normal circumstances. This is a wedding with an elaborate design plan expertly curated by Brooke. As much as it aggravates me that I need to rely on someone else, she needs to be here for these final decisions.

It's getting closer and closer to six o'clock and there's still no sign of Brooke. No call, no text, nothing. This is not like her at all. Hannah's glancing towards the door just as much as I am. Tension builds in my chest. *Caleb Foley, if you fuck up this wedding because you forget to show up at a meeting, so help me god.* She gave me so much shit before I even messed anything up, and now she's half an hour late.

"Caleb?" Baxter looks at me like it's not his first attempt at getting my attention. I need to focus. Hannah is flustered and needs guidance. I may not have Brooke's experience working directly with brides, but I'm not about to fuck this up for her—for us. I'm livid with her right now, but also growing concerned about why she's not here. "Hannah was asking what you thought of this one." He points to a place setting on the table. It's a classic setting with a clear light blue charger that has a ruffled rim and gold edges. On top is a simple white plate for the entree and a patterned salad plate. What had Brooke called it in the design plan? *Relaxed elegance.*

I brush my sweaty palms against my jeans. "It's beautiful but...what do you think about swapping out the patterned salad plate for white and using this one for the entree?" I swap the plate with one from another setting a few places down. "The design on this plate will get lost under the salad course, but the entree plate has the design on the rim and will work nicely with your menu."

"I love that," Hannah says. "Do you think Brooke will be okay with it?"

"You still haven't heard from her?" Jennifer asks, clearly annoyed. I'm seething that Brooke's left me on my own here, but I can't let them see that.

"Brooke will love it," Baxter says, buying me time to get my frustration in check.

"We could use that salad plate for the farewell brunch," I say. "It'll bring the overall design through to the end of the weekend."

"We definitely need Brooke's input before we confirm. She totally gets my whole vision," Hannah says, looking at Jennifer. Hannah may be anxious at Brooke's absence, but Jennifer is mad.

"Where is she anyway?" Jennifer asks.

"I'm sorry she's not here," I say, pulling out my phone in the hopes of a message from Brooke. "This isn't like her."

"She's never missed a meeting here," Baxter says. "I'm sure she has a good reason."

"I hope she's okay," Hannah says.

Jennifer scoffs like maybe she doesn't have a similar hope. It makes me wonder what I was thinking when we dated. And why she acted so cheerful at our initial meeting.

I've worked with plenty of clients who'd be in a complete panic if their planner didn't show. I would have assumed Hannah would be one of them. She's not in a panic, but she is unsettled. I can't believe Brooke's completely ghosted us without so much as a call. She better have a good excuse. If there's something wrong, I don't want it to mess anything up for either of us. I dig my phone out.

"Oh, she just texted me," I lie. "Her car broke down across town and she didn't have service. She apologizes for not being in touch sooner."

"Service does suck over there," Jennifer says, reluctantly. Baxter nods.

"I'm glad she's okay," Hannah says. "Can we send her pictures of what we're thinking?"

"Sure," I say and start snapping.

We finalize the place settings for the reception and move on to the rehearsal dinner and farewell brunch. After an hour, we're finally done.

Baxter walks Hannah out. Jennifer and I following.

"Funny that Brooke hasn't gotten back to you since you sent her those pictures," Jennifer says.

"I'm sure she's dealing with getting a tow," I say. "I'll check in with her tonight."

For the last hour, I've been willing the meeting to end so I can drive to Spencer Soirees and find out what was so important that Brooke missed this meeting. The second it's over, I head across town.

It's a miracle I'm not pulled over for speeding as I fly down Post Road, and another miracle that I don't hit any red lights. It's after rush hour, but you never know what kind of traffic you'll run into in this part of town. The only car in the small lot behind Spencer Soirees is Brooke's. She *is* here.

Heat rises through me and my chest pounds. I wish I had the doors on the Jeep so I could slam one shut and release some of this pent-up frustration as I exit my car.

Instead, I take deep breaths as I walk, hands clenched into fists at my sides. I climb the front steps and knock on the door. I wait a minute before grabbing the doorknob and turning it. It's locked. I knock again and something shifts in me, but I can't pinpoint the emotion.

I pace the front porch, glancing up and down the street. Where the hell is she? Maybe she stepped out to grab dinner nearby. There are enough restaurants in this town that you could dine out once a week all year and never eat at the same place. But Brooke wouldn't do that when she was supposed to be meeting with a client.

From the corner of my eye, I see something inside the office through the bay window. I put my head and hands to the glass to get a better look. My anger evaporates so quickly, I shiver. It's been replaced with fear.

Shit.

Curled in the fetal position on the floor is Brooke. My heart plummets, bottoming out in my stomach. My chest pounds for an entirely different reason.

"Brooke!" I bang on the window. She moves her head less than an inch. Or am I imagining it? I focus on her mouth and then her stomach for any sign of breathing. I bang on the window again.

She stirs a little and holds out her hand, singling for me to stop banging. If she doesn't like that, she sure as shit isn't going to like it when I break the fucking door down.

"Brooke, what's the code?" I yell through the glass. She cracks one eye open slightly, like it hurts to look at me. *Gee, thanks, Brooke.*

"The code to the door, Brooke. I need the code or I'm going to break this window," I yell, voice shaking. She holds up nine fingers, then two fingers, then five, then three, and finally seven before she closes her eyes again.

I run to the front door and enter the numbers. The door creaks open and I dart to her. "Brooke," I say, kneeling beside her. "Are you okay?" Obviously, she's not okay.

She presses her index finger to her lips and makes a soft shushing sound. "Please whisper," she says. "Your voice is making my head hurt."

"So, it's a normal day?" I place a hand on forehead. Her temperature feels normal. "What's wrong?"

"Migraine," she says shakily. "Bad one."

I blow out a breath. Just a headache. "I thought you were hurt. I've got some Tylenol in the car." I move to get up, but she grabs my arm.

"Caleb, if I could roll my eyes right now, you'd be in for it," she whispers slowly, as if the sound of her own voice is painful, too. She takes deep slow breaths. "This is well beyond the power of acetaminophen."

"What can I do?" I'll do anything to make her feel better,

and that thought hits me right in the feelings I've been ignoring.

This is more than just a headache. There's barely any color in her face. Her freckles contrast harshly against her skin. I hate seeing her like this.

"I need to go to urgent care," she says slowly.

"Okay, I'll take you."

She shifts to get up and groans. "I can't get up yet. Can you turn the lights off? And in the kitchen back there, there might be an ice pack in the freezer. Could you check?"

I turn off the lights and head to the kitchen. A minute later, I sit next to her empty-handed.

"No ice pack, I'm sorry."

Brooke groans. Not the annoyed groan she often gives me but a long drawn-out groan of real pain. Like simply existing hurts.

"What can I do to help you feel better?"

She hesitates. "You can't."

That can't be true. There's got to be something.

"I'll do whatever you need me to do. What do we have to do so I can get you to urgent care?"

"You're going to think it's weird."

"I'm okay with weird, Brooke." I shift so I'm sitting cross-legged next to her. She's still in the fetal position, curled toward me. I brush some of the hair that's fallen on her face behind her ear.

"Can you take the tip of your fingers and press them into my temple kind of hard?" She points to the left side of her head. I scoff quietly. That's not weird. I'd do much weirder things to help her right now.

"It helps, I promise," she says.

"Okay," I say, looking at her on the floor. She's using her hands as a pillow. "Brooke, that can't be comfortable. Here, I'm going to move you so you can rest your head on my lap, okay?" Her eyes and nose scrunch like she wants to protest, but she nods. I slowly move her closer and rest her head on my thigh. I take my index and middle fingers and press them into her temple. "Is this okay? Are you sure I'm not hurting you?" She lets out the softest sigh of relief. It's music to my ears.

We sit together on the office floor while I massage her temple like she asked, and I bask in the feeling of having her this close to me. She's always been so independent and self-reliant. It's jarring to see her like this.

After about twenty minutes, she musters up enough energy to move. As soon as she sits up, she grabs the trash can under desk and vomits. She keeps apologizing as if that's going to scare me away. *Please.* I help her get cleaned up and take the trash out before we leave.

Each step makes her wince as we walk out of the office.

"Brooke, let me carry you," I say.

"Carry me? I don't need you to carry me," she protests through deep breaths, barely able to open her eyes. "I can walk on my own."

"Just because you can, doesn't mean you have to."

We make it off the front porch and the setting sun hits Brooke's face. She groans and winces more. Before she can protest again, I scoop her up with little effort and carry her in my arms.

"Fine," she says, resting her head against my chest. My heart's beating so hard I'm afraid it'll make her head hurt more. "But don't you dare tell anyone about this. I'm a strong, capable woman."

"Yes, you are. Your secret is safe with me." Though I'd like the whole world to see her in my arms. I carry Brooke to her car. There's no way I'm taking her in the doorless Wrangler.

From the back of the car, she assures me that she'll be fine, but I'm not convinced. Should I be driving to the hospital instead? Calling her mom? Or at least Maddie? She says all she needs is a shot of something for the pain and a pill for the nausea.

By the time we arrive at urgent care, she's a little steadier on her feet. As much as I want to carry her, I don't want to hurt her pride. Still, I wrap my arm around her waist and walk her inside. She doesn't protest this time.

Brooke is quickly whisked away by a nurse and the sounds of the receptionist scrolling through social media keep me company in the waiting room.

I'd suggested acetaminophen. The most basic of all the pain medications, it's practically a placebo. What a fucking idiot. Sitting next to her on the floor, I got a closer look at her face. It was twisted in pain, her freckled nose crunched, eyes squeezed shut. Her skin lacked its usual glow and rosiness. Even with the lights off, she could barely open her eyes. I've heard people talk about having a migraine attack, but I'd always thought they were just bad headaches. Not this. This was much worse. I never want her to have to go through it again.

While I wait, I read through WebMD and Mayo Clinic resources on migraines. It's a neurological condition and yeah, it's way worse than your average headache. Some people only get them a few times a year, but others get them a few times a week. God, I hope that isn't the case for Brooke.

After thirty minutes, Brooke finally walks into the waiting room, and I take a full breath for the first time since I saw her through the window. I rise to my feet so quickly, I almost trip over my own two feet.

"Brooke," I say with a sigh. "You're okay?" I meet her halfway across the room. There's some color back in her cheeks. Thank god. It takes all my willpower to keep my hands at my side. To not touch her.

"I'm okay." She nods, her lips curling up slightly. "Embarrassed, but I'm okay…I'm so sorry, Caleb."

I shove my hands in my pockets. "Sorry...why are you sorry?"

"For having a migraine attack...throwing up in front of you..."

"And for missing the meeting with Hannah at Warehouse Rentals?" I ask with a smirk.

I'm met with wide blue eyes and parted lips. She had no idea she'd missed the meeting.

"Shit, shit, shit! Caleb, oh my god." She blinks back tears but quickly shakes them off. "I never miss a meeting. Do you have any idea how many meetings I've pushed through with a migraine? And I couldn't even do that for my biggest client ever. This is terrible. I need to call Hannah. Oh my god, if my mom finds out—"

"Hey, *hey*," I place my hands on her shoulders. "It's okay, I told her you were having car trouble. Come here." She's so worked up, I go against everything I've been trying not to do since I've been back and pull her close. I expect her to be tense in my arms, but she falls into me, wrapping her arms around my torso and tucking her head into my chest. Her head's in the perfect spot for me to rest my chin, but I hold back. I settle for inhaling the sweet smell of her hair. I've never held her like this. If I'd done things differently, I could have been doing this every day for the last five years. Fuck. There's no denying what I feel for her anymore, but I make myself pull away.

"Brooke, you have nothing to be sorry for," I say, looking into her glassy blue eyes. "You had a migraine attack. I've become something of a migraine expert in the last half hour, and it's not your fault. I'm sorry I didn't leave the meeting sooner to make sure you were okay. C'mon, let's get you home."

Chapter 15

Brooke

It's not your fault.

I'm fighting back tears. Again. Mom's voice fills my head—she has strong opinions about when it's appropriate to cry. And I've already gotten sick in front of Caleb today, I won't add crying to the mix. In the short time I was with the doctor, Caleb took more interest in my diagnosis than Mom ever has. From her, I get nothing but critiques of all the things I could have done wrong to trigger a migraine attack. I'm not drinking enough water. I should cut out gluten. I'm not getting enough sleep. I'm sleeping too much. I'm being dramatic.

It's always my fault.

When I was younger, I always seemed to have an attack when there was something important on Mom's agenda. She'd have to leave a client meeting to pick me up from school. Or find coverage at the agency. I started pushing through them instead of acknowledging the pain. Barely keeping it together until I was alone. Once I was, the pain was unbearable.

My strict routine is all an effort to avoid migraine attacks. My neurologist says the underlying reason is a highly sensitive nervous system. It's another thing Mom says sounds fake. One slip-up—a missed glass of water or an extra glass of wine, missing a meal because it was a sixteen-hour wedding day or exerting too much energy schlepping wedding supplies—and I've got a migraine attack on the way with her on my case.

I'm lucky Mom didn't stay late. It's been months since I've had an attack that bad. I took my medication the moment that dull throb began, but the pain wouldn't subside. I resigned to waiting it out on the office floor. By the time the nausea crept in, if I so much as lifted my head, I'd be sick. My phone wasn't anywhere near me. By then I'd already forgotten about the meeting, so I curled into a ball on the floor. I'd feel better eventually or someone would show up and take me to urgent care. I hadn't expected that person to be Caleb.

He was still there, at urgent care, waiting for me until I was done. Through the small window on the door between the exam rooms and the waiting room, I could see him focusing on his phone, a crease between his brows.

I feel worlds better. Now I'm just exhausted. That's what I blame for the threat of tears as Caleb drives me home.

We pull into the driveway of my little rental. It's small but it's mine. It's a light gray Cape Cod style home with a light pink door and window boxes full of petunias and geraniums. But my favorite things are the white hydrangeas out front and the blue ones out back.

"Thanks, Caleb," I say, turning toward him as I play with my seatbelt. Stalling. "You didn't have to do all this tonight. I could have gotten myself home."

"Of course you could have, but I don't mind," he says, turning off the car. It brings me back to the drives home after country club weddings. He was always watching out for me. He's contemplative for a moment. "Brooke, what would you have done if I hadn't shown up?"

"Wait it out, I guess. Hope that I would have felt better

before my mom came into work in the morning. She doesn't take my migraines seriously."

"She doesn't take the fact that you could barely move without experiencing excruciating pain seriously?"

"She..." I don't know where to begin. How do I explain that for all she's taught me, for all she's done for me, raising me on her own, Mom doesn't want to be bothered with anything that isn't perfect? I bite the inside of my bottom lip and try to put together some kind of answer. Caleb must sense I'm dying for a subject change because he provides one quickly.

"Hey, are you hungry?"

"Starving," I admit.

"Let me make you dinner. I'm sure I can whip something up with whatever you have."

My face twists into a grimace. "I don't think I have anything that can be turned into an acceptable meal." The last time I did any kind of legitimate grocery shopping was...well, I'm not sure. There's wine in the fridge and peanut butter and crackers in the cabinets. Other than that, it's anyone's guess. "I'm not much of a cook. I live on takeout and girl dinner."

He laughs, unbuckling his seatbelt. "You have no idea what I'm capable of. Challenge accepted."

Caleb hops out of the car and I follow, wanting to find out exactly what he's capable of. By the time I open the car door, he's there holding his hand out to me. I take it. Only because I'm still feeling lightheaded. Not at all because the gentlemanly gesture of helping me out of the car and the offer to cook for me makes me feel like my legs might give out.

Caleb follows me into the house, carrying my bag. He insisted. *Just because you can, doesn't mean you have to.* I rarely have anyone other than Maddie and Jordan over, unless you count Mom showing up uninvited, letting herself in with her emergency key. It's never actually an emergency, but her unexpected drop-ins mean the house is always clean and tidy.

I drop my keys on the entry table. Entry is a loose term for where I'm standing. The stairs are right in front of the door; take one more step and you're in the living room.

Caleb stands outside the door, holding each side of the frame, my bag hanging from one hand, and leans in.

"Are you coming in?" He rakes his hand through his hair, taking a step inside. Maybe it's the post-migraine fog, but he's acting weird. He drops my bag on the table. "Kitchen's back here."

We walk toward the back of the house to the kitchen and little dining nook. For someone who doesn't use it much, I love my tiny kitchen. It has black and white linoleum floors and white cabinets. They're outdated enough that they almost pass as a vintage design choice. All of the tabletop appliances, including the microwave (my favorite), are light blue to match the SMEG refrigerator. The window behind the sink looks out to the little patio, my backyard, and Mr. Edwards' side yard. Whenever I see him working on his garden, I run out to help.

Caleb makes himself right at home in the tiny kitchen. He has to—he practically takes up the entire space. He opens cabinet doors and pulls out drawers, rifling through my sad excuse of a pantry.

"Wow," he says.

"Don't act so surprised." I cross my arms and lean on the counter. "I told you there's not a lot to work with here."

"Maybe in terms of ingredients, but for someone who isn't much of a cook, you have decent cookware." He holds up a light blue enameled Le Creuset cast iron skillet. Oh, that. He's unknowingly picked up on something I'd like to forget.

"I thought it'd be cute because it matches the refrigerator."

"Ah," he says with a smile. "So, it's for the aesthetic?"

"Naturally," I say, stifling a yawn.

"Why don't you go rest while I figure out what to make?"

"Fine." I yawn, in earnest this time. "Don't burn down my house, please."

It's hard to rest, knowing Caleb's in my kitchen. Cooking. For me. I bury my face in my hands, concealing the thrill and embarrassment I'm feeling even though I'm alone. My stomach twists and turns. From hunger, surely. Maybe I should have lied when he asked if I was hungry.

I'm still not convinced he'll manage to find anything to work with. Laying on my bed and staring at the ceiling, I try to remember the last time anyone cooked in my kitchen. It's been months. I roll onto my side, facing my closed bedroom door. I'm starving, but I'm also so tired. My eyes slowly close. I drift in and out of sleep for half an hour, every few minutes hearing a noise from the kitchen or seeing a shadow in the hall.

An amazing aroma, buttery and rich, pulls me from tossing and turning. Did he manage to scrounge up something that wasn't expired? I push myself off of my bed, catching a glimpse of myself in the mirror. *Yikes*. My hair is a matted mess on one side. My skin is more pallid than I'd like, and the light film of mascara under my eyes isn't helping. Not what I'd pictured for our first meal together at my house.

I had been picturing what that would be like, hadn't I?

Since Jordan had to go and send me that photo, Caleb's occupied more and more of my thoughts. I can't even bring myself to finish watching *The Bear*. I wipe the mascara from under my eyes and throw my hair into a claw clip. Still not what I pictured, but an improvement.

My stomach grumbles as I walk down the short hall and remember the way his shirt hugged his arms as he rolled those pigs in a blanket.

I have to shake whatever this feeling is. Caleb and I can never work. First of all, my mother would kill me, and there's no second of all if I'm dead. Caleb is all the wonderful things I remembered from years ago and, apparently, so much more. But the ideal match for Judy Spencer's daughter he is not. Not that she has a good track record of finding a match for me.

God, if Mom even knew Caleb was here! What if she drives by? Or stops by unannounced? I'm brought out of my spiral when I enter the kitchen. Caleb's setting the table, shirt sleeves rolled to his forearms with a dish towel thrown over his shoulder. The combination does something else entirely to my stomach.

He managed to find placemats and napkins. I may not cook, but I do entertain. My table linen collection is unmatched. There are water glasses and a pitcher placed in the center of the small wood table. I continue watching him set the table and a smile breaks through, despite my efforts to keep my shit together. There's a swelling in my chest that could rival the Grinch's on Christmas morning. Caleb's adjusting the placement of a napkin when he spots me. "You're up," he says, smiling. "Perfect timing."

"You didn't have to do all this," I say as he pulls out a chair for me. "I usually eat dinner right out of whatever I heated it up in."

Caleb gasps. "You mean to tell me that the renowned Brooke Spencer doesn't do a full tablescape for every meal? What will the brides-to-be and their overbearing mothers think when they find out?"

I raise my brows with a smile. "Since it appears you found the fancy placemats, I'm sure you won't be surprised to know that I do, at the very least, use those regularly. Full tablescapes are reserved for only the most important guests."

"Ah, of course." He grabs two plates from the counter. "I can only hope to be one of those guests one day."

"You're dreaming, Foley," I tease.

"You have no idea what I dream about, Spencer."

Before I can come up with a retort and make the part of my body that is suddenly aching to calm the fuck down, Caleb places a plate on the table in front of me. We lock eyes. "You made grilled cheese?"

"Yup." He sits down across from me with a satisfied smirk on his face. "You weren't lying…there wasn't a lot to work with. This was the best I could do."

"The best you could do? It's my favorite."

I pick up one of the triangles on my plate, cheese oozing from between the bread. I take a bite and the audible groan that escapes me is more suggestive than I anticipated. So much for keeping my shit together.

"I know," he says, pleased with himself. He rests his elbows on the table and his smile, with that damn dimple, reaches his eyes. I want to chide him for being so smug, but this sandwich is so damn good that I can't. He has every right to be smug. It's been years, but he remembers.

"You clearly already know this," I say. "But this is amazing." I take another bite, but he hasn't moved to start eating his. I think he might be blushing. "What? Stop smiling like that!"

He shakes his head and looks down at the plate in front of him. "Nothing," he says, finally picking up a triangle. "It's no Duchess, but I'm glad you like it."

"It's better."

Caleb stands outside my front door. Lingering like maybe he doesn't want to leave. Maybe I don't want him to. But where could this go? Our parents hate each other. Who knows what Caleb's parents think of me. The migraine is messing with my head more than it usually does. Five years ago, he made his feelings clear and ran away. Quite literally, if you count speed-walking to the nearest exit.

But something is holding us both here at the door, dragging out the conversation like we don't want the night to end. The events of the evening shattered the walls I've been holding up to keep Caleb out. We've had such a lovely night together, falling back into easy conversation like we were back in his car before he'd drop me off at home.

"Thanks again, Caleb," I say, leaning on the banister. "For helping me tonight and making me dinner."

"Anything for you, babe." He winks.

I can't help but laugh. "Shut up." I'm getting used to the nickname, especially because the way he said it feels different. "I'll reach out to Hannah tomorrow to apologize for missing the meeting and text Baxter to confirm the details you covered."

"Sounds good…" He trails off.

"What?"

"I have a confession to make," he says, sheepishly.

I hold my breath. I'm so not ready for this confession.

"I found your Monica Geller closet."

Shit. Shit. Shit. Not the confession I thought it would be. Not the confession a part of me was foolishly hoping for. This is so much worse. I take a step back, putting space between us. Space I was about to close if this confession had been something different.

"My what?" I ask, knowing full well what he's talking about it.

"The room next to your bedroom…shit." He rakes a hand through his hair. "I'm sorry…I was looking for the bathroom and stumbled in there."

"Caleb, that room…you shouldn't have…" I grab on the

door to steady myself, forcing him to back up. "Caleb, you should go."

"Brooke, I..." Before he can finish, I close the door and lock it.

Chapter 16

Caleb

WALKING INTO BROOKE'S HOUSE FELT LIKE WALKING INTO A magazine spread. Not one thing was out of place. It was beautiful but still felt lived in. Lived in by an extremely tidy, brunette control freak, but lived in. It felt *so* her. Shades of blue with pops of pink accents. Classic but fun. Fresh flowers on the coffee table and in the kitchen.

There was a time when I thought about what it'd be like to take Brooke home. I thought about it a lot. This wasn't exactly what I'd pictured before I'd left for California, or while I was there, or since I've been back, if I'm being honest with myself. What I'd pictured over the years involved heading upstairs to the bedroom.

When Brooke padded down the hallway from the kitchen to the bedroom on the other side of the house, I made a mental note to strike the stairs from my fantasy. Even if I had squashed any real chance at being with her years ago. That's when it occurred to me that this was the first time I was cooking for Brooke. She had the burgers at the wedding a few weeks ago, but even though I'd done that for her, it wasn't cooking *for* her.

Again, it wasn't how I'd pictured it. What I had in mind included a trip to the farmer's market for all the right ingredients. Making one of her favorite meals, but better than she ever imagined it could be. We'd have a romantic meal and then I'd carry her to her bedroom down the hall.

She hadn't been lying about not having ingredients. What did this woman eat? In the vintage SMEG refrigerator, for the aesthetic I'm sure, I hoped to find something semi-fresh to work with. Digging through the cheese drawer I found a single wedge of gruyere cheese and a few slices of American. That was a start. It took some rummaging in the freezer, but I found a sourdough loaf. I could work with this. I've done more with less. But I needed the key ingredient for a perfect grilled cheese. More rummaging. Through the cabinets this time. Deep in the back I found it. Hellman's mayonnaise. And there was still an entire month before it expired.

I fired up the burner and warmed up the seemingly brand new Le Creuset skillet. It looked like it'd never been used. Why would someone who never cooks have such nice cookware?

While I waited for the pan to warm, I walked back out to the living room. I was snooping. I couldn't help myself, I wanted to see more of her space. Who she is when she's not making color-coded documents, checking off lists, and generally being amazing at her job. There was a small desk in the corner with a stack of notebooks, a to-do list on top. She's organized at home too, even where no one can see her. I headed back to the kitchen to start cooking but stopped when I noticed another room down the hall, next to the one where Brooke was resting behind the closed door. This door was closed, too.

I knew I shouldn't continue snooping around, especially right next to her room. If she caught me, I'd say I was looking for the bathroom—though another door in the hall clearly led to the bathroom. Whatever. She thought I was an idiot anyway.

I just needed another peek at something about Brooke Spencer.

The small room was a complete mess. It gave Dad's office a run for its money. Bins and boxes stacked along the walls. Some closed, others overflowing with papers and random items that looked like wedding decor and supplies. It was like that episode of *Friends*. The one where Chandler discovers Monica's secret messy closet in their apartment.

Not so perfect and tidy, Brooke. Even when we were younger, I remember her being so poised. She might be a few years younger than me, but I swear she behaved a lot more maturely than I ever did. We'd be in a room full of grownups and she acted like more of an adult than most of them. Like a little child actor who grew up on set and attended Hollywood parties. Sometimes her mask slipped, especially if Judy wasn't around. When Mom watched us while Judy and Dad were working a wedding, the mask wasn't even there. She could be a kid.

Since I'd been back, I'd only seen a small glimpse of this Brooke. Hadn't noticed a single flaw. I was getting the buttoned-up, capable career woman. Sexy as hell, but always professional and polished. I worried this was who she was now, putting her even further out of my league than she was before. Too good to ever settle for the caterer, the help. Not when she was surrounded by wealthy clients with sons, brothers, friends who could give her so much more than I ever could.

But this, this mess, told me that the Brooke I remember, the one I got to see every once in a while, was still there. Somewhere underneath the polished persona and the organized life, there's a perfectly messy version of her.

I stand outside Brooke's door. The door she shut in my face. Feeling even more distant than where we started weeks ago. I linger at the door. I hadn't wanted to leave. I wanted to stay and talk to her. She could read the phone book and I'd listen.

But I had to go and confess that I'd been snooping. The moment I mentioned that room, she froze and all the color that had finally returned to her cheeks completely disappeared. I don't know what I stepped into by bringing it up, but whatever it was, it wasn't good.

My Uber picks me up to grab my car from Spencer Soirees. Mom and Dad had been missing Wendell, so he spent the day with them. I hop in the Wrangler to go pick him up.

If walking into Brooke's house felt like a magazine spread, walking into my childhood home is the opposite. My parents have lived in this large ranch-style house since before I was born. It's not messy, but it's not tidy either. Every inch of wall space is covered with art. All the bookshelves filled to the brim. Each surface has something on it: picture frames, decor, piles of papers Dad will get to eventually. It's cluttered, colorful, and eclectic. It's home.

When I open the door, Wendell's in the entryway. He regards me with a bark, turns, and walks away. I hear Mom singing an ABBA song in the kitchen, over the noise of washing dishes. Dad sits at the kitchen table reading something on his tablet. He's always been the cook and Mom's always been the dishwasher.

Mom stops her singing. "There you are. Wendell was getting worried."

I give her a peck on the cheek while she continues scrubbing. "You mean you were worried, Mom. I don't think Wendell concerns himself with me at all."

"Lynne," Dad says, looking up from his tablet. "I can take care of the dog. Let the poor guy be."

"Am I the poor guy?" I ask. "Or Wendell?"

"Paul, we need to focus on your health and Caleb needs a friend."

"I have friends," I say.

Mom takes off her dishwashing gloves and joins Dad at the table. "I know you do, sweetheart. But you're busy and Wendell can keep you company."

"I'm not sure he enjoys my company...and I'll have you know I was hanging out with a friend tonight."

Mom's honey brown eyes light up behind her glasses. At this point in the summer, her olive skin has developed a tan from her daily outings with the neighborhood walking club. Yes, walking club. They even have matching t-shirts. "Tell me." She pats the chair next to her, signaling me to sit. "How's Joey doing? Dad's been worried about him going on his own."

"I wasn't with Joey, but he's doing okay. Busy. I think he misses the Market. I was with...Brooke."

"Oh," Mom says, turning to Dad.

Dad puts down his tablet. "Brooke, huh? Were you working or..."

"We had a rentals meeting, but she missed it," I say. I tell them about her migraine attack and making her dinner. I leave out the part about the closet and how her mood completely shifted. They nod and ask questions like it's any other friend and not the daughter of their industry rival. It seems so absurd to me now that Brooke and I used to be scared our parents would find out we were friends.

"I have to tell you both something. In college and after, when I was still living here and working for you, Dad, or picking up shifts at the country club, Brooke and I were kind of friends. At least when we worked the same weddings." My parents give each other a sidelong glance. "I mean, I know we'd been friends before...when you used to work with Judy. Then all of a sudden Brooke and Judy were gone. But later, when we ended up at the same weddings, it was like nothing had changed."

They give each other those glances again. This time with knowing smirks plastered on their faces. "What?"

"Oh, sweetheart," Mom says with a laugh. "We knew that."

"You did?"

"Son, you think we didn't notice the spring in your step when it was a Spencer Soirees wedding at the club?" Dad smiles.

"Remember how he'd always spend extra time on his hair those days?" Mom asks with a laugh.

Dad laughs even more loudly. "He went through so much hair gel!"

Geez. These two.

"I can't believe you knew…and didn't care? I was so worried you'd find out and be mad." But had I been worried? I hadn't cared if anyone knew Brooke and I were friends. But she did. She'd been terrified of Judy finding out, and I went along with keeping our friendship quiet because I hated the thought of her being upset. But I was scared of Judy finding out, too. Scared she'd find a way to keep Brooke away from me. I took care of that all by myself.

"Caleb, we don't have any problem with Brooke. I missed her too, when…well, you know," Mom says, glancing at Dad.

"Actually, I *don't* know," I remind them, hoping they'll finally tell me what happened between them and Judy.

"I think it might be time to get Wendell home," Dad says, getting up from the table. Not finding out then. Got it.

Chapter 17

Brooke

Don't go to bed angry. I've heard the advice in one too many wedding toasts. The adage is meant for couples, partners, and newlyweds—not a single twenty-nine-year-old—but I try to follow it, and despite my best efforts, I'm going to bed angry tonight. Mad at Caleb. Frustrated with myself. And furious with my mother. Because I'm never able to unpack when it comes to Mom, I always focus my anger elsewhere. I should've purchased the padlock I thought about getting when I last closed that stupid door.

And Caleb. Snooping around like that. I want to say I wouldn't have done the same thing if the roles were reversed. But that's not true. I would have loved getting a peek into what Caleb is like now. So much about him feels different. But so much feels the same. He's still playful and kind. He's not lacking direction like he used to, and that new air of confidence is sexy. And the cooking. I didn't know a grilled cheese could taste so good.

What had I been thinking, hoping for a different kind of confession? I read the signs wrong once before, and here I am doing it again. How pathetic. Why did he have to look so damn good standing at the door? He made it clear how he felt about me years ago. His quips and jokes that feel so much like flirting are just fun and games. He's not serious about me. He wasn't then and he isn't now. But I'd wanted him then and, despite myself, despite my mom, despite my perfect plan for my life, I still want him now.

We'd had such a nice night but for that room. That fucking room and all the shit in it.

I stare at my phone. He texted an hour ago.

> Caleb: I'm really sorry about tonight.

What can I even say to him? *It's okay, you only opened the door to the second greatest heartache of my life? Don't be sorry, you didn't know the secret I've been hiding from you. The thing I've been pretending never happened.* No, I can't tell him any of that. That would mean having to tell him everything. And reliving the fallout.

I'm going to need reinforcements in the morning.

"Good morning, sunshine," Maddie chirps, letting herself into the house with her emergency key. Too many people have easy access to this place. I pad over to greet my friends at the door, shoulders sagging.

"We brought coffee and croissants from Soundview," Jordan says behind her.

"Mmmm, the almond ones?" I ask, eyeing the brown bag she's holding.

"Obviously! This momentous occasion calls for only the best pastries this side of the Long Island Sound." Jordan hands me a coffee. "Americano with oat milk and a splash of brown sugar syrup."

"*You're simply the best*," I sing to her, attempting to make myself feel better before we unpack the mess that is my life. Literally.

Maddie laughs. "Are you quoting Tina Turner or *Schitt's Creek*?"

I shrug. "Both."

Jordan holds up another bag from Soundview. "Got sandwiches for later, too."

"Alright, B," Maddie says, clapping her hands together and scanning my living room. "Where's the clipboard? What's the plan? How are we tackling the closet of doom? I'm assuming you have a checklist? A timeline? Where is it?"

Jordan eyes every surface looking for a signature Brooke Spencer checklist. Coming up empty, she looks at Maddie, then to me.

The girl who has a plan for every scenario doesn't have a plan for this. I blow out a long breath, my eyes and nose beginning to sting. Mom's voice in my head keeps the tears at bay once again.

"No plan, no checklist. I have to face it head-on."

"Oh Brooke, if you weren't about to burst into tears, I'd be giving you so much shit right now." Jordan pulls me into a hug, and I melt in her arms.

"That is why you're *such* a good friend," Maddie teases, and wraps her arms around the two of us. A few tears fall while they hold me, but I don't let them see. I shake my head and our group hug dissolves.

We put the sandwiches in the kitchen, and I hope they don't notice the pan *I* never use on the drying rack.

"Okay, let's do this."

We walk down the hall to what Caleb called my Monica Geller closet. Tears still threaten to burst, but I smile thinking about that. He's not wrong. It's very Monica of me to have a secret messy room in my otherwise pristine house. I'm still grappling with my feelings around Caleb snooping and seeing this room, but right now, I'm glad for the humor.

I open the door. Jordan and Maddie stand behind me, waiting.

Oh god.

It's worse than I remember. And Caleb saw this. How mortifying. A few months ago, in a fury of anger and disappointment, Mom helped me pack up all the boxes. The gifts, the cards, the special-ordered decor, the unsent invitations—and the dress. I'd forgotten about the dress, with its lace that matched my bride's earlier this summer. I can't see it from where I stand outside the room, but I know it's hanging in a garment bag behind a stack of identically gift-wrapped boxes. Williams-Sonoma signature paper. I know it well. The various wine glasses. Twelve red wine, twelve white wine, and twelve champagne flutes. More than anyone ever needs.

Mom refused to hire movers or ask anyone for help. Even when sweet Mr. Edwards next door offered, she shooed him away. It was just the two of us schlepping boxes and bags from the car into the house. Once we got it all in, I shut the door and haven't opened it until today.

"Okay," I say, rolling my shoulders back like I'm going into battle. It sure feels like one. An emotional one. "Um…" I turn around to Maddie and Jordan. "I don't know where to start."

"Lucky for you," Maddie says, stepping into the room, assessing the situation. "I'm an expert at post-breakup purging. I'll admit, post-broken *engagement* isn't going to be as easy, but we've got this. Is there anything you want to keep? You got some fancy shit at that bridal shower. It shouldn't all go to waste because Judy meddles too much and Kent's a schmuck."

"I'm with Maddie." Jordan follows her into the room. "I'm more of a burn-it-all-down girl, but you really wanted some of this stuff at one point, right? Let's start there."

With my friends in the room, it's not so scary. I cross the threshold and turn in a small circle, taking inventory.

From the outside, the bridal shower was perfect. Mom had the Spencer Soirees office transformed for the occasion. Office furniture removed and put in storage for the weekend. Rentals brought in to accommodate over fifty guests for a tea luncheon. Cocktails and appetizers outside on the front porch. It'd been a beautiful late April day. One of those days that made you feel like spring had finally arrived.

I hate being the center of attention. It's one of the reasons I love being a wedding planner. I'm part of the excitement, but all eyes are on the couple instead of me. It's my job to blend in and remain unseen. Afterward, I'm celebrated and thanked for doing an excellent job. The right amount of attention and praise.

The expensive bridal shower was only a small taste of what was to come. Mom had an over-the-top wedding planned for me and Kent, though neither were what I wanted. What I wanted rarely mattered to Mom, but planning kept her off my back. It made her happy. I'd learned long ago that life's easier when she's happy, when she's in control and ensuring things are to her liking. That everything is perfect. Which it all was... until it wasn't.

I don't even remember what most of this stuff is. Gifts from the registry we made, mostly with suggestions from Mom. She insisted on accompanying us to Williams Sonoma and then to Crate & Barrel. Kent even gave her the login to our accounts. Each item on that list was picked in preparation for a life of hosting holidays as husband and wife in Kent's modern, cold, way too big home. What could I possibly want to keep?

My eyes land on something light blue.

"The cookware," I say, pointing. "The nice Le Creuset stuff."

Maddie and Jordan look at one another, eyes wide.

"Brooke, you don't cook," Maddie says. "Like at all."

"Do you even know how to turn on your stove?" Jordan asks.

I hadn't told them anything about yesterday. I sent a message on our group text last night, *Cleaning THE ROOM tomorrow, need you both!* They'd been hounding me to deal with it, so they didn't ask why I was suddenly so eager to clean it out.

"I…might cook…one day," I say. "And no, of course I don't know how to turn on the stove, but it can't be that hard."

"Okay, what's going on, Brooke?" Maddie's arms move to make a W and don't stop moving as more words tumble from her mouth. "Out of nowhere, you're ready to clean out this room. We get here and there's no plan. You! Brooke Spencer. Who always has a plan for everything…nada! Now, out of all the expensive gifts you got at your bridal shower, you want to keep the cookware because you *might* learn to use the stove and cook…one day?"

I'm failing to come up with any excuse to throw them off the scent of what prompted me to tackle this trauma today. Any other reason that I'd want to keep it. The skillet Caleb had christened making grilled cheese was the first engagement gift Kent and I received last fall, from some distant relative of Kent's whose name I can't remember or never bothered to learn. It made its way into the kitchen well before things went to shit.

They might buy the same excuse I gave Caleb yesterday. It's better than getting into the whole truth right now.

"You got me. It's for the aesthetic. They go with the vibe of the kitchen and match the skillet I already opened. They should all live happily together, remaining as clean as the day they were made."

"Okay…" Maddie says, eyes studying me. "That makes a lot more sense."

Phew. It's not a lie. They *should* all live happily together.

They're too pretty. I may not cook, but I know quality when I see it.

"These are so fucking heavy," Maddie says, carrying a box to the kitchen. "I'll find a spot for them. Might have to rearrange your fancy napkins though."

"Don't you dare!" I say.

When I turn to Jordan, she's staring me down with an ear-to-ear grin on her face. She bites into an almond croissant, getting crumbs all over the floor and shakes her head.

"What?"

"Caleb was here, wasn't he?" she whispers. God, she's good. Jordan has always known how to read people. I swear sometimes she knows what I'm thinking before I do. She has this sense. She watches people and knows what's coming next. And she's there to capture it, whether you like it or not. It's why she's such a damn good photographer.

"Please don't tell her yet," I plead.

"He cooked for you, didn't he?" She smirks.

Jordan can read people but she's not a mind reader. "How did you know that?"

"You've never had any interest in cookware." She takes another small bite of the croissant. "And I saw the pan on the drying rack."

"He did cook for me," I say, grinning. "Grilled cheese."

"Shit, like the good old days."

"I know."

"Did you…?" She raises her perfectly sculpted brows twice in quick succession.

"No! Absolutely not!" I grab the croissant from her and take a bite. It melts in my mouth so deliciously I'm not even mad that I'll have to vacuum up the crumbs. "I had a migraine attack at the office, he helped me and brought me home. We talked for a while and ate grilled cheese like we used to. Then he left, but not before telling me he *accidentally* went into this room."

"Shit."

"Yeah, shit."

"What's shit?" Maddie walks back in to grab another heavy box.

"Soooo much shit in this room," I say, grabbing one of the smaller boxes, a set of ramekins maybe. I follow Maddie out of the room, mouthing *please* to Jordan.

Chapter 18

Caleb

I make my last trip up the stairs and into Hamilton Homestead, carrying a large bin filled with containers of prepped ingredients. We've got two hours until service begins for tonight's reception. The Hamilton Homestead is the historic home of some American revolutionary whose name I can't remember. Not Hamilton himself, but maybe he stayed here once and that's how it got the name. I'll leave keeping track of historic buildings to Joey. While it's beautifully restored and does make for a picturesque wedding, the kitchen leaves a lot to be desired. Lucky me.

Joey's helping tonight, and he's thrilled to be back with the Foley's team. Dad overcommitted this summer and we need more help than we have. I might even be able to convince Joey to come back full-time. I have a feeling it won't be too hard.

Joey and the team already have the catering tent set up, and when I walk through the venue and out the back, he's finishing up with the fire marshal.

"All set, Foley," the fire marshal says. One less thing to worry about. "You've got one of the cleanest operations I've seen, and I've seen it all."

Brooke would be impressed. If she were actually talking to me.

I delegate setup whenever I can. It's one of the more grueling parts of the job. I pushed against it for so long, but cooking really is my passion. As a kid, I loved cooking with Dad. He'd pull a chair to the counter and let me crack eggs, chop vegetables, and mix ingredients. I had a julienne down before most kids were allowed to hold a butter knife. Though I loved it, by the time I was an angsty teenager, I no longer wanted to follow in his footsteps. I wanted to do something, *anything* else. I spent my early twenties picking up enough credits at UConn-Stamford to graduate, then bummed around town hoping to figure things out. I also hoped that such behavior would convince my parents that handing over the business to me was a bad idea.

The summer I dated Jennifer, things changed. We were never going to be anything serious, not when I wished I was sneaking around with someone else. But her family's reaction to us was the wakeup call I needed to get my shit together. I applied to culinary school the next day. I couldn't deny it any longer. I loved it and was pretty damn good at it.

This wedding grind, however, is already getting old. Schlepping supplies and food in and out, cooking under the sweltering sun, breaking down at the end of the night. Every wedding, I'm thinking about how much easier it was in San Francisco. Weddings were still a grind, but being the head chef at a venue with my own kitchen was a hell of a lot easier.

Today, I want to get into the makeshift kitchen at the venue and get to work. Finish prep, fire off the entrees, and focus on executing a great service. Anything to get my mind off Brooke and how royally I fucked up. Right as we were getting back on solid footing. I keep going back to the moment I decided to open that stupid door. I thought it was a mess of boxes, Brooke's little secret that she isn't as perfect and organized as she wants the outside world to think she is. I got that wrong. Yeah, I crossed a line, but she went ice cold on me in an instant. Something more is going on. We have another planning meeting with Hannah and Preston next week. I have to figure it out and apologize before then.

Cocktail hour is in full swing by the time I notice Jordan with her camera. She's buzzing through the outdoor garden, taking candid photos and posing groups of friends together. Inside, as the band does soundcheck, the flower girl and ring bearer are dancing in front of the stage on the black and white checkered floor.

"Jordan!" I call over the noise of instruments tuning and vocalists warming up their voices. I wave my hand in the air signaling her to come over. She gives me a sideways glance. I point to the kids who are dancing like no one is watching. Carefree and having the time of their lives. The band must be done with their soundcheck by now, but they keep playing for the tiny audience.

Jordan notices the kids and walks over, swapping the camera in her hands for another one hanging from the straps crisscrossing her back. She crouches down at the edge of dance floor, snapping candids of the little dancers. They hold hands, trying to spin in a circle but stumble over their own feet. Their giggles are infectious.

"Thanks for the heads-up," Jordan says, scrolling through the shots she captured. "The bride is going to love these. They're her niece and nephew, twins."

"No problem." I shift my hands into my pockets and rock on my feet, trying to figure out how to ask Jordan about Brooke.

"Whatever you want to ask me about Brooke, Caleb, just

ask it," she says without a glance at me. She's occupied with switching out her camera lens. "I've got a reception to shoot and you've got a meal to serve."

Damn, she's perceptive. "I don't know what I did. I mean...I do. I shouldn't have been looking around, but I thought it was cute she had this secret messy closet. As soon as I mentioned it, a switch flipped and she went back to hating me."

"Brooke has never hated you, Caleb," she says, shaking her head. "Upset you rejected her, sure. But she's never hated you."

Rejected her. *Fuck.*

"I didn't...I...it's complicated," I mutter. "I don't know what to do."

"Listen, I know why she's upset," she says, pausing like she's choosing her words carefully. "But it's not my story to tell."

"Whatever it is, she's not going to tell me. She's not returning my texts or emails. Even the ones about work. You know that isn't like her."

She sighs, clearly exasperated by me. "During your snooping, did you take a second to look around that room?"

"Yeah, I mean, it was a lot of boxes. Gift boxes and random wedding supplies and stuff."

"And does that remind you of anything?"

I'm so utterly confused. "Weddings?"

"You're a smart guy, Caleb. You'll figure it out. Now come on, introductions are going to start any minute."

Am I a smart guy? Because I feel pretty fucking dumb. Brooke's life is work, how is knowing it's wedding stuff supposed to help me?

Hamilton Homestead's proximity to residential neighborhoods means the wedding's over at ten o'clock. Which means an earlier night for me and a less exhausting day tomorrow. Thank you, local noise ordinances. Dessert was set at nine, giving the team plenty of time to clear plates, clean, and pack up before the reception is even over.

Joey and I watch the last few songs from the corner of the room. The bride and groom are in the center of the dance floor with guests crowded around them. Arms flailing everywhere. I scan the room to be sure we've cleared everything. A few feet away from me, our wedding coordinator organizes and packs up the gifts for the bride and groom to take home. The table is covered with boxes and bags wrapped in various pastel shades. There's one large Crate & Barrel shipping box. I also spot the Williams Sonoma gift wrap that makes an appearance at all of these Fairfield County weddings.

"Shit," I say a little too loudly, remembering where I last saw that wrapping paper.

"What?" Joey asks. "I thought we got everything. What'd we forget?"

Jordan walks by us, heading to the dance floor.

"Nothing. Can you handle the rest of the night? I'll owe you one!" I clap Joey's shoulder and jog to catch up to Jordan. "Tell me what venue Brooke's working tonight…please?"

She groans, rolling her eyes. "You're so desperate."

"I'm well aware," I say. "Please, Jordan?"

"Alright, if you can correctly guess the last song, I'll tell you where Brooke is."

"Oh c'mon!" I plead.

"Caleb, it's not that hard. You've been to enough weddings to figure this out," she says, sly smirk on her face.

"You know what it is, don't you?"

"Of course I do," she says. "I've got to be strategically positioned on the dance floor to photograph it. That's your only hint."

Okay. Last song of the night. Usually, I'm barely paying attention by that point. Hell, I'm lucky if I can hear the music from whatever terrible kitchen I'm stuck in at any given wedding. "Don't Stop Believin'" is an obvious choice. Or this could be a "Closing Time" crowd. But Jordan has to be on the dance floor in a specific spot.

"'Shout'!" I yell. "It's 'Shout'!"

Jordan shushes me and shakes her head. At least she's genuinely smiling a little. She doesn't seem to hold the same grudge against me that Maddie does. I'll take that win. "Congratulations, Caleb Foley, you are officially a jaded wedding professional!"

"Yeah, yeah, where is she tonight?" I need to run to wherever she is and apologize for being such a complete and total dipshit. And to find out if what I think that room is all about is true. I should have never unfollowed her socials. I had no idea they were set to private when I did.

"She's at home, Caleb."

It's a Saturday in early July. Home is the last place I expect Brooke to be.

"Thanks, Jordan. Good luck out there." I gesture to the dance floor as the band begins the first notes of "Shout," guests roaring with enthusiasm. "Looks like you're going to need it."

I run to my car.

Chapter 19

Brooke

IT'S A PERFECT SUMMER NIGHT. IT WAS A STUNNING DAY, TOO. Warm but not humid. The sky a gorgeous blue scattered with puffy white clouds. By evening, the temperature has cooled down and the mosquitoes are miraculously at bay. The perfect day for a wedding.

Kent and I were the perfect couple. Or so I'd thought. We were great on paper and even better in pictures. Mom loved Kent. How could she not? He checked all the boxes on her eligible bachelor list. She'd hand-picked him for me. Plucked him like he was a Ken doll in the Barbie aisle. Though I hadn't known that at the time.

We may have looked perfect on the outside, but we were putting on a show. I wish I could say that I didn't know what Mom saw in him when she set us up, but they were all the same things I saw and liked at first. He was a good-looking guy, if not a little cookie cutter. Had a successful, well-paying job in finance, but wasn't a total finance bro. Smart and charismatic. And, less important to me but hugely important to Mom, he came from what she considers a good family. By *good* she means *wealthy*.

I spent our whole relationship trying to be the perfect girlfriend. Then the perfect fiancée. I went to the country club dinners and had superficial friendships with the wives of his friends. I created a version of myself that fit into his life instead of being myself and creating a life together.

We didn't work, but that's not what hurt. It was the aftermath.

It's the reason I didn't want to take on a wedding tonight. It's what kept me at home, away from anyone who might remember the date and the tacky over-the-top save-the-date Mom insisted on sending. The relief on Kent's face when I called it off made that part easy, though his ego took a bruising. I'm so much happier to be sipping sauvignon blanc in my sunroom instead of at my own wedding reception right now. Relieved to not be marrying Kent. But I still had to mourn the day and process the fallout.

A knock on the door makes me jump, spilling wine on my summer nightgown. Who the hell is at my door this late? Maddie and Jordan are both working, and I don't know for sure, but I'd guess Mom is wallowing somewhere about the grand wedding reception she had planned. I check my doorbell app, thankful I have the blinds pulled down so I can hide. Honestly, who comes over unannounced anymore?

I look closely at the night vision on the screen and my heart skips at least two beats.

Caleb.

I haven't spoken to him in days. I haven't figured out what to say to him about my reaction—or overreaction—and shutting the door in his face like a petulant teenager. I owe him legitimate information about work and I've been completely ignoring him. That's not like me at all. The day after Kent and I broke our engagement, I booked two new clients, ran a wedding rehearsal, and prepped a venue for the next day's wedding. I should be able to find my way through this.

It's now or never, I guess.

"Caleb, what are you doing here?" I ask, through the app.

"Hey, you're here," he says, relief filling his voice. "Could we talk for a minute?"

I look down at my floral, objectively not at all sexy, cotton nightgown. My hair is pulled in a messy topknot, and I've already completed my skincare routine for the night.

"I'm in my pajamas," I say.

"And I'm in a greasy, sweaty chef coat." I watch him look down and take stock of the mess. "Actually..." He unbuttons the coat and takes it off. The crisp white shirt he's wearing underneath rises to show his toned stomach as he pulls his arms out of the sleeves.

"Whoa," I say.

He smirks directly at the camera and drops his coat onto the grass. "Excuse me?"

Shit. I didn't realize I'd been holding the talk button.

"Brooke," he says. "Are you going to let me in?"

I pad to the front door and open it wide. I hope the dark hides the heat in my cheeks. Surely he can't see my heart thumping in my chest, right?

"Hey, babe." Caleb smirks, leaning on the doorframe with casual confidence.

I want so badly to roll my eyes, but I can't. Caleb is here. And happy to see me despite me ignoring him when we have actual work to do.

"Hi, Caleb." I smile, feeling exposed in my nightgown as he gives me an excruciatingly slow once-over. The floral print is something my grandmother would have worn, and the thick straps and overall silhouette give off major '90s mom vibes. There's a ribbon woven through the trim for heaven's sake! But when his eyes finally meet mine, I swear he's biting the inside of his lower lip.

"What?" I ask, my cheeks even warmer.

"Nice pajamas. Is that vintage JCPenney or—?"

"Shut up," I cross my arms over my chest as if that's going to hide the embarrassment that is this dowdy nightgown.

"I'm kidding, Brooke. It's cute and exactly what I picture you wearing to bed."

Cheeks on fire. "You picture what I wear to bed?"

He pushes himself off the door frame to stand, shoving his hands in his pockets. "No, I, uh, just meant that they seem like…um…on brand for you."

A laugh escapes me. A JCPenney circa 1996 floral nightgown is absolutely on brand for me. I am who I am.

"I'm kidding, Caleb," I say. Though I'd like to know the real answer. "Come inside. You're going to let a bunch of bugs in and then you'll have to stay to kill them all."

He follows me into the house and closes the door. "You can't kill them yourself?"

"I can, but I'd prefer to have someone else do it." I walk to the kitchen and Caleb follows. "Mr. Edwards next door would, too. Last time I saw one of those disgusting millipede thingies that get away super fast, I yelled so loud he came over in his walker with a baseball bat. He thought I was being robbed. I killed it myself but then he had to rest here for an hour to gather the strength to go home. I told him he shouldn't be trying to rescue his single female neighbor at the age of eighty-four."

"Poor Mr. Edwards. He was probably milking it so he could hang out with his single female neighbor."

"He gets to hang out with me every Monday. We have a standing date to garden together. Plus, he only has eyes for the late Mrs. Edwards. It's sweet, actually." I lean back on the counter and cross my arms again. The only armor I have for this conversation. "What are you doing here, Caleb?"

"Brooke," he says, running a hand through his hair. It's more disheveled than usual, wavy pieces falling across his forehead. The summer sun has lightened it a bit. Some people pay good money for those highlights, it's not fair. "I had no idea what I was looking at in that room. I didn't realize."

"Did Jordan tell you?" I ask with more bite than I intend, even though she wouldn't tell a soul. That girl is a vault. "I know you two were working the same wedding tonight."

"She didn't, but I figured it out. I think. I shouldn't have snooped around your house. I don't know, it's just...this home feels so you, and I wanted to see more of it. I thought I'd just found your secret disorganized room. You're always so polished and organized, I thought it was your...I don't know...like I said, your Monica Geller closet."

"It kind of is, or *was*, in a way," I say.

"We haven't talked in years, Brooke, and I needed to be so far from this place. I didn't keep up with what was happening back here, I stayed off socials and barely talked to Joey. I had no idea you'd been married—"

"I wasn't," I say quickly, looking at the floor. "We didn't make it that far."

"Oh." He sounds relieved.

I look into his honey brown eyes. "Today was supposed to be our wedding day."

"Shit."

"Yeah..." I say. "Shit." We hold each other's gaze. Is this the part where I tell him everything? He's looking at me like it is. Like he wants to know. "Are you hungry?" I ask.

"Starving."

Chapter 20

Caleb

It's no wonder she's home tonight. Everything in that room was Brooke's. She was hiding items from *her* own wedding. Her almost wedding. A wedding that was meant to be today. And here I am, sitting in her kitchen, asking her about it when all she probably wants to do is forget.

Brooke places a bowl in the middle of the kitchen table. "May I present...girl dinner," she says, gesturing to the bowl of popcorn topped with chocolate chips. I give her a questioning look. "Just try it."

"Someone really needs to teach you how to cook." I grab a small handful and try it. I don't hate it. "God, Brooke, I'm such an asshole," I say, dropping my head into my hands on the table.

"Yeah." Brooke sits down across from me and slides a beer in my direction. "You are..."

Geez. I didn't expect her to completely agree. Though, as kind as I've been to her lately, I'd also been a huge asshole at one point. Jordan's words about rejecting Brooke are fresh in my mind. It was so complicated, I don't know how to explain any of it.

"...sometimes." Brooke takes a sip of her wine. "But not because of this. How would you have known?"

"I don't know but I still feel like an asshole."

"I appreciate the apology. If it makes you feel any better, I'm relieved to not be Mrs. Kent Chadwick right now."

Kent. Fucking. Chadwick. Is she kidding? It takes every part of me not to spit my large sip of beer across the table. She laughs as I struggle to swallow.

"You've got to be kidding me. Kent Chadwick? I haven't thought about him in years. You were going to marry *him*? He was the fucking worst. Remember how awful he was at the country club?"

Her face twists into a grimace. "Yeah..." she says before taking another sip of wine.

I am utterly baffled. Kent's the eldest son of Mr. and Mrs. Chadwick. No first names. We weren't allowed to call any of the members by their first names, so to me they simply didn't have them. Kent was, probably still is, a spoiled country club kid who treated staff like they were there to serve him. I guess technically we *were* there to serve him. We were there to give the members the best possible experience. After all, they paid a lot of money to be members of an affluent social club. But Kent was always a fucking prick about it. At least his parents had some manners. They said *please* and *thank you*. I doubt Kent ever uttered either of those words to staff.

Kent and Brooke. Engaged. To each other. It's a knife to the chest. He's exactly the kind of guy I worried she'd end up with, but that doesn't keep an emotion that feels a lot like jealousy from coursing through me.

I look at her in that nightgown that's somehow adorably sexy on her, despite being the most conservative nightwear I've ever seen. Her wavy brown hair is pulled into a disheveled topknot, pieces falling in her face. Not a stitch of makeup on. Beautiful.

Until I found her on the floor of Spencer Soirees and took her to urgent care, I'd rarely seen Brooke Spencer with a hair out of place. I like that version of Brooke, the version she puts on when she steps outside her door. But I more than like this version. So perfectly imperfect. Kent Chadwick didn't deserve a moment of her time, let alone an engagement and everything I'm trying not to think about that comes with that.

"Why, Brooke?" I ask as calmly as I can manage.

"There is…" She releases a long breath. "A lot to unpack there."

"We don't have to talk about it," I say, though I desperately need the answer.

"No, it's okay." She gives me a half-hearted smile. "What better time than now?" She glances away and I follow her gaze to the digital clock on the microwave. 10:45 p.m.

"You're thinking about what you would have been doing right now…at the wedding? Picturing the timeline in your head?"

She looks back at me and smiles.

"Well, what is it?" I ask, leaning back in my chair. "Tell me about the grand plans for a Spencer wedding."

"Grand plans," she says with a laugh. "That was part of the problem. My mom has had my wedding planned for at least a decade and was probably plotting for me to get together with Kent for even longer. Maybe not Kent specifically, but someone like him."

I tip my beer bottle in Brooke's direction. "Classic Judy."

"Classic Judy. It made her so happy, planning the wedding. Everything she wanted for me, the things she never had. The engagement party was over the top…that's where most of the stuff in the closet came from. That and the bridal shower. But that was nothing compared to what she had planned for the wedding. Right now, we would have been getting ready for a sparkler exit, obviously, and fireworks over the green at the country club."

"No, not the country club," I groan, hanging my head down. "I thought they didn't allow sparklers."

"Oh, you know Judy convinced them to do it. *Just this once*," she says, doing an impression of Judy. "Would you expect anything less than the country club for Kent Chadwick? You'll be relieved to know that the wedding wasn't going to be in the ballroom because that wouldn't fit the four hundred guests my mom and the Chadwicks were expecting. They were going to tent over the golf course. It was all my mom and Kent's vision. He didn't contribute much, but when he did, Mom fawned over every terrible idea he had like he was the first groom to ever show interest in wedding planning. Things she would have told any other couple not to do. Anything I asked, like a smaller guest list or having my favorite flowers, was ignored because it didn't fit her vision. But I wanted my mom to be happy."

"You're too good to her, Brooke."

"She's done so much for me, Caleb. I owe it to her," she says.

I disagree, but I hold my tongue. I've never liked Judy and nothing she's done this summer is changing that opinion.

"How did you two get together in the first place?"

"Matchmaker Judy. Set us up on a blind date. Spent weeks talking about this guy who'd be so great for me. Never mentioned his name and I didn't even think to ask until right before he picked me up. If she'd told me, I wouldn't have agreed to it. He picked me up in his Cybertruck."

"No," I groan. "You're lying. Getting me back for being such a dick." A fucking Cybertruck. Come on.

She laughs, and the smile that comes with it is worth hearing about Kent and his Cybertruck.

"I know, red flag."

"The reddest."

"He was actually pleasant and nice. He even said *thank you* to the waiter at dinner."

I scoff. "I don't believe you."

"I wouldn't believe me either if I hadn't heard it myself. It turned out to be an okay first date. And we had good dates afterward. He even promised to never drive me in that car again."

"What a gentleman," I say, rolling my eyes.

"Before I knew it, my mom and I were going to the club with him and his parents and…I don't know…it was nice. She wasn't on my case as much and I was happy enough. Last fall, we were at the club for dinner and Kent stands up, clinks a knife against his wine glass, and asks everyone in the dining room for their attention. He makes this grand speech about how perfect we are together and the perfect life we'll have. Then he's down on one knee in front of me with this absolutely obscene ring. I should've known that second it would all be a disaster, but I looked at my mom. She had a huge smile on her face and she was crying. So I said yes."

Happy enough. She deserves so much more than happy enough.

"What do you mean you should have known?"

"I don't know," she says, tilting her head in thought. "I know I'm surrounded by weddings all the time, but I've never thought much about getting proposed to. I knew at that moment it was all wrong. The country club, so terrible. When he was on one knee and said 'will you marry me,' it gave me the ick."

"Him getting down on one knee gave you the ick? I thought that was the ultimate romantic grand gesture." That's so Brooke now that I think about it. She's always cared more about the connection than the fanfare.

"I was sitting there in the middle of the dining room with

women in pearls that I didn't know grabbing my hand to look at the ring and telling me how lucky I was. It was my mom's dream, not mine. Suddenly I knew exactly how I'd want to be proposed to."

"Oh?"

Her cheeks flush but she continues. "I don't want to be put on some pedestal. I want to be standing face-to-face with the person I'm going on this enormous adventure with. As equals. I know it's supposed to be romantic or whatever, but if I ever get the chance again, it won't be like that. Weddings and romantic proposals are great, but marriage is about creating a life together. And…never mind. You don't care about how I would want to be proposed to."

Oh, but I do care. I care a lot. I can't form words because my heart is in my fucking throat, so I give her a look that says *just tell me*.

She looks down and plays with her hands.

"…definitely not in front of dozens of watching people. In public is fine, but not some big grand gesture. Like a secret, no one around even knows it's happening. And not at a fucking country club."

Noted.

I'm imagining standing face-to-face with Brooke. Asking her that question. I hope she can't tell that my heart is about to pound right out of my chest.

I figured I'd ask someone that question eventually, but I've never put much thought into the proposal. My work-life balance in California was shit and didn't allow for much more than casual hookups or friends with benefits. Not to mention being hung up on the woman sitting across from me.

I like what she's saying. Going into marriage together.

"You'll get the chance again, Brooke," I manage to say, shaking away the daydream.

She looks at me with a soft smile and shrugs. "We'll see."

Brooke Spencer is full of surprises. I always imagined she'd be a hopeless romantic. If she'd told me she had her whole wedding planned, it wouldn't have shocked me one bit. Until tonight, I would have bet she had a secret box containing a full color-coded itinerary with everything planned down to the minute. A secret Pinterest board at least.

"My mom's convinced I'm a ruined woman. That I'll never get married, as if that's the worst thing in the world. Rich, coming from her. She never married but made a good life for herself. For us. When I called it off you would have thought Kent died, the way she behaved. According to her, I not only ruined my life but hers too. She seems to have gotten over that for now, thankfully. Wedding season is keeping her occupied."

"That sounds like a very Judy reaction. When did you call things off?"

"In April, after the bridal shower. It was an awful day. Well, it was the most beautiful bridal shower I've ever seen. Some of my mom's best work. Don't ever tell her I said that."

I draw an X over my heart. All her secrets are safe with me.

"I sat there opening gift after gift, trying to imagine my life with Kent and…I couldn't picture anything. My brain wouldn't go there. I'd been playing fiancée for months and I never once thought beyond the wedding day. When I tried, I panicked. All these guests I barely knew, friends of the Chadwicks. The wives of Kent's friends. Thank god Maddie and Jordan were there. Kent came at the end and everyone, except the two of them, fussed over him. I couldn't fake it anymore. I kept it together until the guests left. Once they did, I called it off."

"Was he an insufferable asshole about it?"

Brooke raises her eyebrows. "What do you think?"

"I hate that fucking guy."

"He was relieved, but I injured his pride a little bit." She takes a breath as her eyes meet mine. "Caleb, I'm sorry I overreacted the other night. How my mom handled things made me feel like a complete failure. Having all of it tucked away in that room, I could pretend it never happened. And then you opened it."

"Brooke," I say. "You're not a failure for calling off a marriage you didn't want to be in."

"I know," she smiles, weakly. "But I appreciate you saying that. I should be thanking you. Jordan and Maddie helped me clean the closet the next day. Returned some gifts, donated things, burned the dress. I kept the rest of the Le Creuset though."

I look at the stove. "Ah, it's all making sense now. You don't cook though, Brooke."

But I do.

"So everyone keeps reminding me…it's for the aesthetic, remember?" She laughs and I want to bottle it up so I can listen to it over and over.

"Of course, the aesthetic."

"Maybe I'll learn one day," she smiles. "If I can find a good teacher."

Me.

My mind is a mess of emotions, regrets, dreams. I've messed up so many things in my life and I certainly ruined any chance of anything more than friendship with Brooke. Friends. We can be friends again.

Why doesn't that feel like enough?

Chapter 21

Brooke

AFTER I UNLOADED ALL OF MY BAGGAGE ON CALEB, WE SPENT another hour catching up on what we've been up to for the last five years. We talked about everything: work, friends, exes. Everything except that Warehouse Party. I almost brought it up, but my heart's been through enough this week. It's starting to feel like we're friends again and that's not worth jeopardizing. Especially with the tremendous amount of work ahead of us.

Waking up the next morning, I feel lighter than I have all year. I brew myself some coffee and I head upstairs to the small bedroom I turned into an office. I painted the room a colonial blue and got a bright pink couch. Bookshelves line one wall, filled with old bridal magazines and books. Usually my Sundays are sacred, but I've got too much to catch up on after a week of ignoring Caleb.

I settle at my antique writing desk and get to work. Labor Day weekend is six weeks away, and even with the Quincy wedding looming, I have five other weddings to get through first. Off-season can't come soon enough. I'll have a few weddings in the fall, but my calendar is completely clear

December through March. If I'd married Kent, we'd be doing a belated honeymoon in January. I should book a trip with Maddie and Jordan. Get away from the worst New England months.

After I catch up on tasks related to this Saturday's wedding, I focus on the Quincy wedding. For an event of this size and importance, planning has been fairly straightforward. *That* makes me nervous. The only guarantee in event planning is that something will go wrong. The closer the wedding date gets, the harder it is to troubleshoot any issues that arise. If I have any hope of proving to Mom how capable I am, I need to anticipate challenges before they become real problems.

Despite the entire staff being in the office on Tuesdays, they're my most productive day. Something about the chaos of the office helps me concentrate. I put on my headphones and focus on the next wedding. It's in five days—an eternity in event planning.

Tuesdays are also the weekly staff meeting. We review upcoming weddings, discuss new client prospects, and go over general housekeeping. It's crammed with two dozen women occupying every possible surface. Judy doesn't subscribe to work-from-home flexibility. She regularly tells us she didn't pay rent through eighteen months of a global pandemic just so everyone could work from home in their sweatpants when it was over. But in the same breath, she complains there are too many people and why can't we figure out a way to fit everyone that doesn't require someone sitting on the floor. Whenever she goes on this tangent, she reminds me and Maddie of Miss Hannigan complaining about being surrounded by little girls.

Maddie whispers over her computer, "Little girls, little girls, everywhere I turn I can see them." I stifle a laugh as Mom emerges from her office.

I mouth *stop* to Maddie.

"Brooke," Mom calls across the office. The room falls silent. "Do you have something to share?"

"Sorry, Judy," I say, ignoring the snickering assistants. All this weird boundary does is make newer staff laugh at the absurdity of it. It's obvious they have yet to see Judy's harsher side. If they had, they'd be a lot more terrified of her.

One by one, each lead planner provides updates on their weddings. We troubleshoot any hiccups as a team. When it's my turn, I share details for the upcoming weekend. And since the entire staff is so invested both professionally and personally —they all follow Hannah Quincy's socials—I share updates on her wedding, as well. The assistants are vying for one of the coveted spots working on-site at their favorite influencer's wedding. When I mention that I'll be sharing assignments next week, they're buzzing like kids at a birthday party who found out it's time for goody bags.

"I can't believe Foley's is working with us!"

"Did you see the reel Hannah posted today? She was wearing the cutest dress."

"I'd die to work her wedding."

"I want to see that hot chef."

Judy clears her throat. Loudly. The assistants quiet, pressing their lips into thin lines.

"Ladies, some decorum please. Brooke will make her staff recommendations and share them as discussed. It is unprecedented that we're working with Foley's; they're lucky to be included in such an esteemed vendor team. And none of you should be setting your sights on a chef, whether he's attractive or not. You're Spencer Soirees planners and should be aiming higher than that." Her gaze lands right on me like she knows Caleb's been to my house. Twice.

"That's all, ladies," she says, turning on her heel and retreating to her office.

"Why are your cheeks on fire? You look like a tomato," Maddie whispers to me as the meeting ends. "What's wrong with you?"

"Nothing," I say through clenched teeth.

"Coffee run?" Maddie asks.

I grab my phone and follow Maddie out the door. I can't get out fast enough.

"God, she acts like we're the royal family or something and we must be chaste until marriage. Heaven forbid we consider a man who uses his hands for his work. A working-class man, not for a Spencer Soirees girl." Maddie is talking and walking fast ahead of me. "If you ask me, Judy could use a quick romp with a working-class man. Have him take those calloused working hands and work her…"

"Maddie!" I abruptly stop walking. "Do *not* finish that sentence. That is my mother."

Maddie turns and begins walking backwards. "Am I wrong?"

"No…but gross."

I catch up and we walk to Old Post Coffee, the eclectic local coffee house that's been here since I was a kid.

"So, Brooke, are you setting your sights on a certain hot chef?" Maddie opens the coffee shop door. "Because I'm still mad at him for what he did to you."

I shush her. "Someone might hear you, and no, I am not. We're work acquaintances who are…I don't know…maybe becoming friends again. That's all! But Judy cannot know that, Maddie. As far as she's concerned, I'm begrudgingly working with Caleb and hating every minute of it."

She holds her hands up in defeat. "Alright, alright."

I give her an overdramatic eye roll and we order our coffees: iced oat milk latte with brown sugar syrup for me and a double Americano for Maddie. Even though the last thing Maddie ever needs is more energy.

"So, you and Caleb are friends?"

"Yes," I say, focused on twirling my drink in a large circle to mix it while avoiding Maddie's hazel eyes. "We're friends."

"You don't have any feelings for him anymore? Because it was a lot of work picking up those pieces after he left."

"Feelings," I scoff. She might be on to me, but it's not like whatever I'm feeling for Caleb is going to become anything. Something might feel different now, but he could've made a move last night and didn't. No, nothing can happen. I hate keeping my feelings from her, but I'm not prepared for her wrath if I admit anything, especially if nothing would come from it. I'll keep lying to myself instead. "No, no feelings."

By the time we've returned, coffees in hand, most of the staff have left for meetings or site visits. Mom's in her office with the door closed. That's odd. She usually likes to keep her eyes and ears on her staff. I settle at my desk to update the Quincy wedding weekend timeline and think about which staff should round out my day-of team for each event. Definitely not the snickering assistants. They're way too green.

Their excitement over the pseudo-celebrity wedding does give me some newfound excitement of my own, though. I'm elated to land this account, but I'm not fangirling like they are. Hannah, while an extremely popular and successful influencer, is simply another young woman planning a wedding.

It always helps to look at my brides this way. Whether they're an influencer with brand deal money or the girl next door who's splurging on a wedding planner, they're all women planning their most important day *so far*. I've never liked the idea of a wedding day being the most important day of someone's life. There are so many special moments ahead, waiting to be enjoyed. It's this somewhat lackadaisical attitude about wedding days that Mom hates. To her, it *is* the most important day of a woman's life. But I like to think my approach is what makes me so great at my job. Yes, your wedding day is a meaningful milestone, but it's also just a party celebrating the love two people have for each other with the people who love them.

Maybe that's also what helped me on Saturday night. Confessing to Caleb that I'd been engaged on what was supposed to be my wedding night. It was just a party. A party that was *so* not my taste or style with people I didn't know and who didn't know me, let alone love me.

I may not have put much thought into what an engagement looked like, but I *have* thought about what my perfect wedding would look like. Not often, because when your mother is Judy Spencer, the wedding you envision isn't an option. But I allow myself to think about it for a minute. Something small, no more than fifty people. Unless my husband-to-be comes from a large family. In that case, I'll bump it up to seventy-five, no more. There's a boutique hotel nearby with a stunning restaurant that opens up to a cobblestone courtyard filled with trees and string lights. Or there are some beautiful properties in the backcountry with modern farmhouses or renovated barns. There'd be a short, meaningful ceremony outside, followed by a family-style dinner and dancing. Lots of dancing. I'd wear a simple white dress without a single stitch of lace. Surrounding me and my fiancé would be only the people we love.

Of course, this fantasy will never happen. I can't decide what's worse—marrying the person I love and having an over-the-top wedding planned by my mother, or not getting married to the person I love at all.

Chapter 22

Caleb

WENDELL WAKES ME BY LICKING MY FACE. MAYBE HE'S FINALLY starting to like me, or the sound of my phone buzzing is annoying him. I forgot to set it to Do Not Disturb before falling asleep. I'd been preoccupied with thoughts of Brooke and that floral nightgown as I fell asleep, and if the certain stiffness I'm experiencing is any indication, I was having similar thoughts while I slept.

I grab my phone from the nightstand. Notification after notification from Brooke. They're about the Quincy wedding, but my mouth breaks into a smile at the thought of Brooke thinking about me before nine o'clock in the morning. Even if it is about work.

My thoughts of Brooke are interrupted.

> Joey: Hey man, remember how you owe me a favor?

> Caleb: Redeeming that already?

> Joey: I need a sous this Saturday. Harold's wife is in labor early, Gianna's on vacation, and Garrett doesn't know what the fuck he's doing.

> Joey: You're the only one I trust to help.
>
> Caleb: I'm your third choice? Ouch.
>
> Caleb: What are the chances of Garrett figuring out what he's doing before Saturday? It's my only weekend off all summer.
>
> Joey: What if I told you a certain brunette wedding planner would be there?
>
> Caleb: I don't know what you're talking about.
>
> Joey: Nice try. After you rushed out the other night, Jordan filled me in.
>
> Joey: C'mon, it was fun working together again.
>
> Caleb: I'll think about it.
>
> Joey: See you Saturday!

Obviously I'm going to help Joey. Last weekend had been like the old days when we were both sweating our asses off working for Foley's. I miss having a partner to work with. I think he does, too. Going out on his own is more demanding than he anticipated. I also miss working with Dad. Getting away from town for a while was what I needed, but I worry I missed too much time working alongside him.

I've seen glimpses of Brooke in action already. At the first Quincy meeting, the night of the burgers, that wedding she did with Joey at the beginning of the summer when I'd resisted the urge to dance with her. Her clipboard energy is pretty fucking hot—I wouldn't hate seeing more of it—and I want her to see me in my element. Though Joey bossing me around isn't exactly ideal. *Shit.* He's absolutely going to take full advantage of being head chef and having me as his sous. Whatever, I'll take it. I'm ready to give off all the *yes, chef* energy.

> Caleb: Don't tell her I'm going to be there

> Joey: You don't tell me what to do, sous. I tell you what to do.

> Joey: (But you got it, man)

> Caleb: I'm already regretting this.

Dad's been back in the office more. It's nice seeing him where he's supposed to be. His energy has been up lately and he's been doing a little work. Mostly administrative—the kitchen's too chaotic—but the way he's deep in documents with a smile on his face tells me he's happy. I tap my knuckles on the open door. "Hey, Dad."

"Caleb!" he booms and pushes himself out of his chair.

"Don't get up." He doesn't listen. I walk around the desk and give him a hug. Lingering for longer than I used to. The summer schedule has kept me busy and away from my parents more than I would've liked, but they insisted I focus on work. Get them through the summer catering schedule while Dad recovers.

Foley's is everything to them. All he ever wanted was for me to follow in his footsteps and take over one day. I should be grateful, but it was suffocating having my life planned out for me. Even when I was accepted to culinary school, I wasn't ready to fully agree to my parents' plans, but they gave me the space I needed to figure it out.

When I started at the wedding venue out in San Francisco, it was for the experience Dad wanted me to have in order to take Foley's to the next level. What he didn't know was that on my days off, I also worked at one of my instructor's restaurants. It was while working there that everything clicked. It finally felt like I belonged in the kitchen.

Foley's is where I grew up, but I wanted my own restaurant; a cozy place where people can gather and enjoy a good meal.

Right when I'd gathered up the nerve to tell my parents my idea, Mom called to tell me about Dad's heart attack. It was time to come home.

"You've been busy here," he says, shifting through papers on the desk. Invoices and schedules I left for him last week. His desk is a lot cleaner. Took me a full day and a few hundred dollars at the office supply store to organize the mess. I even started a color-coded filing system that Brooke would approve of.

"Sure have," I say. "Part of me thinks you had a heart attack just so you could get out of working this season." I force a laugh. Making jokes is the only coping mechanism Dad and I can handle. "It's been grueling here."

"I may have booked a few extra events hoping this was the summer you'd be coming home," Dad says with a wink.

"Thanks for that."

"Are you surviving the Spencer women?" he asks, raising a brow.

"Something like that," I say. "Haven't had to deal with Judy much. I'm not used to sharing control, but Brooke is great. A perfectionist, but I'm getting used to it. We're getting along well." I look down in an attempt to hide the smile growing on my face.

"She has to be to survive her mother. I didn't want to get into it in front of your mother." He sighs, staring into space. It's a look I know well. He's choosing his words carefully. "Judy's a bit of a narcissist, Caleb. And she's done some pretty questionable things over the years."

Dad's far from a mental health professional, but as soon as he says it, the pieces fall into place. Judy dismissing Brooke's chronic migraines. Judy making the broken engagement about her. Judy pushing Brooke to be perfect in every way. Whenever Brooke shows an ounce of autonomy or makes a mistake, it's somehow a personal attack on Judy.

"What do you mean?" I want to know more from him about their dynamic. In those early days, Dad and Judy were building their businesses alongside each other. He saw a lot of Brooke. *We* saw a lot of Brooke.

Dad folds his hands together on the desk. "I always felt bad for Brooke. Judy doted on her, it was sweet at first, but Brooke became Judy's little doll. Always dressed up, behaving like an angel, quiet when she was supposed to be quiet. Performing for adults when Judy wanted, following her direction. Your mother and I couldn't understand it. You were throwing tantrums, generally rowdy. We chalked it up to the difference between girls and boys, but as time went on, I noticed Brooke walking on eggshells around Judy. Reading the room and Judy's mood, behaving accordingly when she was only a kid."

"I don't remember any of this. I remember Mom watched Brooke a lot when you worked weddings with Judy."

"Well, you were young yourself. Whenever I could, I'd bring you both home to our house. The poor girl needed a break. Remember what you two played the most?"

A memory pops into my head so suddenly it nearly takes my breath away: Me grabbing a toilet paper roll from the bathroom and wrapping it around Brooke to make a wedding dress. Arranging stuffed animals and action figures to be wedding guests. I laugh to myself. "We played wedding. Over and over."

Shit, this goes further back than I realized. I've married Brooke Spencer dozens of times.

"You made your mother be the officiant," he says.

"I remember." I smile, remembering a young Brooke wearing Mom's veil.

"Oh, she loved it. I'd get home and she'd tell me the vows

you'd made up. It seems like she's come out the other side. Judy's a damn good wedding planner, I'll admit that. Brooke is, too. I just hope she's found some happiness. She's had a hard year."

"She told me about Kent."

"I should have told you," he says with a heavy sigh. "Judy went around town swearing everyone to silence about it. For Brooke's mental health, she said. I'm sure it was good for her, but Judy never cared a lick about anyone's mental health. She made the whole thing about her. Asking everyone not bring it up to Brooke. Meanwhile, she'd tell her sob story to anyone who would listen."

"That's what Brooke said. I do think she's happy, Dad. At least happy to not be married to Kent Chadwick."

"I always hated that kid."

I laugh. "Me too."

There's a tightness in my chest I can't shake. Different from the warm swelling ache I've grown accustomed to whenever I'm near Brooke. Hell, whenever I think about her. This is tight and hot. I'm white knuckling my way around the traffic circle on my way home. And I'd like to tell the car with the *please be patient, new driver* sticker that just cut me off to fuck off.

I'm fucking angry.

Angry for Brooke. Furious with Judy. Upset with myself.

Brooke's so smart, confident, capable. She works so hard to be the perfect daughter to Judy.

How could someone take advantage of her? How can her mother completely disregard a chronic condition? How can she make her daughter's broken engagement all about her? How can Brooke continue to work for her? How does she not see it?

I'm home and parked, but my hand still grips the steering wheel with all my strength. I have to channel this anger and frustration. As soon as I enter the house, I grab Wendell's leash and he comes running to the door. We head toward the marina so I can try to make sense of things. Running's always cleared my head, but Wendell can't keep up on his short legs so a walk will have to do.

I'm not sure what's next for me after this summer, so much of it depends on Dad's health. But I am sure of one thing: I'm spending the rest of this season making sure Brooke knows she's absolutely remarkable.

Judy got into my head years ago. Our paths didn't cross often, but when they did, she barely acknowledged my existence. She sees me as the help. Someone beneath her. The same way some clients do—never good enough to be part of their circles. Pretty rich coming from someone else in the service industry, someone who started with nothing. But Judy always saw herself, and therefore Brooke, as better than.

I thought I knew how much Brooke would do for her mom's approval back then, but I didn't know the half of it. She's not looking for approval, she's looking for love. She'd go so far as to marry someone she didn't love because it made her mom happy. She deserves so much more than that. She deserves unconditional love.

Telling myself Judy would never approve of me for her daughter is a mantra I've lived by for years. That only solidified when Jennifer's dad berated me for dating his daughter. He'd caught us making out behind the paddle hut at the country club. Such a cliché.

I let that fear push Brooke away five years ago.

It wasn't because I didn't feel the same when she kissed me. God, I wanted to kiss her back. But I thought I wasn't good enough for her. That I didn't deserve her. Maybe I didn't.

Fuck, I did completely reject her. I pushed her away like a fucking coward.

Maybe I don't deserve her now. Maybe she won't let me in that way after I left her standing at the edge of the dance floor that night. But I see the way her cheeks fill with color when we're together, and calling her "babe" feels right. She's even stopped rolling her eyes whenever I say it.

Fuck it.

I'm still not perfect, but I'm going to make it my mission to be perfect for her.

Chapter 23

Brooke

"Tits up!" I wink, sending the bride and her moms down the aisle. All three are crying to varying degrees and I'm beginning to tear up myself. It's so beautiful to see all that love exploding from someone's eyeballs.

I dab the corners of my eyes. I can't help but think of my mom and my own cancelled wedding. She'd never cry tears of happiness walking me down the aisle. The only tears she cried over the whole ordeal were about what it all meant for her. I don't have time for those tears right now, though. There's work to be done. Twenty minutes until the ceremony is over and guests fill the pavilion for cocktail hour.

I walk back to the venue, clipboard in hand. The sun shadows a Caleb-looking shape ahead of me.

"Did you just say 'tits up' to the bride?" he asks, eyes wide.

"Caleb!" I whisper-yell. The string quartet playing the processional music is loud, but I don't need guests hearing Caleb say *tits*! "What are you doing here?"

"Well, Mrs. Maisel, Joey needed a last-minute sous, so here I am." Here he is all right, chef coat hugging his thick arms.

"You've watched *The Marvelous Mrs. Maisel?*"

"Of course I have. Something about a commanding woman does it for me."

I look down at my clipboard to hide the flush in my cheeks.

"What other crude language do you use in front of your clients?"

I give him a light smack with my clipboard and start walking ahead of him to the pavilion. He quickly catches up, walking with his hands in his pockets.

"If you're lucky, you'll find out at the Quincy wedding. Until then, those are my secrets to keep." Wait until he sees the bush-to-bush demo.

"Looking forward to getting lucky," he says with a smirk, dimpled cheek looking as good as ever. "Babe."

I fake a groan because, as annoying as it was at first, I've grown to like it. I only wish he actually meant it. "Shouldn't you be helping Joey? Cocktails start in fifteen minutes, and for some insane reason, Joey agreed to passing ten different hors d'oeuvres."

"Oh, I know. I've been wrapping pigs in blankets for hours." He stops walking when we get to the venue's small kitchen. It's literally bursting with too many cooks. "I just wanted to say hi."

"Hi, Caleb."

"Hi, Brooke."

He smiles and turns to the kitchen. I hug my clipboard against my beating chest and watch him walk away. How does he work in a sweltering kitchen with three other cooks in the middle of July wearing jeans that hug his ass like that?

"Brooke, my eyes are up here." Caleb's turned around to stare at me, smirking, pointing a finger to his face. Shit. I have to focus. I'm at work, damnit.

"Get to work, Caleb!" I yell before turning on my heel to oversee cocktail hour.

Guests quickly fill the pavilion and swarm the bars as

soon as the ceremony ends. My team immediately swings into action, grabbing the ceremony chairs from the beach and dismantling the chuppah while I help the photographer facilitate family photos. Tonight, that requires asking passersby enjoying golden hour at the public beach to get the hell out of the shot. The pavilion can be rented, but the public beach cannot. I've tried. I'm used to managing it, though. This is my third wedding at Beachside Pavilion this summer. Last year, I had five. I've mastered the art of politely ruining someone's beach evening on behalf of my clients.

My favorite thing about this venue is the location. The view does all the hard work. It's low tide, making the seascape even more striking. Tide pools dot the sand, dozens of sailboats glide along the cotton candy horizon, and you can see the path to the lighthouse off the coast.

My least favorite thing about this venue is the chairs. They're terrible, clunky ballroom chairs that belong in a dated country club, not a venue that opened less than five years ago. I wish someone had thought to consult us before the town opened the building and purchased two hundred ugly chairs. Thankfully, tonight's clients decided to rent better seating.

The night continues according to my timeline. Before I know it, the bride and groom are cutting the cake and it's smooth sailing from here. I stand at the edge of the room watching the guests.

"Come here often?" Caleb asks.

"As a matter of fact, I do." I smile up at him, somehow charmed by the lamest pickup line ever. I've barely seen him tonight. Except for the dozen or so times I made an excuse to peek into the kitchen. If he didn't already think I was a micromanager, he definitely does now.

Instead of laughing at guests and critiquing dance moves like we used to, we enjoy a comfortable silence. Until glass shatters on the dance floor and we both spring into action to clean it up.

These goddamn chairs.

Another reason I hate them so much is because the venue contract requires that if rented chairs are brought in, the original ugly chairs have to be returned to the ballroom from the storage closet. As a full-service wedding agency, this responsibility falls to me. And because I'd been distracted by Caleb fucking Foley all night, I let my support staff leave already. I'm stuck handling this tedious task alone.

The catering team's still here cleaning the kitchen and packing up. I could ask for help, but they've been on their feet as long as I have, maybe longer. And I haven't been in a hotbox kitchen for the last six hours. The band is packing up too, but there's no way I'm asking them. I'd have to give up the slice of cake I snuck into the van for later, and I'm not about to do that.

I'm on my sixth trip out of the storage room when Caleb and Joey emerge from the kitchen. "Yo, Brooke." Joey calls from across the room. "You need some help?"

Oh, thank god.

"Nah, I got it," I say, juggling three chairs. "Only fifty or so more trips."

They don't move.

"Of course I need help!"

We spend the next fifteen minutes moving stacks of chairs out of the closet and back to the ballroom where we arrange them around the tables, as per the contract. We're almost through the task when Joey steps out to take a call.

With most of the chairs in the ballroom, Caleb and I can both fit in the storage closet to grab stacks at the same time.

I've been able to carry three at a time. Caleb has been carrying six. I don't know how many chairs Joey's managing, because I can't take my eyes off of Caleb's muscled back each time he lifts a stack. He makes it look effortless. I feel like I'm going to pass out.

A loud, sudden bang startles me and I drop the stack in my hands. When I turn to see what caused the noise, I realize that the storage room door slammed shut.

"Shit," I say. "I've got it."

I grab the door handle, turn it down, and push. Nothing. I turn the handle up and push. Nothing. *Shit.* Behind me, the stack Caleb's holding hits the ground.

"Is it stuck?" He walks over. The storage room is long and narrow. I try to step aside to get out of his way but there's nowhere to go.

I keep trying the handle. "Yeah, I think so."

Caleb comes up behind me, his breath warm on my neck, and reaches for the handle, grazing my arm with his fingers. The heat of his body is at my back. My heart rate increases steadily, and I'm sweating more than I was five minutes ago.

I shift a little so he can try the door, bumping into his solid chest. He turns the handle up and down as I try to push the door with my body weight. Nothing works.

"Shit." Caleb exhales. "It's really stuck."

I turn around to face him. He's so close we're almost touching. He could step back but he doesn't. His eyes are wide, and one hand is all but pulling out his brown hair. Little beads of sweat dot his hairline, making his waves curl a little.

"Caleb, are you okay?"

"Um...yeah...." He swallows and his chest heaves, eyes darting around frantically. His skin pales. He's definitely not okay. "I think I might be claustrophobic."

I try not to laugh. "You *think*?"

"Okay, yeah, I a*m* claustrophobic." His voice shakes. "But I didn't know it until right now. Are you going to give me shit about it?"

"Caleb," I say, resting my hands on his chest. He looks side to side like he'll find a secret escape from this godforsaken storage room. Stupid ugly chairs. I rise to my tiptoes—I changed out of my heels hours ago. Cupping his cheeks in my hands, I turn his head. "Look at me."

I take a slow breath in. Then a slow breath out. Slow breath in. Slow breath out. Caleb grips my wrists lightly to anchor himself. His warm touch is distracting. I lean back on the door to steady myself. He mirrors my breathing. In...and... out. In...and...out.

I've never seen him like this. Scared. Vulnerable. Needing me.

"It's going to be okay," I say, my palms still on his cheeks. A strand of my hair has fallen into my face, and I fight the urge to move it. I don't want to let go. I don't want to stop touching him. "I left my phone in the ballroom, but Joey will be back any minute. Okay?"

"Okay," he says. It's all he can manage. His dark brown eyes pierce into mine. I can see the golden specks in his irises. We continue the deep breathing and he doesn't look away. Minutes pass. He doesn't move to break physical contact. Slowly, color returns to his cheeks and his body relaxes.

"Better?" I ask.

He takes another deep breath and removes his hands from my wrists. He steps closer, placing one hand on the door behind me. The other brushes the hair off my face, but he doesn't let go of it. He twirls it between his fingers, my gaze following his hand. His hands. Maddie's words about hardworking calloused hands pop into my head. I inhale and make a sound that gives away what his closeness is doing to me.

"Brooke," Caleb whispers, voice thick.

I swallow slowly and his eyes watch my throat. Time seems

to slow as his face moves closer to mine. Now I'm the one who can't breathe. He looks at my lips and leans in. They're so close to grazing mine. I close my eyes and it feels like I'm tumbling backwards. Losing all sense of purchase.

Shit.

I *am* tumbling backwards—the door behind me has swung open. Joey catches me as Caleb stumbles right onto the floor next to us.

"Oh, *shit*!" Joey helps me stand, and I dust myself off. "Sorry, Brooke."

He offers Caleb his hand and pulls him up. "Sorry, man."

"The door jammed," I say, feeling hot and flushed. From the fall or from the way Caleb was looking at me, I don't know. The way he said my name. He's never said it like that before. Like it means something.

"Yeah…" Caleb mumbles, raking his hand through his waves and shuffling his feet. "We…uh…we were just trying to open it."

"Dude, I told them to fix that door," Joey says. "I was here two weeks ago and the groomsmen helping at the end of the night got stuck in there."

Caleb scoffs. "Thanks for the heads up, man."

"I'll call the venue manager in the morning and remind her," I say. I might have a word with her about the chairs, too.

Joey looks back and forth between me and Caleb, like he's caught us doing something wrong. A knot twists in my stomach. I'm a rule follower who always has a plan, and it's been a long time since I had a plan that involved Caleb.

"Brooke, we can wrap this up if you want to get out of here?" Joey says, making steps toward the storage room.

"Yeah…uh…sure, okay," I say, but my feet stay planted. I look at Caleb and the pained expression on his face. I want to ask him what almost happened in there, but I can't. Not without risking my heart again.

"Um…so yeah, great wedding guys!" I turn and dash to the ballroom to grab my phone. Thank god I didn't dismiss the rest of the staff until after the van was loaded. I need to get far away from Caleb. Screw my post-wedding routine, I need to get home and take an ice-cold shower. I don't know what to make of what just happened. Either Caleb had been moments away from kissing me or he was about to pass out on me post-panic attack.

I don't know which one I want it to be.

Chapter 24

Caleb

BROOKE DARTS AWAY LIKE THE BUILDING'S ON FIRE. AS IF SHE felt the heat building in my chest and needed to flee from it as quickly as possible. I sag into one of the nearby chairs and bring my fist to my aching chest.

Is this how she felt when I left her at the Warehouse Party? The thought that I could hurt her this much crushes me completely. She probably felt worse because she'd actually kissed me. And I hadn't kissed her back. *Fuck.*

The memory of that night has lingered in the back of my mind for years. Now it pushes its way to the front.

Everyone knew I was leaving, and the party was an unofficial send-off. By midnight, there was only one person I hadn't said goodbye to. I hadn't been able to keep my eyes off of Brooke all night. She barely left the dance floor, dancing and singing to her heart's content. It was the first year Judy didn't attend and Brooke was relishing in it. She kept catching me glancing. I kept looking away.

Finally, she left the dance floor and came over to me. I needed to say a quick goodbye and leave. Even if it'd kill me to do it. I was moving in a few days, and nothing could ever happen with Brooke for roughly two dozen reasons. But once she was finally standing in front of me, I couldn't bring myself to say goodbye.

Her skin was dewy from dancing, cheeks a perfect shade of pink. The hairs around her face curling. She was a little tipsy and it was a lot adorable. I don't remember the theme that year or what she was wearing, only that she looked beautiful.

"Hey," she said, blue eyes sparkling through those dark lashes.

"Hey," I replied.

A long pause.

We spoke at the same time. "Brooke." "Caleb."

An awkward laugh was all I could muster. I should've left then.

Brooke spoke first.

"Caleb, I know you're leaving." She placed a hand on my chest and lifted herself to the balls of her feet. "But I've wanted to do this for a while." I should have stopped her, but I couldn't. Her soft lips brushed mine. Warm and smooth. I savored the feeling for one devastating moment, before I came to my senses. The senses that told me that as much as I wanted this, I couldn't let it happen. Not now. Maybe not ever.

"Brooke," I said, gently rocking her back on her heels. Her eyes were suddenly glassy, I hoped it was from the alcohol. "You don't want to do this."

"Yes, I do, Caleb."

I winced at those words. She'd regret it in the morning; I was sure of it.

"You do, too," she said smiling, reaching for my hand.

I pulled it away. Her lips parted, eyes welled with moisture. I did. God, did I want it. But I could either break her heart now or later. It'd be easier to do it now.

"I don't, Brooke," I said and took a step back.

"What do you mean you don't?" Her voice cracked. "You do, I know you do."

The music blared around us, but she spoke loud enough that people were staring. Maddie joined the fray.

"I'm sorry if I was lead—"

"Leading me on?" She blinked at me in disbelief. "Caleb, you drive me home every night, we talk for hours in your car. Then you look at me the way you do. The way you were looking at me a minute ago. I know you feel something for me."

I felt too much for her. That was the problem.

"We're just friends, Brooke," I said, avoiding her eyes. The lie tearing at my heart as I told it.

She huffed out an agitated laugh. "Friends?"

"Yes, friends." I wanted to take it back, but I couldn't. It was better this way.

Brooke took a step back and shook her head.

"No, we're not, Caleb," she said. One single tear fell from her cheek. "Not anymore."

I couldn't look at her. Not when my hands shook and my eyes stung. I turned away from her and left.

I shake away the memory and follow Joey into the storage room.

Joey turns abruptly, dropping the chairs in his arms. "Dude!"

"What?"

"What the fuck do you think you're doing?"

"Um…helping you with these fucking chairs, asshole," I say, passing him to get into the storage closet.

"Go after her!"

"What?"

"Go. After. Her." Joey enunciates each word. "Were you or were you not kissing Brooke in here before I opened the door and interrupted? Sorry about that, by the way."

"I wasn't kissing Brooke," I say. I wish I had been.

"But you were about to, right?"

"Maybe...I don't know...whatever." I pull at my hair. All my resolve from earlier in the week is gone. "It's for the best. Look how she ran out of here. Like you saved her from making a huge mistake. I thought there might be something between us again, but I was wrong. Brooke deserves better than me, and her mom might actually disown her if she ever found out she'd so much as kissed me on the cheek."

"Oh, for fuck's sake, Caleb. You've got to get over this idea that you aren't good enough for her. Why, because her mom's a nightmare and Brooke's the only one who doesn't see it? Who gives a shit! Brooke put herself on the line five years ago and you fucked that up. It's your turn now buddy." Joey points a finger to the door. "Go!"

"But she ran, Joey!" I protest.

"Of course she ran, that was fucking awkward. But I saw you two tonight. I saw the way you look at each other. You're down bad for each other. Just like you used to be. Stop trying to pretend you're not. I'm only going to say it one more time...go after her."

"Fine." I toss my hands up in defeat. It can't hurt worse than it does now, can it? I'm gone for her, but I'm not convinced she is for me. "If this goes to shit, it's on you."

"I'll take that risk. Now get out of here! I've got these fucking chairs."

I drive by Brooke's street three times before I can bring myself to turn. I park in front of her house and walk up the driveway. It's humid and muggy out, cicadas buzzing loudly. The outdoor light by the garage barely emits any light, and even if this all goes wrong, I'm replacing that bulb.

"Brooke," I call from a few yards away. She's grabbing something from the passenger side of the van.

She jumps and turns around. "Jesus Christ, Caleb! What the hell is wrong with you? You're supposed to go out of your way *not* to scare women at night. Unless you're here to kill me, in which case I should remind you about Mr. Edwards."

This is off to a great start. I'd parked in the street so as not to alarm her by pulling into the driveway, only to scare the shit out of her anyway. "I'm sorry, I wasn't thinking."

She sighs, closing the passenger side door. "No shit."

I rake a hand through my hair then shove my hands into my pockets, rocking on my heels. Brooke leans back against the van, arms crossed over her chest, on guard.

"It's okay," she says. "I mean, it's not *okay*. Please don't do it again, but thanks for apologizing."

"Brooke—"

"Caleb, what are you doing here?"

My turn to put myself on the line. Now or never.

"I have to apologize for something," I say, looking into her eyes. They're tired from the long day but still have that spark I love. "A few things actually. I'm sorry about what happened back at the venue, I—"

"It's okay. I mean it, this time it's okay. You were having a panic attack, I helped you through it and whatever that was… after…it's fine, don't worry about it. I know how you feel about me, Caleb. It's…it's…okay."

"Brooke, no." I step toward her, slowly closing some of the space between us. The knot of anxiety in my chest gets tighter. "I don't think you have any idea how I feel about you. How I have felt about you for a long time. And that's my fault. I'm not sorry that I almost kissed you…I'm sorry that Joey interrupted us. I'm sorry I didn't kiss you."

She pushes herself off the van. Her lips part but words don't come out.

"And I'm sorry I didn't kiss you back five years ago." I force the words out before I lose the nerve.

She releases a quiet scoff. "You didn't just not kiss me back. You told me you didn't want me. That you didn't have feelings for me. That we were just friends." She winces at the memory, looking at the sky. Looking anywhere but my eyes.

God, I don't deserve her. Not after that. But I'm going to try. I take another step closer. Another risk.

"Those are the worst lies I've ever told," I say.

She shakes her head. "Lies? Caleb, you can't be serious. You pushed me away so easily. It sure felt like the truth."

"Brooke, look at me please," I say, reaching for her. She holds up her hand and I step back. "I've done it all wrong when it comes to you. I thought I was protecting you."

"Protecting me? From what?"

"From me, Brooke. I couldn't let anything happen between us. All I wanted to do was kiss you back that night. To stay here and be with you. But all I could think about was how bad I was for you."

"Caleb," she says with a sigh, finally looking at me, her eyes filled with sadness. "How could you have possibly been bad for me?"

I blow out a breath. "You know how I was back then. And you know what your mom thinks of me. She's always looked down on me. I thought I was helping you not make a mistake you'd regret...I knew how much her approval meant to you, and you know she'd never be okay with you and me.

"Not kissing you back was the hardest thing I've ever done. I've wanted you for years. Not kissing you each night when I dropped you off...it broke me little by little every single time. I couldn't stay here and not be with you."

"That's why you left?"

I nod, looking down at my feet. "If I couldn't have you, I

had to get away. I had to make something of myself and hope you'd still want me by the time I did."

"Couldn't have me? I threw myself at you, in front of everyone. You could've had me!"

There's a lump in my throat. "You don't actually think that, do you, Brooke? Your mom...she had a plan for you, and I wasn't a part of it. I'm not someone like Kent."

"That's a good thing, Caleb," she says flatly. Her eyes well.

Fuck. I can't make her cry. I reach for her hands and this time she doesn't stop me. Hope rolls through me. "When I saw you at the party...the exact place I'd fucked it all up. God, Brooke, I almost melted onto the floor when you bumped into me. I don't know if it was because you looked fucking amazing in that leather skirt or just the pissed-off look on your face. I already knew about the Quincy wedding. Even though you were furious with me, and I committed to acting like a jerk, I couldn't wait to work with you all summer. Even if you were going to hate me the whole time."

"I don't hate you, Caleb." She squeezes my hands. "I could never hate you. Though, I *am* a little mad at you right now."

"I can handle mad," I smile. All I want to do right now is finally kiss her, but I need her to understand. "For so long, I let my insecurities dictate my choices. My whole life, I felt like less than. I let how other people saw me get in the way of being with you. I'm so sorry, Brooke. For all of it. I'm dying to make it up to you, if it's not too late."

I pull our hands to my mouth and kiss her knuckles. She draws in a breath, and I force myself to keep my feet planted. She's rarely at a loss for words.

I take a step and close the space between us, unlacing our hands and leaving barely an inch between our bodies. She's glowing under the soft light of that pathetic bulb.

I gently cup her cheeks like she cupped mine in the closet. "Is it too late?"

She shakes her head and grabs my wrists. "No, it's not too late."

Relief pours through me.

"I'm going to kiss you now...is that okay?" I ask, my finger hooking her chin. I need my mouth on hers more than I need air, but only if she wants this too.

She nods.

I want to devour her and savor her all at once. I brush my lips gently against hers. She parts her lips ever so slightly for me, slowly deepening the kiss. She tastes sweeter than I ever could have imagined. Like buttercream frosting.

Brooke reaches a hand to my neck, pulling our bodies closer, my hips pinning her against the van. I coax her mouth open more and stroke my tongue against hers. I kiss her softly, carefully. She lets out a soft moan that's nearly my undoing. God, I want to make her do that again. Need to make her do that again. Her arms wrap around my neck with no sign of letting go. I pull back, biting her bottom lip. When she moans softly again, I pull away completely, breaking the kiss.

Her flushed face. I did that. This time for all the right reasons. Before I can fully take in the sight of her, she pulls me back to her, crushing her lips to mine hungrily. I laugh against her mouth at her eagerness. It's everything I was trying to keep in control. I can't believe I ever thought this was a bad idea. I pull away again. Her hands drop from my neck, but I catch them before they fall.

"I thought you wanted to kiss me." She frowns, pulling our entwined hands back so I stumble closer to her.

"All I want to do is kiss you, Brooke. You have no fucking idea."

She pushes her lower half against mine. "That's all?" She smirks.

"No, that's not all." I can't deny it when she can feel every inch of what I want to do. No more lying to Brooke.

I press my body against her again and before she can draw our lips together, I cup her ass and lift her, pinning her against the van. I don't think I've ever held anything that feels as good as Brooke's ass in my hands. She wraps her legs around me, locking her ankles at my back. She makes that fucking sound again as the friction of my jeans rubs against her, her black work dress riding up her thighs. *Christ*. She rests her elbows on my shoulders and digs her hands into my hair. I could die here.

"Caleb?"

I breathe into her neck. "Yes?"

"Let's go inside," she says.

Fuck. So much for savoring.

Brooke giggles against my lips as I carry her to the front door. That sound and the warmth of her body against mine make it hard to control myself. I need to let her down so she can unlock the door. But first I push her against it and bury my face in her neck.

"Caleb," she scolds. "Mr. Edwards has a direct line of sight to my door. Sometimes he checks to make sure I'm home safely if he knows I had to work."

I suck her neck before putting her down. "I don't give a shit who sees us, Brooke."

She unlocks the door and pulls me through the house, looking back at me as we approach her bedroom. She laughs at the sheepish and probably downright goofy expression on my face. Before she can turn away, I pull her into my chest and wrap my arm around her waist. I get completely lost in her. Her freckled face, her wavy hair falling, her soft curves. All of it.

"What?"

I tuck a loose tendril behind her ear, tangling my hands in her hair and caressing her cheek with my thumb. So many freckles. I need to kiss every last one.

"Just…you," I say, my smile growing wider.

She looks away, embarrassed. "What *about* me?"

"I…" I rest my forehead on hers. "…really like you." I step forward, pushing her backwards until her legs hit the bed. "And I'd like to kiss you more."

She hooks her hands around my neck and pulls, tumbling us onto the bed. "So…kiss me."

Say no more, babe.

I don't hold back this time. I crash into her, coaxing her lips apart with my tongue. Her knees move apart, and I settle into her. Her hands move into my hair, pulling me impossibly close. It's frantic and frenzied. It's perfect. She rocks her hips against me while our mouths crash against each other, barely breaking for breath. God, she wants me as much as I want her.

I run a hand up her soft thigh—her dress already bunched at her waist—and under her lace underwear. My fingers brush inward. When I feel the texture of coarse, short curls, I let out a low groan of want I've never made before.

At the sound, Brooke stiffens beneath me. *Shit.* Too fast, too aggressive. Immediately, I stop and push myself off of her.

"Shit, I'm sorry," I say, sitting back on my heels. "I should have asked before going any further."

"No, it's okay." She hides her face under her hands. "I mean, verbal consent is always a good idea, but I was definitely showing you consent. It's just…is it okay if we slow down a little bit?" She pulls her dress back down.

Relief rushes through me. I lie on my side next to her, propping myself on my elbow.

"Brooke," I say, pulling her hands away from her face. "Of course, it's okay. You don't have to ask if it's okay. I always want you to tell me what you want even if…especially if it's to slow down or stop."

"Thank you. I'm sorry. It's been a long day, and I want to, but…"

"Hey, you don't need to give me a reason," I say, playing with her hair.

"Okay," she smiles, face still flush.

"Do you want me to leave?" *Please say no.*

"What? No!"

"Thank god," I put a hand to my chest and roll onto my back. "I mean, I would have, but it would have been devastating."

She smiles. "I'd like you to stay, Caleb."

"I'd like to stay, Brooke."

She has a sweetly devilish smile on her face.

"What?!"

"I have a whole post-wedding routine that I won't scare you with tonight, but there's one thing I can't miss."

"Okay…"

She jumps from the bed. "I'll be right back."

I stare at the ceiling. Brooke's soft, feminine room. Brooke's bed. *Finally*.

Minutes later, she's back with a paper plate covered in tinfoil and one plastic fork. "How do you feel about wedding cake?"

That's why she tastes like buttercream.

Chapter 25

Brooke

I WAKE UP WITH THE ACHE OF REGRET. I LET MYSELF GET IN THE way of having an amazing night, but I wanted it all to be perfect. As soon as Caleb's fingers skimmed beneath my underwear, I panicked. How could I have explained it to him? *Caleb, now that you know what girl dinner is, I'd like to explain an everything shower to you. Because having sex with you for the first time requires an everything shower.* I was gross and sweaty from working and hauling ballroom chairs. And I haven't gotten a wax in who knows how long.

Now I'm in bed with Caleb curled around me—something I've fantasized about. A lot. He toys with the hem of my nightgown, tracing circles on my thigh. It doesn't have to be perfect. I can get up to quickly brush my teeth (an absolute requirement) and we can spend the morning how we should've spent the night. I'm about to stealthily visit the bathroom when my phone rings. Caleb takes his hand off my thigh and searches for his phone on the nightstand. But it's not his phone.

"It's your mom." He hands me the phone. The screen says JUDY—you can guess who insisted on that—with the picture she selected.

I groan.

Caleb laughs. "My thoughts exactly."

The last thing I want is for anything to interrupt the pure bliss of this morning and how I'd like to spend the rest of it. Leave it to my mom. I consider silencing the call, but there could be a client emergency.

"Hi Mom," I say in a put-on, chipper voice.

"You sound like you're still in bed. We have breakfast scheduled, dear. You didn't forget, did you?"

"Breakfast?" I shift out of Caleb's embrace so fast I almost kick him right in the groin, which also seems interested in picking up where we left off. *Sorry*, I mouth.

"Yes, I'm picking you up."

"Right, sorry. I didn't forget, I just…I, um…overslept… ah…breakdown took a while last night, I didn't get much sleep."

Caleb grabs my waist from behind and plants kisses on my shoulder. Distracting me entirely.

"Mom, I'm a little beat. What if you head to Soundview and pick up coffees and croissants to go, and we can catch up here? That'll give me a few minutes to get myself together." I shoot Caleb a hopeful look over my shoulder.

"No, dear. I'd like to breakfast there like we planned," she says, voice filled with annoyance.

I shake my head and Caleb's eyes drop in disappointment.

"Of course, I know how much you love eating there. Okay, I'll see you in…exactly how far away are you?"

"Ten minutes."

"Ten minutes?!"

Shit.

Caleb's hands fly off my waist. All I want is for their firm grip to be on me again. He's up from the bed and searching for his jeans.

"See you soon." I end the call.

"I'm so sorry," I say, getting out of bed. I walk over to Caleb as he finishes putting those fucking jeans on. What I'd give to be the one taking them off, rather than him undressing when we finally agreed to stop making out and go to sleep. What the hell is wrong with me? "I completely forgot she's picking me up to go out for breakfast. I usually check my calendar before I go to bed, but we were…ya know…and oh my god, if she sees you here…I mean maybe you're dying to leave, and we haven't talked about anything…"

"Hey, *hey*." He gently grabs my arms and my hands land on his chest. He smiles wide and pulls me flush against him. "You do not need to be sorry. The last thing I want to do is leave. What I want to do is get you back in that bed for a long while and then cook you breakfast, but I agree that it wouldn't be ideal for your mom to see me here."

My core aches at his words. *Damnit, Mom.*

He gently presses a kiss to my forehead.

I sigh, breaking away from him to check the time on my phone. She'll be here any minute. I try not to panic. We walk to the door. Caleb grabs the handle, then stops and turns to face me. I don't want him to leave but also, I need him to leave.

"Brooke, I do want to talk about this, and we will, but what I want you to know right now is that I *am* going to get you back in that bed. Very soon."

He grabs my face and kisses me deeply, slowly. It's intoxicating.

"Is that a promise, chef?" I ask, with a smirk.

"Yes, babe, it is."

I'm going to kill my mother.

"Hellllooooo," Mom sings, letting herself into my house with her emergency key. I need to change the locks as soon as possible.

"Hi, Mom!" I yell from the bathroom. "I'll be right out."

I don't need to see her to know she's walking through my living room like a forensics agent. Taking stock of what is or isn't clean. Checking if the frame she gifted me is still where she suggested it'd look best. Taking a finger and swiping it across the mantel to check for dust. She won't find any. It's spotless.

"You know dear," she says, raising her voice so I can hear her down the hall. "I think I saw Caleb Foley in that awful car of his as I turned onto your street."

Shit. "Did you?" I ask, emerging from the hallway. It's amazing how presentable I manage to make myself in the five minutes I had between Caleb leaving and Mom arriving. Thankfully, Soundview is a casual neighborhood eatery, and I can get away with athleisure and a baseball hat—the only option for the tangled mess that is my hair this morning. No doubt she'll have something to say, even if it is Spencer Soirees branded. *Hats are not ladylike, dear.* Maddie ordered them for the staff after a lot of negotiation with Judy.

"I wonder what he's doing in this part of town?"

I shrug.

"Perhaps he's been demoted to deliveries," she says. "Makes me worried about him leading the Quincy wedding."

It shouldn't worry her at all. Foley's has always had glowing reviews. With more pouring in since Caleb's been back.

I need to make absolutely sure she doesn't suspect anything, though I don't know why she would. This isn't going to help my cause when I have to tell her the truth. If I tell her. I don't *have* to tell her. But I've rarely kept anything from her. She always gets it out of me.

"I've got it under control," I say. "Caleb's a pain in the ass to work with but, as much as I hate to say it, he knows what he's doing." My stomach turns telling this lie. Feeding into her narrative.

"Exactly like his father," she says.

Caleb was right. She's always looked down on him and anyone else who doesn't fit her absurd standards. That's why he thought he'd be bad for me.

I'm getting ahead of myself. Caleb did confess some pretty big feelings last night, but that doesn't mean I have to make Judy aware of whatever is happening between us. At least not yet. Not before the Quincy wedding. Not before Mom retires. Nothing can jeopardize that.

Despite its name, Soundview Café doesn't have a view of the Long Island Sound. It's tucked in a sweet residential neighborhood on Soundview Avenue, which leads to a street that leads to another street that *does* have a Sound view. Once a local grocery store, it's now a quirky place loved by locals. Tables of all shapes, colors, and sizes fill the cozy room, each with several mismatched chairs around them. You can spot someone who isn't a regular because they'll claim a table before placing their order at the counter. That's not how it's done at Soundview. Order first, then find a seat.

On a summer Sunday, it's packed. The outside patio is filled with families brunching or couples with their dogs. We get in line to order.

"Morning, Judy!" one of the cashiers calls from her station.

"Judy, how have you been?" a diner calls from her table.

"Is that Ms. Spencer?" an older gentleman asks, looking up from his paper.

This is exactly why she loves to come here. She's a local, but maintains a schedule of appearances that gives her the illusion of local celebrity.

We order, and while Mom says hello to her adoring fans, I take my iced coffee to find us a spot at one of the large communal tables. When I sneak a look at my phone, there's a text from Caleb.

> Caleb: I'd like to invite myself over to make you dinner on Wednesday night. A real dinner this time. With fresh ingredients provided by me.

I'm smiling at myself as I text him back.

"Brooke."

I drop my phone on the table. When did Mom sit down?

"I hope you're posting some of last night's wedding on the Instagram page, dear," she says. "You forgot to last night."

Shit. I never forget to post. Mom eyes me, bringing her coffee mug to her lips. "Who was the photographer? Was it someone new? I hate that you try out these young up-and-comers. They don't know what they're doing. Did you forget to explain to them that we expect to receive the sneak peeks as soon as possible?"

It *was* a new photographer. A brilliant new photographer who knows exactly what they're doing. They sent over photos late last night. I'm not about to lie and throw someone getting their start under the bus. One mistake and you're off the Spencer Soirees recommended vendor list. She's ruthless.

I'll have to throw myself under the bus this time.

"I was going to, but I read something the other day about the algorithm. About Sunday morning posts getting a lot more engagement versus late on a Saturday, so I thought I'd try that. I can find the article if you want to take a look." A white lie that I hope my boomer mother will accept.

"Interesting," she says, tapping her chin. "Well, I'll leave that to you zillenniums to figure out."

"It's zennials, Mom."

"That's what I said." She takes a long sip of her coffee,

holding out her pinkie like she's an extra on *Bridgerton*. "Make sure you're staying on top of things, Brooke. I have a lot to consider come the end of this season."

"Of course, Mom," I say.

"Now, dear. The Quincy wedding, it's only four weeks away. You still have quite a bit of work ahead of you, and I think Mr. and Mrs. Quincy would appreciate my expertise on the day of, so I've rearranged my schedule to make myself available for the next month of prep and the entire wedding weekend."

I knew this was coming, so it shouldn't surprise me. If I hadn't been so distracted lately, I might've been more prepared. After all, the Quincys are one of the wealthiest and most influential couples of a certain generation in town. Naturally, she wants to be there. Their social status isn't something I care much about at all, but she does. She cares a lot. Of course she has to be there herself to mingle with them and micromanage me.

Her hands-off approach had been too good to be true. Now we're going to have a problem. Not only because I'm not sure I can look at Caleb without giving all my feelings away.

For the last couple of years, Mom's managed business operations and slowly stepped back from planning weddings herself. She still plans a small handful each year, usually a couple her age on their third or fourth marriage. Or sometimes the child of a friend of a friend.

But one of the lead planners always works alongside her. That took a lot of convincing on my part. I played to her ego, told her that it wasn't fair I got to learn so much from her. The rest of the staff should get a chance to learn from the best. Meanwhile, I bribed the planners with promises of covering the weekends they wanted off.

Mom's always been a talented wedding planner. Now she's a little too old school for most clients. She still writes out her timelines *in cursive*—I'm not sure some of the interns can even read them—and makes photocopies to distribute. She insists on calling vendors to confirm details, despite their preference for texts or emails. She even leaves voicemails. Long ones!

I might joke about being too old for the wedding industry grind, for the setting up, breaking down, standing on ladders, lifting heavy boxes. But she really shouldn't be doing most of that, even if all the work she's had done suggests she's younger. All that aside, it isn't the physical nature of the job that's the issue. It's her unwillingness to adapt to change that puts the agency at risk.

The poor planner stuck with her is the one keeping the event on track. Typing up a timeline and sending it out to all of the vendors. Following up the phone calls with the emails and texts Mom refuses to send. And day-of, well, anyone would think Mom's a guest. She refuses to wear all black—an agency policy that doesn't apply to her. She dresses like a guest and mingles with them. *It's networking*, she told me once. Networking with a glass of champagne in one hand and a canapé in the other. This behavior is exactly what I expect from her at Hannah and Preston's wedding. That and critiquing my every move.

"Great," I say, as cheerfully as I can manage. "I'm sure they'll appreciate that."

"Now bring me up to speed." She claps her hands quickly. "And tell me when your final walk-through is so I can be there."

So, I do. Over coffee and almond croissants, I update her on the progress I've made, the work with Caleb, and the outstanding tasks. All so Mom can have all the information she needs to micromanage me all Labor Day weekend long.

On Tuesday afternoon, I pull up to Hannah's home. The house is much more modest than I anticipated. I've seen bits and pieces on Instagram. It's still a million-dollar home, but it's on the more congested side of town. It was hardly the sprawling backcountry estate I conjured up in my head.

"Come in, come in." Hannah waves me inside. "It's so good to see you," she says as we hug. I look around the stunning modern farmhouse-style home. Very Instagram-worthy. Hats and jackets hang on pegs on the foyer wall. Shoes and flip-flops are scattered on the floor next to tennis rackets and beach bags. Following Hannah to the kitchen, I notice boxes stacked in the dining room (wedding gifts or PR packages) and a dirty plate and coffee mug in the living room. Influencers, they're just like us!

"One month to go," I say. Not to get right down to business, but also to get right down to business. It's the height of wedding season, and for the first time in my career I'm overwhelmed. It's not something I'm used to, and I don't like it. "How are you feeling?"

She hesitates before answering, "I'm a little anxious if I'm being honest." I've dealt with my fair share of stressed brides. Everyone has a moment, or three, of major stress during the planning, especially as the date looms closer and closer. Nothing I haven't seen before.

"Logistics-wise, we're in a great place," I offer. "Tell me what you're stressed about." Showing my clients that I have control over everything usually eases most of their concerns.

"Oh, I'm sorry," she says, shaking her head. "I feel good about how it's all coming together. It's, well, I just found out *The New York Times* is sending a reporter to cover the wedding. We were planning to submit after the wedding, but one of the editors follows me and thought it'd make a great piece." She can barely contain her smile.

"They don't usually do that," I say. I should know. Mom

has tried for years to get that kind of coverage. We've had weddings in the *Times* before, but couples submitting their story for a short writeup is entirely different from sending a reporter for a full piece.

"I know, I almost can't believe it. It could be incredible for my brand, but it's stressing me out a bit."

It's stressing me out, too. This could be what changes everything. Mom seeing my work bring in this level of publicity might finally convince her that she's leaving Spencer Soirees in good hands—great hands. This wedding weekend needs to be better than perfect. I discreetly brush my sweaty palms on my dress under the table. Hannah can't see even a hint of nerves from me.

"That's so exciting, Hannah!"

"You and Caleb are going to kill it," she says with a smile, clasping her hands together on the table. "But it's a lot."

"I get it," I say, because I do. Mom's going to be even more on top of me once she learns about this. "Let's review things from start to finish and you'll feel a lot better, I promise."

It's going to make me feel a whole lot better too.

Chapter 26

Caleb

When I stop by my parents' after closing the market, Dad's already gone up for the night, giving me a chance to talk to Mom. This afternoon, I was organizing more of Dad's office when I came across a box of old photos from the first Foley's location. In it, I found a photo of Mom and Judy. All this time, I'd been looking to Dad for answers. I'd been going about it all wrong.

"It was a long time ago, honey," she says, making herself comfortable on the upholstered rocking chair across from me. The light gray fabric where she sits is worn from years of her rocking back and forth. There's an indent in the rug where she pushes her foot for momentum.

When I think of Mom, this is what I picture. Glasses perched on her nose as she reads or works on her knitting projects. As a kid, I'd play at her feet. Lining up Hot Wheels or organizing baseball cards. Once, I got too close playing with my Hot Wheels cars and almost lost an eye to a knitting needle. Tonight, I sit across the room, on the floor with my back against the sofa, far away from the legitimate danger.

"Was it really that bad?" I ask.

She takes a deep breath and places her knitting in her lap.

"At the time, it felt like the worst thing that could ever happen. I've lived quite a bit since then and, well, it wasn't the worst thing ever, but it was bad enough that I don't blame your father for his part in this rivalry."

I shift against the couch. Nervous for what I might learn. It was enough to ruin a friendship between my parents and Judy. Could it affect things with Brooke?

"We met Judy shortly after we opened the market. You remember that first location, the small one in the plaza by the old video store? You were eight or so by the time we moved locations. She came in, Brooke in tow, and the three of us hit it off right away. She was a new wedding planner and looking for caterers. Dad was building up the catering offerings. I thought it was serendipity. It was wonderful for a while, for a few years, actually. Dad and Judy did so many weddings together that we started talking about going into business together, building out to be a full-service operation. They handled the weddings and I did the books and kept the business organized for both of them. Judy never paid me, but we were able to all work together, so what was a few unpaid hours?"

She stops rocking and turns all of her focus to me.

"Caleb, I need you to know I've always trusted your father. You know how much I love that stupid man. And you know how much he cares about me. We've always had a solid marriage."

I laugh, thinking of my first night back home. It was clear they were used to being alone. But they've always been like that. I was used to it, living with them.

"I'm well aware, Mom." I laugh.

"Oh, you catch us kissing one time, my goodness, Caleb. How do you think you got into this world?!"

I drag my hand over my face. No one wants to think about

their parents and *that*, but the love they have for each other is something I want one day. "Mom," I groan.

"Anyway," she says, pushing her foot to rock again. "Judy began to find ways to cut me out of conversations and meetings. I didn't notice it much at first. The books and back end of things took a lot of time. And I had you to deal with. You weren't the easiest child."

"Also well aware of that."

"Brooke was usually around, too. I was busy enough. But folks started coming into the market, asking how I was doing. I thought people were being kind because we were so busy with a wedding almost every weekend." She laughs. "We thought one wedding a weekend was busy. Look at things now—at least two or three."

"What I'd do for one wedding a weekend," I say. Walk away from the business my parents built and buy a whole new property, that's what I'd do. But that stays tucked away for now.

"I started noticing how they were asking, the looks on their faces. It was pity. They felt bad for me."

"Why would they feel bad for you?" I'm so focused on Mom that I barely hear the faint creak of the floorboards, the padding of feet. Mom looks behind me.

"Dad!" I hop from the floor. I was so close to finally getting an answer. He's not going to let this conversation continue.

He settles on his armchair, right next to Mom. "I'll tell you why." He will?

"I thought you were sleeping." I sit on the couch and pick my beer up from the floor.

"How can I sleep when your mother is taking an eternity to explain that Judy Spencer convinced the whole town that I was leaving your mother for her?" He says it like he's reading a weather report, not dropping a bomb about the mother of the woman I'm completely falling for.

My eyebrows nearly hit my hairline. "She what?"

"Paul, must you be so curt?"

"Yes," he says, serious for a beat before letting out a small laugh.

"Anyway," Mom says, rolling her eyes at him. "One of our regulars came in one day before the morning rush and told us about the rumors."

"Margaret Edwards," Dad says. "She was a sweet lady. Grew up in town and knew me since I was a kid. Didn't believe a word of what she heard and wanted to make sure we knew."

"Like I said, honey, at the time it felt like the greatest betrayal. The worst thing to happen." She grabs Dad's hand and they share a smile. "But we've been through a lot together, haven't we?"

I see Dad squeeze her hand from where I sit. He takes his eyes off Mom and looks at me. "Judy weaved some elaborate lies. I forget most of them now, but when we came out from under it, I vowed that Foley's would just be us. Family."

I swallow the knot in my throat. He tried to expand Foley's with someone else so they could be full-service, and it backfired.

"How did she come out unscathed? How could she go on and have such a successful business?" There's a fire burning in me, and I want to have some words with Judy Spencer. About my parents. About Brooke. About her superiority complex.

"Caleb," Mom says, her voice as sweet as the word. "We stopped being angry about it a long time ago. There were more lies, something about how Dad was interested in her but she wasn't interested in him. It doesn't matter anymore."

"And she was a damn good wedding planner," Dad says.

I scoff.

"Think of the people you've worked with, Caleb. The clients you've had. People can be good at their jobs and be assholes."

He's not wrong, but I'm struggling to understand how he can defend her.

"I won't let you be angry about it. Don't let it ruin things with you and Brooke," Mom says with a knowing smile.

Me and Brooke. What could they know about me and Brooke?

A laugh erupts from Dad, jolly and loud. "Look at him, Lynne. I told you he didn't think we knew."

I feel my ears turning pink. I'm thirty-two and embarrassed about a girl in front of my parents. This house makes me feel like a teenager again. They look at me with smug smiles. They know and they don't care. Well, they do care. They're happy.

Finally, I have the answer. An answer I have to keep from Brooke. This would break her. She's got blinders on when it comes to her mom, but how can we move forward without the truth? I've spent years lying to her. I can't replace one lie with another. Not when I know in my heart how far this will go. It always has been and always will be Brooke.

"Does Margaret Edwards still live in town?" I ask, changing the subject.

Mom sighs. "She passed away a few years ago. Her husband comes in sometimes, picks up her favorites. It's sweet."

"Any chance, he lives near Brooke? Near Black Rock?"

Dad ponders. "I think he does."

Chapter 27

Brooke

I TURN AWAY FROM THE FULL-LENGTH STANDING MIRROR IN THE corner of my bedroom and grab another dress from the pile of clothes strewn across my bed. The pile that I've already tried on. I feel twenty-four again, trying to find a way to make the same boring black work dress look irresistible. Hoping that Caleb Foley walks out of the kitchen, stops in his tracks, and falls in love with me.

As I put on my blueberry stripe Nap Dress, I hear the buzz of my phone. I slide my arms through the ruffled sleeves and answer the video call. "Hey, Maddie."

"Oh good, you're alive," she says, sarcasm coating her voice. "And dressed. So why aren't you here?"

"Why aren't I where?"

"Brooke, where the hell are you?" Jordan pops into the frame and I get a closer look at the seascape behind them. The blue sky. The sand. The sound of small waves crashing. *Shit.* I was supposed to meet them at the beach for pizza and wine.

"I...um..." I eye myself in the mirror, willing my reflection to provide a convincing excuse. "I can't go out," I say, and fake two coughs. "I'm sick."

Jordan rolls her eyes.

"Very funny, B," Maddie says. "Your hair is curled and you're wearing makeup. Got a hot date or something?"

Yes, but I'm not ready to tell them that. Caleb will be here any minute and I haven't told them anything. I'm not ready to tell them what will maybe—hopefully—happen tonight. If I tell them, Jordan will uncharacteristically squeal for joy and want more details, which I do not have time for. Maddie will drive right over and swear on her life to murder Caleb in his sleep if he so much as thinks about hurting me.

"Hot date? Me?" My attempt to be nonchalant is not convincing. "Something came up with the Quincys and I have to run to an emergency meeting. It literally *just* came up when I was about to walk out the door, or I would have texted." From my window, I see Caleb's Wrangler pull into the driveway. "Sorry to miss pizza and wine. Gotta go! Love you guys!" I hang up.

It's not lying if I plan to tell them soon. Somewhere Jordan can squeal without terrifying small children, and I can make sure Maddie has plenty of space for her emotions. Maybe one of those rage rooms where they give you a baseball bat and protective goggles so you can smash shit to smithereens. Yes, that's the perfect place.

I give myself one last glance in the mirror and shrug. This will have to do. My black work dress did the trick a few nights ago, maybe I don't have to worry so much about everything going exactly to plan.

My phone buzzes twice, back-to-back.

> Jordan: If you're with who I think you're with... have fun!

> Maddie: You got some 'splaining to do

"I know I'm not a professionally trained chef, or even a mediocre home cook…but I'm pretty sure Cacio e Pepe doesn't have eggs in it."

"It doesn't," Caleb says, standing over the stove.

"So why do you have eggs in here?"

Caleb places a kitchen utensil that I don't know the name of on the blue Le Creuset spoon rest. With the carton of eggs in one hand, I'm on my tip toes trying to reach the bacon at the bottom of a green reusable Foley's Market grocery bag. Caleb moves behind me, gently grabbing my hips and resting his chin on my shoulder. "Breakfast, Brooke." He kisses the nape of my neck. I almost drop the bacon back into the bag at the touch of his lips on my skin. "The eggs are for breakfast…" He turns me around and pulls me into his chest. "…tomorrow." With the bacon and eggs in each hand, I wrap my arms around his neck and give him a playful smile.

"Oooh," I say with a hint of sarcasm. "That's a little presumptuous of you, chef."

He raises a brow. "Is it?"

"Maybe. Depends on how good dinner is, I guess."

Hands digging deliciously into my hips, Caleb lifts me onto the counter.

I squeal, eyes wide. His warm, calloused hand is on my neck, pulling my face to his. He kisses me hard. Opening my mouth with his tongue. I moan in return and draw him closer. Dinner is almost ready, but I'm ravenous for something else. Without breaking the deep kiss, he takes the eggs and bacon from my hands and places them on the counter. My hands now free, I claw my fingers through his soft, thick hair. We're all tongues and teeth. I keep him pulled close. I can't get enough of him. This need and hunger that's been bubbling below the surface for so long is not going anywhere until it's satiated.

Ding

A timer for some part of our meal goes off.

Caleb pulls away slowly, dragging my bottom lip between his teeth. Ending that kiss is one of the crueler things he could do right now. My chest heaves. He's quite literally taking my breath away. Caleb reaches to turn off the burner.

"Fuck dinner," he breathes onto my neck. *Thank god*.

I wrap my legs around his waist. Resting his forehead on mine, he runs his hands under my dress from my knees up my thighs. Goosebumps pebble my skin. He slows as he reaches the curve of my hips. I run my hands through his hair again, and I stare into his honey brown eyes, pleading for more with heavy breaths. He toys with the hem of my underwear and nuzzles my collarbone. My breath hitches when he brushes a thumb over the damp fabric between my legs. A proud chuckle rumbles from him. My head tips back against the cabinet as he places languid kisses up my neck then sucks lazily below my ear.

Heat pools in my core at every heightened sensation. The warmth of his body against mine. The pressure his fingers make against me. The taste of the IPA he's been drinking in my mouth.

As soon as he walked in the door, I knew we wouldn't make it to dinner. With his nose, he pushes down the ruffled straps of my dress, peppering kisses along the way. His thumb circles me through my underwear, over and over and over. Teasing me so thoroughly. I need more. Now. I grab his shoulders and grind against him. His lips curl into a smirk. He doesn't hesitate, pushing my underwear to the side, sliding a finger inside me. I gasp at the relief of finally feeling that pressure, but it's not enough. "More," I beg, moving against his hand. He kisses me forcefully and adds a second finger, working his fingertips in slow, measured movements back and forth inside me. This is what I so desperately need.

"Brooke," he says, a question.

"Yes," I pant.

"Can I ask you something?"

"Now?"

His fingers keep working in perfect rhythm. "Did you stop this from happening the other night so you could um… groom?"

I *am* going to have to explain an everything shower to him. I can't form words to answer. Not with the heat burning inside me. Not with my cheeks flaming. "This is…nice," he sighs, breath warm against my neck. "But I need you to know that… nothing could ever stop me from touching you…from tasting you."

A throaty moan escapes my lips. *Words, Brooke. You have to say words.* "I just wanted it to be perfect," I say, breathlessly.

Caleb's fingers still and he withdraws them. I feel empty. Before I can protest, he grabs my ass under my dress and lifts me off the counter. "Brooke," he says, carrying me out of the kitchen and down the hall to my bedroom.

He puts me down in front of the standing mirror in my room. He turns me to face it and stands behind me. My dress is a wrinkled mess, straps pulled off my shoulders. My skin is blotchy and red from Caleb's touch. I'm thoroughly disheveled.

"You." He slowly pulls the hair off one side of my neck and kisses me in that spot below the ear. I lean into his touch.

"Are." He fists the fabric at my waist with one hand and drags my dress to the floor. In the reflection of the mirror, his eyes darken when he finds me braless under the dress.

He groans deeply. "Fucking." He cups my breasts from behind, thumbing my nipples.

"Perfect." He drags one hand down my stomach and toys with my center. I lean my head back against his chest and close my eyes.

"Uh-uh," he whispers in my ear, his voice thick. "Eyes open. Look at you." We make eye contact in the mirror. I am stripped bare, and Caleb is fully clothed behind me. But I don't feel exposed. Not with Caleb. I feel wanted, safe, comfortable.

He's hard against my back. I reach my hand between us, feeling him over his jeans. The breath of his groan blowing more pleasure against my neck. The slow movements he makes bring me closer to the edge. My legs shake, I reach my free arm behind me, wrapping it around Caleb's neck to steady myself.

"I've got you, Brooke," he whispers, wrapping one arm around my middle, cupping my breast and teasing my pebbled nipple with light touches. He sucks on my neck and the burning inside me builds. Stronger and stronger. Until my legs are about to give out from under me.

"I'm…" I breathe, watching him touch me in the mirror.

"Beautiful," he says, and release crashes over me. Waves of pleasure rolling through as my legs shudder, giving out completely. Caleb's grip keeps me from falling. He caresses me through it, until I can stand on my own again.

I don't have words, so I turn and kiss him feverishly.

We move to the bed and I melt into it, worn out from the pleasure. I don't know how much more my body can take. Caleb reaches behind his back and pulls off his shirt with one hand. *God, that's hot.* And as I watch his toned, tanned torso—the man has abs for days—move as he unzips his jeans, I tell my body it will take whatever he gives it. He kicks off the jeans, but not before grabbing a condom from the back pocket. I swallow slowly as I take in his size under his navy boxer briefs. He grins like the devil and crawls over me. He holds his weight up with his forearms, but I grab the waistband of his boxers and pull him on to me.

"Brooke," he brushes my lips. We're chest to chest and it's heaven. I move my hand between us to touch him.

"Uh-uh," he says, flipping us effortlessly so I'm on top of him. I give him a questioning look. "Tonight's all about you."

"Is that what you want?" I ask.

Another devilish grin. "What I want is for you to take my boxers off and get on top of me."

"Yes, chef," I tease, and grab the condom from his hands. I shimmy down his body and release him from the boxers. *Whoa.* Boxers on the floor, I crawl over him, stopping to take him in my mouth.

"Christ," he groans, and it makes me ache. I've never had that urge to make someone come undone like he did to me. Suddenly, it's all I want to do. I swirl my tongue around his tip before taking him fully in my mouth again. "Brooke, I'm trying so hard to make this last," he says, pulling away and hooking a finger under my chin.

I'm the one with a devilish grin now. This isn't like me. Watching myself come in the mirror. Needing to taste him. Taking the condom and rolling it on him now. But it all feels natural. Something about Caleb makes me release any inhibitions.

I straddle his thighs and grind myself against his length. It's already earth-shattering and he's not even inside me. Caleb takes one arm and rests it behind his head, looking like a goddamn Abercrombie model. The other grabs my hip and moves with me.

"Sorry," I sigh. "This just feels so good."

"Brooke, don't you ever apologize for that. All I want is to make you feel good."

If he makes me feel *this* good now, I can't imagine what I'm in for.

I grab him and rise on my knees. His hands find my hips, nails digging in, and he lifts me. Slowly, I lower myself onto him, my breath catching as he fills every inch of me.

He rises to kiss me, grabbing my neck, hands in my hair. The shift drives him deeper. I didn't think that was possible. I close my eyes and see stars.

Our lips crash, tongues tangling and sucking. It's messy. It's perfect. I rock in a steady rhythm, and he thrusts into me perfectly in time. He must do a thousand sit-ups a day.

With every beat, pleasure coils, my breath is tight and hot in my chest. He pulls my hair at the base of my neck, tilting my head back. His lips sucking below my ear. I never want this to end, but the tension aches for release.

He pulls away and I push his torso back on the bed.

"Fuck," he moans.

I rest my hands on Caleb's chest, and he uses his strength to thrust harder as I ride him. Harder. Deeper. He brings a thumb to my throbbing clit, rubbing in time with movements until my muscles clench and contract around him, pulsing with the satisfaction of my climax. As the pleasure rolls through me, Caleb's fingers dig into my hips. He finds his release and moans my name.

Chapter 28

Caleb

Dad sits across from me, watching me work on the signature dish he insists I haven't perfected yet. I have. It's one of our most popular catering appetizers. Crabbies. Mom found the original recipe in some magazine in the early '90s and made it for a dinner party. It was such a hit that it's been on the menu ever since. The recipe's gotten some tweaks over the years but it's not hard to master: Mix crab meat, old English cheddar cheese, and some spices, spread on English muffins, cut into triangles, and bake.

So we're at the Market kitchen with Dad micromanaging each step. He's enjoying every second of it. I'm trying to focus and not give him anything to comment on, but that's proving difficult when all I can think about is Brooke.

Leaving her house this morning was agonizing. But last night was heaven. By the time we got around to leaving the bedroom, dinner was unsalvageable. Some chef I am.

"Hungry?" I asked her, looking at the eggs and bacon on the counter.

"Starving," she said, giving me a sly smile, her cheeks turning pink. She'd put on an oversized white t-shirt and pink-striped boxer shorts. No bra under the thin fabric of her shirt. I don't know what I did to deserve that.

"Are you blushing, Spencer?" I teased, letting out a laugh. She buried her face in her hands.

"Yes, you are!" I pulled her close. She fit so perfectly against me. When I held her then. When we were in bed. I traced the freckles on her face with my thumb. "What are you blushing about?"

"Shut up." She smacked my arm. "I don't know…I…I haven't done anything like that in my kitchen before. Barely even made out in here."

All I hear is *made out* and *kitchen*. Before I could hear any more about anyone else touching her in this kitchen, I kissed her soft, swollen lips. I felt her smile against my mouth and her pert nipples against my chest.

"Babe," I said. I meant it sincerely, that term of endearment was now all hers. "You're about to do a lot in this kitchen that you've never done before."

"Oh?" she said, biting her lip.

"Yes." I kissed her forehead. "Like learn how to make scrambled eggs and bacon."

She smirked. "And after that?"

"I have some ideas." And I did. A lot of them.

"Like what?"

"Well," I whispered in her ear, skimming my fingers across the waistband of her shorts. "For starters, I haven't gotten to taste you yet."

She dropped her face into her hands and groaned sweetly.

"C'mon, time for food," I said.

Cooking with Brooke was a…disaster might be too harsh, but she certainly would have been berated by a culinary instructor. We lost four eggs to cracking mishaps, and there was nearly a small grease fire with the bacon. After that, I gently suggested she set the table. We'll start smaller next time—how to boil water small. Or I'll just cook for her all the time. Nothing would make me happier.

But my daydreaming about all the things I want to cook for Brooke is interrupted.

I hear her before I see her. "Caleb Foley!"

I raise my brows at Dad across the table.

"Hello, Maddie," I glance sidelong toward the bakery counter. Ali, our bakery apprentice, blocks Maddie from getting into the kitchen. "You can let her back, Ali."

"See," Maddie huffs at Ali. "I do know him."

Dad chuckles as Maddie stomps into the kitchen, her hands in fists at her sides. I swear she's about to walk right up to me and slap me in my face until Dad clears his throat. She stops in her tracks.

"Maddie, this is my dad, Paul Foley. Dad, this is Maddie, Brooke's best friend and Spencer Soirees planner."

"Nice to meet you, Mr. Foley," she says tersely, shaking his hand before shifting her gaze back to me. "We need to talk. About you know who…" She looks at Dad. Like he'd ever miss this. She doesn't know enough about Paul Foley. I give him a shrug.

"It's been quite some time since we've had a wedding planner waltz in here on a mission. I'm intrigued," Dad says. It's been decades. I think about Judy waltzing into the old location and how different Brooke is from her mom—her opposite in almost every way. I have no right to feel it, but pride grows in my chest. For all she's been through, Brooke's kind, smart, beautiful, and so much more. And for some baffling reason, she likes me.

"I'm talking about…" She glances at Dad again before covering her mouth with her hand. "Brooke."

"You can say whatever you need to say in front of him."

"Ugh, fine…" she says, literally stomping one foot. She blows out a breath and points a finger at me. "Caleb Foley, if you break her heart again, I vow to murder you in your sleep with your own chef's knife and then…"

Dad's chortle interrupts what's obviously a prepared speech. He slaps his hand hard on the table, causing some of the Crabbie triangles to bounce on the baking sheet. Good! I can blame whatever issue he has with this batch on him.

"I think I like you, Maddie," he says. "Please, continue."

"She's my best friend, and I had to pick up the pieces last time. It took her forever to move on. Then Judy set her up with Kent and you know the rest. She's been through a fucking lot. She has to deal with having Judy for a mother and is blind to how that affects her. So, if you aren't all in, get out. Because while I won't hesitate to help put her back together, I don't think *she* can take it." She turns to Dad. "I'm sorry you had to find out this way, Mr. Foley. I know you hate Brooke and her mom, but I cannot stand by and watch Brooke get hurt again."

"Maddie, I can assure you that we don't hate Brooke or her mother. Judy and I have our issues, and I tried my best to watch out for Brooke. Most of what you've heard has come from Judy. I'd keep that in mind since you already know what she's like. I've had my suspicions about how Caleb felt about Brooke for a long time. I'm not surprised by it. In fact, I'm delighted."

"Oh," Maddie says, clearly surprised.

"Brooke's lucky to have a friend like you, Maddie." He looks away from her and his eyes land on me. He's grinning ear to ear. "And I agree with you, if he breaks her heart, he'll have hell to pay. Not just from you. I've got a chef's knife of my own, you know."

Jesus Christ. I throw up my hands in defeat.

"Maddie," I say. "I have no intention of breaking her heart. I promise."

Maddie looks lost. She was obviously expecting more of a fight. "Okay, good." She eyes the knife roll on the table.

"Because those are some good-looking knives, and I'd hate to ruin one of them."

I push the knife roll down the table, away from her. I don't doubt for one second that Maddie would commit assault with a deadly weapon on behalf of a scorned friend.

Dad chuckles when I return from walking Maddie out. He's enjoying this far too much. But if I know him, I'm also in for a lecture. He doesn't take hurting anyone, especially women, lightly.

"What are you laughing at?"

"Oh, the drama of being young. Though you're not as young as you were when you first hurt Brooke. Are you all in, son? You've only been back home since June. Things are moving fast."

"I think...I think I've been all in for a while. I just wasn't ready."

"Ah, I see," he says, waiting for me to say more, but I don't. "And you're ready to face the wrath of Judy?"

"I think I am, but I don't know. She's never been fond of me."

"Caleb, I know you've struggled sometimes with what we do. Thinking folks look at us like—"

"The help," I say. "Yeah, it pisses me off."

"We are the help, son. It's not a bad thing. It's the most precious gift. We help with the happiest moments, the weddings, birthdays, and graduations. They come to us when they've brought home a new baby or when they're visiting a loved one in the hospital. We help the most devastating moments too, the funerals and celebrations of life. And the small moments, when they're having a bad day and need comfort, or received good news and want to celebrate. We help them through the milestones of life. It's a privilege. I'm sorry I haven't imparted that on you enough. I'm proud of the work we do here. I hope you are too."

There's a stinging in my nose. I blink it away.

"Dad, I'm sorry, I never meant—"

"I know, Caleb, I know. I'm proud of you. All you've done and all you're going to do. With this *Times* piece, you're going to be ready for what's to come. Now redo those Crabbies. They look awful." He stands up and is out of the kitchen before I can find any more words.

I spend the rest of the afternoon perfecting Crabbies. With one pinch of salt more than the recipe calls for, I finally get an almost perfect batch. Before I leave for the day, I grab some of the prepared items that Mom mentioned Mr. Edwards likes to drop off to him before going to Brooke's. Whatever kind of day he's having, I can help.

Chapter 29

Brooke

"Yes, I understand that *you're* writing the check, but Hannah and Preston signed the contract so technically *they* are the clients…Hannah specifically told me no surprises…yes…okay…I'll speak with Judy, of course…nice speaking with you, Mr. Quincy."

Maddie dances into the office, *literally dances* to whatever pop song she's hyper-fixating on at the moment blasting in her earbuds, catching the end of an argument I usually have with the mother-of-the-bride.

Maddie tosses her bag on her chair and pops over to her computer. "He's a piece of work, huh?"

"You have no idea." I sigh. "He wants bagpipers at the ceremony as a surprise. Hannah didn't just tell me no surprises—she explicitly said no bagpipers, no matter how much her dad wants them."

She sips her coffee and shakes her head. "I love bagpipers."

"Me too," I shrug. "But not my wedding. He insisted that I talk to Judy about it. Said she'd understand that he has the right because he's paying. Can you believe that?"

"Oh, I can," Maddie says, then puts on her famous Judy

Spencer voice. "And that, girls, is why we always have the couples sign the paperwork and not the parents!"

It's a strict policy. We've all dealt with one too many overbearing parents who try to make the wedding all about them. Under normal circumstances, Judy would stand by her policy. With the Quincys, I'm not so sure. She certainly didn't stand by it when it came to planning Kent and my nuptials.

This is the type of thing that usually sends me into a spiral about Mom and the broken engagement fallout.

"You okay?" Maddie asks. She knows all too well about this particular spiral.

"I'm fine," I say, my usual response, before thinking about it. "Actually," I say, straightening in my chair, "I *am* fine."

"Are you now?" She sounds skeptical.

"Yes, I am," I say, sitting up even straighter in my chair.

Maddie looks at me expectantly.

Play dumb, Brooke. "What?"

She cocks her head to the side, raising a brow. "This is the part where you tell me why you ditched us the other night, why you lied about it, and why in your right mind you're giving Caleb fucking Foley another chance."

Shit.

"Maddie! Lower your voice! Judy's in her office."

"So, you are then?" She eyes me. "Giving him another chance?"

"It's complicated," I say through clenched teeth. "And we can't talk about this here."

"It's complicated?! Of course it's complicated! Bad complicated!"

"Maddie, please," I beg, eyeing Mom's office.

She sits back at her desk. "Fine, but this conversation isn't over."

"Fine." I knew she wasn't going to be thrilled about this. I should have researched those rage rooms sooner. Maddie's always been fiercely protective. She's like that with the people she loves. She's an eldest daughter; Made to watch out for the people she cares about.

She's been by my side since we met, putting all my pieces back together. After Caleb moved to San Francisco. When I broke things off with Kent. I can't blame her for holding onto some anger. If anyone can hold a grudge, it's Maddie. She is an Aries after all.

I scan the room to ensure no one overheard us. It's Tuesday and the room is already filling up for the staff meeting.

"Also!" Maddie pops up, her red curls bouncing. "I'm still mad, but I should tell you that I confronted Caleb."

"You *what*?"

"I told him if he breaks your heart again, I'll murder him. You're welcome."

My jaw drops. Before I can find words to respond, she's sitting again. She hasn't *actually* murdered him though, so I guess that's a win.

My phone buzzes.

> Jordan: Just landed. I would have warned you if I'd known. Thoughts and prayers.

Jordan left early this morning to shoot an elopement somewhere out west. Wyoming or Colorado, I can't remember. It's hard to keep up, but it's definitely some place that involves a ranch. She refuses to give me access to her calendar, but all that matters is that she'll be here for the Quincy wedding.

"Still mad but…" Maddie rolls her chair over next to mine and points to Judy's office. "Who is that?"

She's walking out with a woman who can only be described as absolutely stunning. She's tall with a blunt blonde bob and impeccable style. She looks like she stepped right out of *Vogue* in her definitely-designer-but-not-a-label-to-be-seen outfit.

"I have no idea." I usually know about important meetings

or new client prospects. This woman isn't one of those. Only Maddie and I are paying attention to the runway model walking through the office, everyone else is busy finding a place to sit. At the door, Judy shakes the mystery woman's hand before saying, "I'll be in touch next week."

Judy turns back into the office. Her eyes meet mine in the sea of planners. There's a moment of surprise before she schools her features to a neutral place. What is she up to?

"Good morning, ladies. Let's get started."

The walk-through at the Quincys' isn't until eleven o'clock, which gives me and Caleb the morning to work from my sunroom. Early light shines through the bamboo shades in my favorite spot in the house. This room's at its best in the summer.

It's only been a week since Caleb and I have become… whatever we are, but it feels like we've always been *us*.

Every moment we haven't been working, we've been together. Either here or at his place, sneaking around like teenagers worried our parents will catch us. Though I *am* worried Mom will find out sooner than I'm ready for her to. She's been micromanaging more than usual. Maddie, despite being angry with me, dropped me at Caleb's after work earlier this week in case Mom drove by his house. It's possible I'm a little paranoid. The truth is I'm terrified of having to tell Mom anything when it comes to us. I knew Maddie was going to have some concerns, but I also knew she'd always have my back. Mom I'm not so sure about. Actually, I am sure how she's going to react and it's terrifying. I try not to sit with that thought for too long.

Caleb told his parents about us and they're happy. That's

what he said, *they're happy*. I had a lot of questions, but he knows exactly what to do to distract me.

This morning he's laying across the daybed with his computer perched on his lap, answering emails and preparing estimates. I'm supposed to be preparing an inspiration board for one of next year's clients. Sitting cross-legged with various samples and swatches spread in front of me, it's hard not to watch Caleb work. Chef mode Caleb is my absolute undoing, but this is also extremely sexy. Watching him focus on the screen, scrunching his nose just so and gnawing on his lip without realizing it is making it hard to find the motivation to work.

Caleb's lips curl up into a smirk. "Stop undressing me with your eyes, Brooke. I have work to do," he says, without taking his eyes off his laptop.

I quickly look down at the mess of samples in front of me. "I'm *not* undressing you with my eyes."

He scoffs. "Then what *are* you doing?" He sits up and throws his legs over the side of the daybed.

I look at my watch. "I'm thinking about how much time we have until we have to leave for the meeting."

He leans back, clasping his hands behind his head. I swear he flexes his biceps on purpose. "Oh?"

"Yes." I stand up and pad over, stopping right in front of him.

"C'mere." He grabs my waist and pulls me onto his lap.

"I like this." I smile, my legs comfortably straddling him. "Having you here and working with you."

"Me too," he says, brushing my lips with a soft kiss. "But I'm not sure how much work we're getting done, babe."

I'm officially a convert on the nicknames. Well, only this one. And only when he says it. And only when it's not in front of anyone. If he ever calls me baby, it's over.

He gives my neck a soft bite in that perfect spot. A quiet

moan leaves my lips. I'm desperate for his mouth to be on mine, but he keeps kissing my neck with more urgency. His hands crawl up my torso underneath my shirt until they reach below my breasts. Unable to take it much longer, I run my fingers through his hair and pull his face up to mine. He brushes my lips lightly and then captures my mouth with his. I open my mouth for him and his tongue that I'm so ravenous for.

I roll my hips over the hardness of his jeans in a slow rhythm as he cups my breasts, his thumbs circling my nipples, slowly at first, the pace picking up as our tongues clash.

Caleb pulls his lips away from mine. "And do you like this?" He pinches my nipples lightly before grabbing my hips to guide my rocking. I nod in answer, my short breaths making it hard to speak. If I'm not careful, I'm going to come just from riding him like this.

He lowers one hand to the front of the waistband of my linen shorts. I thank past Brooke for picking this particular two-piece set as he easily runs his hand down the front of my underwear and teases me over the fabric. He's quickly learned how much I love that friction. "Mmhmm, I thought so," he whispers in my ear, moving his hand inside my underwear and torturing me with slow, soft strokes.

"Caleb...we don't...have a lot...of...time." My chest heaves. His finger teases my clit with each word I manage to get out. Caleb buries his head in my neck, kissing and sucking. This, I think, is heaven.

He pulls away briefly. "We have just enough time," he rasps, driving two fingers into me. Pleasure consumes me and I roll my head back, giving him perfect access to that sensitive spot below my ear. His fingers move in and out to the cadence of my grinding against him. I'm slowly falling apart.

He drives his fingers in hard, keeping them inside as he curls his fingertips back and forth. My core is on fire, melting me into his touch. Caleb's thumb presses harder, moving in small perfect circles. My nails dig into his back. He puts his mouth to mine, kissing me fiercely between my short breaths.

I pant. "Caleb, I'm going to…"

"I know," he says, satisfaction in his voice.

He applies the smallest amount of additional pressure with his thumb, fingers still working in time. I unravel completely, my muscles pulsing against his fingers as my climax comes in waves. Caleb's mouth hovers over mine. He continues to work his hands as I come down from the release. My breathing slows to a steady pace.

"Oh my god," I manage between Caleb's kisses.

Caleb pulls back and smiles.

"What?"

"You're glowing," he says, a proud smile on his face.

"That was…" How do I put that into words? How do I reconcile the person I usually am—a buttoned-up rule-follower who always has a plan and is terrified of doing the wrong thing—with the person I am around Caleb? With him, I forget my plan for the day. I don't put all my value in my career. With him, I do things like ignore client work and come from getting fingered in my sunroom before noon.

"Oh my god!"

"I know, that was…"

"No, Caleb. My mom is here." I point behind him. Through the shades, I see her car pulling up in front of the house. I push myself off Caleb's lap.

"Shit." Caleb stands. The front of his jeans are painfully stretched. "What is she doing here?"

"I have no idea!" I attempt to fix my hair and rid myself of anything that screams *I just had one of the most incredible orgasms ever*, and then I remember that Caleb is here. His fucking Wrangler is in the driveway. "Oh my god, oh my god." I pace, keeping eyes on the window. She hasn't gotten out of her car.

"She's going to see your car. What are we going to do? She's going to lose it on me, Caleb."

This. This is why I have plans. And a schedule. When I don't, things fall apart.

"Hey, *hey*. It's going to be ok." He takes my hand, interlacing our fingers together. "We'll tell her that I came over to pick you up for the meeting. Your house is on the way. She might be annoyed, but she's not going to suspect you just rode my hand into oblivion." His lips curl up into what I know now as his signature smirk. Stupid dimple.

"Caleb!" I swat his arm. "That's not funny."

"But it was fun!" He gives me a hurried kiss, and I wish we had more time. That Mom wasn't here so I could show him what else my mouth can do. Outside, her car door slams, her heels clack up the walkway to the house.

"Go wash your hands," I hiss at him playfully.

Caleb inspects his hand and lowers his gaze with a smug smile. "Go change your shorts." *Shit*. I do need to change. I reek of sex.

Chapter 30

Caleb

This short time with Brooke gives me all the confidence I need to face whatever is coming our way. The insecurities I once held to so tightly have unraveled and flown off. Dad's pep talk definitely helped. I still have my own dream, but I see the work we do in a different light.

It's perfect timing as Judy tries her key in Brooke's door. Thankfully, Brooke changed the locks—which she might want to share with her mother. Brooke's still getting changed. If it were up to me, she'd keep those shorts on all day as a reminder of how good we are together. I open the door to find an extremely frustrated Judy.

"Good morning, Ms. Spencer," I say, holding the door open for her.

"Caleb," she says, not surprised in the least to see me. "What are you doing at my daughter's house?" She walks into the living room, crosses her arms, and stares me down.

I'm glad I catch Judy first. Brooke is freakishly calm under pressure when it comes to work, but I have a feeling she wouldn't be so calm under the pressure of her mother possibly finding out about us. *She's going to lose it on me, Caleb.* I make a mental note to unpack that later. I may be feeling confident, but Brooke isn't there yet. Not when it comes to Judy. For Brooke's sake, I play my part.

"We have a walkthrough with Hannah and Preston today. Thought I'd pick Brooke up," I say with a grin. "She's getting ready. I had the time wrong and got here early."

"I know the walkthrough is today, Caleb." Judy narrows her eyes at me. "That's why *I'm* here. You'd do well to be a bit more organized with your calendar."

Before I can respond, Brooke walks into the living room, her cheeks still rosy and her hair disheveled. She's changed into a fitted blue sundress. After this walkthrough, we're picking up right where we left off.

"Hi, Mom!" she chirps. "What are you doing here?"

Judy walks to her with something like concern on her face. "Brooke," she says, placing the back of her hand on Brooke's forehead. "Are you feeling all right, dear? You look a little flushed."

I stifle a laugh.

She pushes Judy's hand away. "I'm fine, Mom."

"You're not having one of your little headaches, are you? Always such terrible timing."

Little headaches. I'm not laughing now. Is she kidding? Surely, she's seen Brooke in the middle of a migraine attack. How could anyone call being curled up on the floor in the fetal position a little headache? I fight the urge to answer for Brooke and tell Judy a thing or two. Holding my tongue is not going to be easy.

"No, I'm not having a migraine attack right now."

"Okay, good. Then let's get going."

"I thought you were only coming to the final walkthrough, Mom. This is just the preliminary site visit," Brooke says.

Neither of us want Judy involved any more than she needs to be. "You don't have to waste your time with this one. Caleb and I have it covered."

"Don't be silly, Brooke. With the *Times* piece, it's imperative that I'm involved in every detail from here on out."

Great.

"The pleasure is all mine Douglas," Judy shakes Mr. Quincy's hand. The Quincys do appear pleased that she's here, and Brooke has Hannah and Preston distracted reviewing some final rental estimates. Judy and the Quincys exchange more pleasantries, discussing a recent heat wave… in August… *how shocking*. It must be exhausting to be Judy. Always putting on a show.

We start the walkthrough with the wedding day and circle back to the rehearsal dinner and farewell brunch. Maddie's here too. I should have brought one of my sous to help take notes and make sure we've got everything covered. The enormity of this wedding hits me as we go through the logistics. It's the opportunity Dad dreamed of for so long. Instead of him standing here, though, it's all up to me. He's not getting the chance to enjoy the accomplishment.

I'm even more invested than I was before. I want it to go perfectly, for my dad and our clients, but especially for Brooke. I want everything to go exactly according to her meticulous plan. Watching her now, running this extremely complicated site visit, is incredible. Our clients hang on her every word, and she has an answer for every question or concern thrown her way. It's incredibly sexy how in control she is.

It makes seeing her lose control with me that much more satisfying.

"Is now a good time to review the guest list?" Judy asks. That wasn't on the agenda for this visit.

"Judy," Brooke says, shifting uneasily on her feet. The dynamic between them is bizarre to watch. To anyone that didn't know them, it'd seem like a typical boss and employee relationship. A demanding boss and an employee trying to get it right. But it's not a secret to anyone here that they are mother and daughter. Brooke calling her Judy throws me off. I can't imagine calling my dad by his first name.

"We've been tracking the RSVPs closely. We don't need to take up everyone's time by reviewing now," Maddie offers.

"Nonsense. There are several VIPs attending and it's important we review to ensure we have all the necessary arrangements in place."

"That's a great idea, Judy," Mr. Quincy says.

We settle at the large outdoor dining table on the patio. Though, patio is an understatement. I'd call this a veranda. A veranda that will hold seventy-five for the rehearsal dinner and another hundred for the farewell brunch. I try to snag the seat next to Brooke, but Judy beats me to it without a glance in my direction. I end up across from her. Brooke pulls out her iPad, opening up the guest list, and we discuss missing RSVPs and important guests.

Just when I think we're finally wrapping up and Brooke and I can go back to what Judy interrupted, Judy shifts the conversation.

"Quite a few eligible bachelors on the guest list," Judy says, looking at Brooke. I clench my fists under the table. When I look to Brooke for her reaction to Judy's unprofessional comment, she's rubbing her temple.

"Oh, yes," Mrs. Quincy says. "We'd be happy to introduce you, Brooke."

Brooke smiles apologetically in Hannah's direction. "Mom...I mean Judy, I'll be too focused on making this day amazing for Hannah and Preston to concern myself with finding a date."

"We were so sorry to hear about you and Kent, dear," Mr. Quincy says. "He's a fine young man."

"Yes, he is," Judy clips, eyes darting at Brooke. "Now, Gage Wilson…I've heard some wonderful things about his family."

Maddie stifles a laugh, trying to cover it with a cough.

"Ms. Spencer, as fun as matchmaking is, I think we should get back to figuring out these final seating details, don't you?" Hannah gives her a sweet smile.

"Yes, of course. My apologies, Hannah." Judy places her hand over her heart. "I want my daughter to settle down and be as happy as you and Preston."

Bullshit.

She moves on to discussing some local politician who may or may not be able to attend at the last minute and what contingencies we'll need in place.

"Excuse me, I'm going to pop inside and use the restroom," Brooke says, leaving the table quickly. Judy continues talking, barely noticing her daughter's rushed exit from the table. I wait a moment to confirm no one cares about my thoughts on the seating. I don't give a shit where anyone sits. All I need are the final numbers a few days before the wedding. I'm not sure why I'm even sitting here. I lock eyes with Hannah. She tilts her head toward the house. I quietly get up from my chair and follow Brooke inside.

When I walk into the kitchen, Brooke is leaning against the massive island with a glass of water, her back to me. The kitchen is big enough that we'll be able to use it for service for the rehearsal dinner and farewell brunch. We'll only need a catering tent for the wedding reception.

"Hey," I say. "You okay?"

"Shit." She places a hand on her chest. "You scared me."

"I'm sorry, I need to stop doing that."

"It's okay. You make my heart jump even when you're not startling me."

Warmth grows in my chest. My heart jumps, too. "Are you okay?" I ask again.

She places the water down and sighs, fixing her beautiful face into a smile. "Yeah, I'm fine. Just needed a minute."

"Brooke, it's me. You don't need to pretend you're fine when you're not. I saw you rubbing your temple at the table."

"I just took my medication. It should kick in soon, I caught it at the start. I mostly needed to get away from Judy for a minute. I promise I didn't know she was coming to this. The final walkthrough, yes, but not this. Now I know why. She's trying to find the next Kent to shoulder all of her hopes for me... I'm sorry you had to hear that."

It's cute that she thinks I'm worried about some finance bro taking her away from me. Now that I've got her, I'm never letting go. What I'm worried about is the way Judy treats her. "I know who some of those guys are, Brooke. I'm not concerned."

Her gaze softens. She raises her hand to massage her temple, but I stop her and put my fingers there instead. Putting a little pressure and massaging like I did the night I found her at the office.

The sigh she makes shouldn't turn me on, but it does. "You're so good with your hands," she says. *Jesus Christ.* All I can do is kiss her forehead while all the blood rushes out of my head.

"I wish she'd stop meddling in my life. Let me live it instead of trying to fit me into this plan she has. I've done everything she wants me to do. I went to the college she wanted me to. I joined Spencer Soirees when she wanted me to. I followed in her footsteps like she wanted me to. It's never enough for her. I don't know what else to do." Her voice breaks with those last words.

"Brooke, is this what you want to do?" I ask. She gives me a puzzled look. "Listen, you're the most talented wedding planner I know. You're incredible at your job, and I love watching you do it. But is it what you want?"

"Yeah…of course it is. I mean, it's what I always wanted to do…?" It sounds like she's trying to convince herself. "I never knew to want anything else, and I *am* really good at it. Not all of us want to run away from the path our parents started us on, Caleb."

Ouch. I wince.

"I don't mean that…I'm sorry. It's so complicated with her. She says she wants me to take over but hangs it over me like I haven't done enough to earn it. Your dad is so excited and proud to hand Foley's over to you, Caleb. He believes in you. He's proud of you. I wish my mom felt that way about me." Her eyes fill with tears. She bites the inside of her cheek, working so hard to keep tears from falling, but a few roll down her cheeks.

"I don't mean to question you. It's just…I…listen, this…" I point back and forth between us and then step closer to her, hooking my finger under her chin. "…it's new, brand new. But we've known each other a long time. I care about you, Brooke, and I want you to have whatever you want. I want you to be celebrated for being the best wedding planner in Connecticut. I want your mom to give you the agency if that's what you want. And because I care about you, sometimes I'm going to ask hard questions. But I'm always on your team. Team Brooke, always."

I lower my face and kiss her, tasting the salt of tears on her lips. The whoosh of a door makes me pull away. I carefully wipe her cheeks. She'd hate for our clients to know she was crying.

Hannah walks in smiling with Preston behind her. "Looks like my mom doesn't need to play matchmaker after all."

Brooke straightens her posture and steps away from me. It's too late to deny anything. We've been caught red-handed. At least it wasn't Judy.

"I knew it," Preston says, grabbing an apple from a bowl on the island and taking an enormous bite.

"Hannah. Preston," she says. "I'm so sorry, we were… uh…"

"Making out in my future in-laws' kitchen?" Preston laughs. "Been there."

I can't help but laugh with him. "Brooke needed a minute."

"Your mom is something else, Brooke," Preston says, chewing on another bite of apple. He barely said a word during the walkthrough and suddenly he's the chattiest guy I've ever met. "I'd need a lot more than a minute if I was working with her, and I've worked with some real assholes."

"Preston!" Hannah scolds him.

"What?" he asks. "You're always saying the guys I work with are assholes."

"Well, they are," Hannah says. "Brooke, don't worry. You weren't here five minutes and I could sense something going on between you. Judy doesn't know?"

Brooke shakes her head.

"Your secret's safe with us," Preston chimes in. "Believe me, we know how complicated families are."

"Thank you, both," Brooke says. "I'm sorry for being so unprofessional."

"Oh, please." Hannah waves a hand in the air. "You needed a minute, and your boyfriend wanted to make sure you were okay. I'd be concerned if there wasn't kissing involved."

"Maddie wrapped things up and we sent Judy off. Told her we'd drive Brooke home," Preston says, clapping my back. "But I'm guessing you've got that covered?"

"I do, thanks."

"Thank you, Hannah, Preston," Brooke says. "We got a lot

accomplished today. I truly can't wait to celebrate you both in a few weeks. It's going to be a beautiful day!"

We still have a lot of work ahead of us to make it incredible, but right now all I care about is making sure Brooke feels okay.

Chapter 31

Brooke

CALEB'S GOT ONE HAND ON THE STEERING WHEEL AND THE other resting on my thigh. I'm so relieved to be driving home with him instead of Mom. Her behavior today was not only extremely unprofessional but hugely embarrassing. She treated an important client meeting like the Gilded Age marriage mart. Hoping to marry me off to the richest bachelor regardless of what I want.

What I want—what I've maybe always wanted—is Caleb. Driving in his stupid Wrangler with the doors off. Working together on my porch. Cooking together in the kitchen. Fine, *him* cooking in the kitchen.

"How's your migraine?"

"Much better," I say with a smile. I did manage to catch it before it got bad. Not only does Mom not have patience for my migraines, but Kent wasn't understanding either. *Mind over matter*, he used to say to me. Like I could simply decide to feel better and, *poof*, the migraine would disappear. I wish. As pathetic as it sounds, Caleb simply asking how I feel makes me feel cared for and important.

"I'm glad," he says, squeezing my knee. "So sometimes the medication works and other times it doesn't?"

"Basically. I know a lot of my triggers…dehydration, red wine, tomatoes—"

"Tomatoes?"

"I know, it's tragic."

Caleb removes his hand from my thigh and rakes it through his hair. His brows knit together in concentration.

"You okay?"

He blows out a breath. "That rules out so many things I can cook for you. Do you know how good my gazpacho is?"

"Aw, babe," I laugh. "I'm sorry to tell you this, but even if I didn't have an aversion to tomatoes, there's no way I'm eating gazpacho. Soup's not meant to be cold."

"Excuse me?" He's so offended, it's cute.

"It's for warming you up on a cold day or warming your soul when you're sad. Not to be eaten cold. Gross."

"You think you know a person," Caleb says with a laugh.

"Anyway, I try to avoid my triggers, but sometimes a combination of things can cause an attack, sometimes it's hormonal. Most of the time the medication does the trick, or I'll need to rest in a dark room for an hour or two. When you found me at the office…that was the worst one I've had in a while. I'm glad you came to check on me."

"I was fuming when I got there. After all the shit you gave me about messing something up." I'm sure he was. I shouldn't have been so hard on him "But when I saw you on the floor, Brooke…I was terrified," he says, his hand finding my leg again. "I'm glad I came to check on you, too."

I rest my hand on top of his and squeeze. He has his eyes on the road, his brown hair blowing back with the wind, looking like a fighter pilot with his aviators on. He gnaws at his lip, and I can't wait to get him home.

"Caleb, what are you thinking about?"

A sly smile stretches across his face. "I want to show you something. Can we make a detour?"

"Sure."

"Great, we just have to swing by my place and grab Wendell."

"Wendell? Who's Wendell?"

Getting out of the Wrangler has gotten a lot easier, but Caleb still gets out of the car as fast as he can to meet me at the passenger side with an extended hand. "You know I can get down myself, right?"

"I know," he says with a smirk, grabbing my hand. "But it gives me a good excuse to touch you."

I hop, literally hop, out of the car. Caleb unhooks Wendell from his harness and clips a leash on his collar.

He's the cutest little corgi I've ever seen. According to Caleb, Wendell's not his biggest fan, but he does seem to like me—he gave me a pretty wet greeting when we picked him up. Poor pup shouldn't be stuck with a human he doesn't like, even if *I* happen to like that human very much. I might just have to steal him.

We're out in the backcountry at a beautiful farm. The drive up was gorgeous. I never get to be the passenger when I drive these roads, so I have to miss peeking at the charming homes and farms in favor of not running my car off the road.

The landscape is lush and green thanks to recent rains (mostly on the weekdays, thankfully). Maybe I can control the weather with my Thursday night pleas to Mother Nature after all. Caleb keeps my hand in his as we walk up the driveway, his other hand holding Wendell's leash.

"This isn't the part where you murder me, is it? I left my pepper spray in my bag in the car."

He stops in his tracks. "Do you really carry pepper spray?"

Do I carry pepper spray? Men. "Caleb, I'm a woman who's often alone late on weekend nights, of course I carry pepper spray."

"Oh."

"So, murder, no murder? I just need to prepare. Make a mental checklist, you know."

"You and your lists. No murder." He laughs, raising my hand to his mouth and kissing my knuckles. "I wanted to show you why I'm hesitant about taking over Foley's. This…is what I want." He gestures broadly to the land around us. There are two houses, one set back up the driveway and one a few dozen yards away, plus a large barn further out. It's all beautiful and picturesque, but I don't understand what he's trying to tell me.

"You want to be a farmer?" I ask skeptically. I know we all contain multitudes, but I never expected one of Caleb's to be farming.

"God, no."

Oh, thank god, I don't think I could be a farmer's girlfriend. Am I even a chef's girlfriend? We haven't yet addressed Hannah calling him my boyfriend. I feel so high school with him and not like a woman who's about to turn thirty. He tugs on my hand to face the smaller of the two houses.

"I want to convert that farmhouse into a farm-to-table restaurant. Maybe I'll use those few garden beds for herbs and greens, but the rest would be local, from other farms. It needs some work, but that means I can make it my own. The main house is in move-in condition. The barn is another story, and I have some ideas, but I'm getting ahead of myself." He grins sheepishly.

Caleb Foley has a plan. And a good one. We aren't too far

out of town, and this area is full of wonderful family farms. It's where everyone comes to pick strawberries in the spring, go apple picking in the fall, or cut Christmas trees in the winter. Where people who know how to cook pick up their CSAs. He's on to something. Especially with his cooking. It's a bit of a risk, but restaurants always are. And there is the whole parents handing over an already successful business with an excellent reputation and years of devoted clientele thing. But it's a brilliant idea.

"Caleb…it's gorgeous. I can picture it. And I can see you doing it." I wrap my arms around his neck and kiss him. Wendell sniffs the grass between us, around us, anywhere within the range of his leash.

"It might not happen, but I wanted you to see it. See why I'm not sure about what my parents want for me. The market and catering are my dad's dream. I know how lucky I am to have been mentored by him, but he wanted to build something of his own and watch it grow. I think he and I are alike in that way. Taking over Foley's feels like getting a fast pass or skipping the line. It's not mine."

"Oh," I say, taking in his words. Would taking over Spencer Soirees be my fast pass? Mom started the business, but it's always felt like it was ours. I pocket those thoughts for another time. "Have you talked to your parents about this?"

He shakes his head. "C'mon, there's one more thing I want to show you."

Caleb pushes the old barn door open. I suck in a breath.

It's stunning. Old and falling apart, but beautiful. And huge. A hundred and fifty people could fit in here and there'd still be room for a dance floor. The beams are perfect for string lights. Or three sleek light fixtures would work beautifully across the ceiling—a large one in the middle and two smaller complementing it. The guest house isn't too far, so if the kitchen were big enough, it could be used for weddings. Barn weddings had their moment—I know many brides who wished they could have a do-over on that trend—but there's something about this space. It's a blank canvas ready for any event design with the perfect touch of rustic, like Beachside Pavilion. It could be transformed into almost anything. Minus the ugly ballroom chairs.

Wendell rushes by me, dragging me out of this beautiful vision.

Caleb wraps his arms around me from behind and rests his chin on my shoulder. "What are you thinking about?"

"Nothing," I lie.

"I see it too," he says, placing a kiss on my temple.

"I don't know what you're talking about," I say, cooly.

"It would make a beautiful wedding venue."

God, it *really* would.

I turn myself around in his arms. "I thought you didn't want that. What your dad wants. To do weddings or catering."

"I didn't," he says with the sly grin again. "But it's possible I've had a change of heart…I like weddings, being part of someone's celebration. What I don't like is having to prep in one place, schlep food and supplies somewhere else, cooking in tents or terribly equipped kitchens. But here…I don't know. It's just an idea."

"What inspired your change of heart?" I ask, trying to keep cool, but I feel my cheeks warming.

"No one…nothing," he says quickly.

I wrap my arms around his neck and lift myself on my toes to kiss him.

"It's a good idea. Thank you for showing me. You need to show your parents."

"I don't know." He sighs. "There are a lot of things I need to figure out. I need to finish the business plan, price out renovations, pull all the documents for a loan…"

"You mean like a long to-do list that feels complicated and

overwhelming?" I smile. Standing here in this man's arms is already my favorite thing but add the opportunity to work together and help make lists, organize paperwork, develop a system. It's almost euphoric. "I know someone who might be able to help with that."

Chapter 32

Caleb

Somehow in the midst of an insane wedding season, this amazing woman is helping me finalize the business plan, complete with projections, mood boards, and sample menus. The details and ideas that were living in a list on my phone are now printed in a binder with color-coded tabs and a cover page.

Brooke sits in my pathetic bachelor pad sublet, helping me put the final details together to share with my parents. For a long time, I focused on doing something completely on my own. But that's not feasible. Instead, Brooke suggested I pitch it to my parents as an extension of Foley's. It'd be mine, but still part of the family. I know they have enough faith in me to hand the business over, but do they trust me enough to expand this way? I don't know.

It's not only them I need. My parents had each other when they started Foley's. I have Brooke helping me put together the business plan, but it's not enough. I haven't voiced just how much I want her to be part of this.

I'm so gone for her. I have been for a while, and showing her the property only made that clearer. The way she walked into the barn and immediately saw the potential. I only realized the possibilities after she came back into my life. This is my dream. Her. Me. Us. All of it. Whether this business plan works out or I end up taking over Foley's as-is, she's the only plan that matters.

She won't leave Spencer Soirees, and she deserves to run it once Judy releases it from her manicured claws. But I'd be the happiest, luckiest man to work with her all season long. To have her by my side, building something together. There has to be a way to make that work. Spencer Soirees can be the exclusive wedding planning agency. No, she can be the exclusive planner. I don't want to work my ass off every weekend night without finding her beautiful smile across the room.

I'm getting way ahead of myself, but I'm hoping that in the back of her mind she's thinking about this, too.

Brooke bites her bottom lip and adds color-coded tabs to the color-coded dividers, and if we weren't about to head to my parents' for dinner, I would push the papers and binders off the table, lay her down on it and bite that perfect lip myself. God, am I lucky.

I insisted on picking up food to bring to my parents' place for dinner. Brooke waits in the car while I go into the restaurant to pick up the takeout. It's not exactly takeout—it's a to-go kit from our favorite Italian restaurant. Pretty laughable when Dad or I could easily whip up this exact meal ourselves. But my gift to Mom is not having to deal with the mess the two of us usually make in the kitchen. We're pretty organized at the Market, but in the comfort of home, our cooking gets a little sloppy. All we'll have to do tonight is boil the fresh pasta, heat the sauce, and assemble the salad. Something even Brooke might be able to handle.

I'm greeted by my favorite hostess when I open the door. "Hi Maria!" I wrap the old woman in a hug. Maria's been the hostess at La Stazione since I was a kid and she's a regular at Foley's.

"Caleb!" She squeezes me tight. "Your order's in the back. Michael will grab it." She nods to the bus boy standing nearby and he heads to the back of the restaurant.

"It's good to see you," I say. "I'm sorry I haven't been in more. It's been a busy summer."

"I know, I know, you kids, always so busy." Her Italian accent is barely detectable anymore. "How's it going with Ms. Spencer? She's here with some tall lady. Another wedding planner, I think." She turns and peeks around the hostess stand. I follow her gaze and spot Judy right away. The blonde across from her is sipping a martini and reading paperwork. She looks vaguely familiar. Instead of twisting in anticipation of my parents meeting the love of my life—something I should probably confess to Brooke—there's a pit in my stomach. Michael returns with our order. "Thanks," I say as he hands me the bag. I turn back to Maria. "It's going well actually. I'm mostly working with Brooke and she's amazing."

"So, I've heard." She winks. Christ, news travels fast. But we'd know if it was fast enough to get to Judy by now, wouldn't we?

"I'll be back in soon, Maria. Promise!"

She kisses my cheek and I head out the door.

"That smells amazing." Brooke grabs the oversized brown paper bag and places it between her feet on the floor of the car. Wendell whines in the back at the smell of bolognese.

I turn and grab Brooke's cheek, angling her to face me so I can kiss her deeply. She releases a soft moan when I swipe my tongue against hers.

"What was that for?" She smiles, lips red.

"Just wanted to," I say, buckling my seatbelt. "So…uh, your mom was in there…"

The color drains from her face. "Shit, we've got to get out of here."

It's starting to get difficult to be okay with the affect Judy has on Brooke. I can't imagine any circumstance in which I'd be so scared and nervous to see my parents. Brooke deserves so much more than Judy has ever given her.

"She was with a blonde woman. Definitely not from here," I say as I pull out of the parking spot and turn onto Post Road.

"Blonde bob? Flawless makeup?"

"Um, yes," I say, glancing quickly at her face while I drive. Her nose is scrunched in thought.

"Oh, well…" she hesitates. "I think she's a new vendor. Some collaboration or something."

"Hmm." It doesn't sit right with me, but I don't tell Brooke that. It's probably nothing.

It's been over a decade since Brooke has been to my parents' home, since she's spent any real time with them. The deep breath she takes as I pull into the driveway tells me she's nervous. She's hidden it well so far.

"Hey." I put the car in park and cut the engine. "My parents are going to love you. I mean, they already do."

"It's just…I spent years thinking your dad hated me, and I haven't seen your mom since I was a kid. It's hard to wrap my head around the fact that they didn't absolutely freak out when you told them about us," she says, straightening in the passenger's seat, like she suddenly remembered something. "What exactly *did* you tell them about us? Are we—"

"Brooke." I unbuckle and turn to face her, taking her hands in mine. I know what she's asking, and I should have given her the answer the first night we spent together. "We're together. You and me. That's what I told my parents and that's what I'll tell the world when you're ready. I understand why you're not,

I won't rush you. But without sounding like a possessive asshole, I can't wait for everyone to know you're mine."

"Yours?" She looks at me through her lashes, cheeks pink, a smile growing across her face.

I smile. "Mine."

"You sound like one of the guys in my romantasy books," she says, grinning.

"Is that a good thing?"

"Yes, it's a good thing." She nods, biting her lip.

This woman. I hook my finger under her chin and lift her face. Her fair skin gives away what she's feeling as her cheeks redden. I lean in and kiss her softly.

"Caleb!"

That's Mom's voice. I lean my forehead on Brooke's and sigh. Mom's always had impeccable timing.

I break away from Brooke. "We'll be right there, Mom," I shout. "Ready?"

"Ready." Brooke smiles so widely it reaches her ears. *Mine.* My chest swells.

"My word, Brooke," Mom says when she lets her out of a hug. She holds on to Brooke's arms. "You've grown up to be a beautiful young woman."

"Thank you, Mrs. Foley," Brooke says with a smile.

"Mrs. Foley!" Mom scoffs. "Don't you dare call me Mrs. Foley, Brooke! It's Lynne, like when you were little."

"If you insist…Lynne."

"I do." She lets Brooke out of her grip and eyes the bouquet of hydrangeas in Brooke's hand.

"These are for you." Brooke hands her the blue flowers. "I cut them from my backyard this morning. Thank you for having me tonight."

"Oh, they're beautiful, Brooke, thank you. Now, now... come in, come in." Mom quickly wraps her arm around Brooke's shoulder. Mom has a few inches on her and holds her in such a maternal way, like Brooke is the daughter she never had. As they walk down the hall, Brooke turns her head back and gives me a smile that says *she really likes me*!

Mom and Brooke sit outside at the patio table while Dad and I put together the meal. Well, I put it together and he supervises. Brooke fell right back in with Mom like I knew she would. The force with which Mom embraced Brooke when we made it to the door looked borderline painful, but Brooke took it in stride.

I drop the fresh pasta into the pot of boiling water. Dad slices the sourdough loaf and throws the croutons onto the salad. I made the executive decision to keep Brooke far away from the meal prep. Baby steps. Once we're settled and eating, I'll share the plan with my parents. They've never given me reason to think they wouldn't support me, but I'm worried I'm about to ruin all their plans. They deserve to step back and retire if they want to.

While the pasta cooks, I take a fresh bottle of wine outside. Mom and Brooke are laughing together, and it's music to my ears seeing the two most important women in my life reconnecting after all this time.

"Dinner will be ready in a few minutes," I say, refilling their wine glasses.

"Thank you," they say in unison, smiling at me. But while Brooke's lips curve into a smile, it doesn't quite reach her eyes. Those gorgeous ocean blue eyes hold a hint of sadness.

"You okay?" I ask quietly while Mom is focused on sampling the new wine.

Brooke schools her features into happiness. "I'm great," she says with a forced smile.

"Okay," I say, though I don't believe her. "Dad and I will be right out with dinner."

My parents each shut their binders at the same time and look up at me. They didn't say a word as I went through each color-coded section. They nodded and flipped the pages. I reviewed the business plan, the loan and mortgage documents, the renovation schedule, and the plan for how I'll still support the Market. My mouth is dry when I finish—from the nerves or all the talking, I'm not sure. I can't get a read on what the looks on their faces mean.

The pit in my stomach brings me back about twenty years when I got caught smoking pot with Joey and his younger brother at a nearby playground after curfew. My dad and Joey's dad drove Mom's Ford Taurus wagon around the neighborhood until they found the three of us lying on our backs on the basketball court, laughing our asses off. None of us remember what we were laughing at, but we all remember the sound of my dad's booming voice shouting our names. They confiscated what remained of the pot and drove us home. Then my parents sat me down at this dining room table and gave me a lecture that involved the dreaded *we're not mad, we're disappointed*. I later learned they took the confiscated pot and smoked it that night...and even later learned that Joey's brother, Adam, had stolen it from their dad.

I take a deep breath and glance in Brooke's direction. After a silence that lasts seconds but feels like decades, Brooke gives me a hopeful smile and squeezes my hand under the table. It gives me the courage to ask them what they think.

They slowly look at one another, and Mom raises her eyebrows at Dad. I envy the way they can have full conversations with just their eyes.

Dad speaks first. "You've talked to the bank and gone over the mortgage with them? The monthly payment breakdown, closing costs?"

"Yes, I've reviewed everything and have a more detailed budget on my laptop we can go over."

Mom's next. "The renovation timeline is pretty aggressive."

"It is, but we've built in a buffer, so even with some setbacks, we'd be ready to open on time."

"You're sure you can get the right permitting for a restaurant?" Dad again.

"I've spoken with the town's planning and zoning committee and started the initial paperwork. I don't expect any delays there, but again, we have a buffer built in."

"What do you think, Brooke?" Mom asks.

"It's a risky endeavor," she says, all business. I hold my breath for what she'll say next. "Restaurants are tough. But Caleb has done all the due diligence in researching and planning. The location is fantastic. It's far enough into the backcountry that you feel like you've escaped the shoreline, but close enough that it's not a huge trip. The proximity to the parkway will attract people from Westchester and the city. Having a casual bar area and a formal main dining area are perfect for a regular night out and special occasions. There are opportunities for events like bridal or baby showers, rehearsal dinners. The local community is supportive. Caleb's already spoken to many of the local farms and they're excited by the idea. Plus, Caleb's an amazing chef, but you already know that."

I can't look at her because if I do, I'll tell her I love her and I want her to quit her job and do this with me. Instead, I squeeze her hand under the table.

My parents look at each other again. Mom gives the smallest nod to Dad. He looks to me and I can see the tears building up in the brown eyes that match mine. *Fuck.* This was a terrible idea.

"Caleb," he says, his voice cracking. "We're so proud of you, son."

What?

In the corner of my eye, I see Brooke's lips curl into a smile.

"You're what?" I ask, mouth agape.

"We're proud of you, Caleb," Mom says, her eyes twinkling. "You put a lot of work and thought into this, which is more than I can say for your father when we got started."

"Hey, that's not fair," Dad says with a laugh.

"Honey, your *plan*, if you could even call it that, was written on the back of four different coasters at some bar downtown one night after a few drinks. It all worked out, but we had no idea what we were doing. This is impressive, Caleb."

"I like how organized this is," Dad says, shifting his eyes to Brooke. "I take it you had something to do with that…and all the different color folders in my office?"

"Maybe a little." She shrugs with a sweet smile. "But the rest is Caleb. You have to see the property. The pictures in there don't do it justice."

"We can't wait to see it," Mom says, still beaming.

We talk more about the plan—there's still plenty to figure out and more questions to answer—but the conversation moves to Mom and Dad reminiscing about the early days, when Judy was still in the picture. We're all ignoring the elephant in the room. The elephant that Brooke knows exists but has no idea how large it is. Her relationship with her mom is precarious, and as much as I've wanted to broach the subject, I've stayed silent. It's still so new between us…but how long can I ignore this?

Brooke picks at her slice of key lime pie, listening to Dad tell one of his many stories of near mishaps and difficult clients. My hand is draped over the back of her chair and I'm not hearing a word he says. I can't when being near her takes over every single one of my senses. She laughs wholeheartedly at a particularly funny part of a story that I'm sure I've heard at least a dozen times. The sound reverberates through my body, bringing a wide smile to my face.

"My mom never told me any of these stories," she says, stabbing the last small piece of pie crust. "It sounds like you worked so well together, I don't understand why you stopped."

"It was a long time ago, Brooke," Dad says. "Best to forget about it."

"Is it really *that* bad?"

My body stiffens as Dad's eyes reach mine. The resolve in his eyes answers the question in mine.

I guess we're doing this.

Chapter 33

Brooke

It *is* that bad. It's so unbelievably bad.

Caleb drives us back to my house with one hand on the steering wheel and the other firmly holding mine. It's a short drive, but long enough for the memories I've kept tucked away in little boxes to open and spill their contents all over.

I'm nine-years-old and Mom takes me to a meeting. I sit quietly in the coffee shop until I see a classmate. We goof around like kids do, and I accidentally knock over a coffee at the table next to us. I apologize and clean up, but Mom yells the entire car ride home. *How could you do that to me? You ruined my meeting. Think of everything I do for you, and this is how you repay me.*

I'm in high school, she compares me to the other girls, mostly the girls from wealthy families. I'm voted to homecoming court, but not crowned homecoming queen. It's my fault. *Why can't you be more like her? You messed up everything by not behaving like the other girls.*

I start working at the agency and Mom praises my work, tells me I did a wonderful job, but follows up with *I could have done much better.* Reminds me that I have her to thank for my career.

Whenever I pushed back or defended myself, she accused me of creating drama, remembering something incorrectly, or said I was too sensitive. I'd end up apologizing to her for one of those things.

Those boxes in my mind must have been filled with glitter. I'll never be ever able to pick up all the tiny pieces and tuck them away again.

Caleb pulls into the driveway and cuts the engine, never letting go of my hand. How can he sit here looking at me like…like *that*? How could Lynne and Paul spend the evening with me, laughing and telling stories, after what Mom put them through? How can they be *happy* that I'm dating their son?

The tears I managed to keep at bay in the Foley's dining room fill my eyes, and I fight to keep them back. I hate crying tears of sadness. Crying at weddings, at movies, and special moments, no big deal. Crying because I'm hurt, never. Mom hated whenever I cried, especially if I was upset or sad. That's for people who are weak.

"Brooke," Caleb whispers. My name was so gentle coming from his mouth. That's all it takes. The tears come storming out. Every little bit that I've tried to hold in. He unbuckles his seatbelt, then unbuckles mine when my hands are shaking too hard to do it myself.

"I'm…so…sorry," I say between sobs. "Please…tell your parents again…I'm sorry."

"Brooke." He holds my face in his hands, wiping tears off my cheeks. "What do you have to be sorry for? You didn't do anything."

"My mom…" I sniffle loudly. God, this is full-on ugly crying.

"Your mom, Brooke. Not you," he says gently, not bothered at all by my ugly tears.

"She tried to break apart your family! It could have gone so differently. Caleb, you're so lucky. They love you so much. Your dad's face when you were taking them through the plan, you should have seen it. You were looking at the pages, but I was watching him…oh my god, we should be celebrating." I struggle for air between the tears and getting the words out. "This is terrible…I'm making it all about me…like she does. Oh my god, Caleb, I'm the worst thing for you. For your family. I need to go."

I move to get out of the car, but Caleb's hand is on my wrist, pulling me back to face him.

"Caleb…please."

"No, Brooke. I'm not letting you walk away. And I'm not walking away from you. I'm not letting your mom get in the way of us. This is about more than what you learned tonight, isn't it."

It's not a question. I nod.

"Talk to me. Tell me what's going on in that beautiful head."

We sit in the car, and I tell him about Mom's behavior over the years. The comparisons, the judgements, the gaslighting, the guilt-tripping. That every disagreement is my fault. All the little specks of glitter in these boxes that will never be closed up again. It's a relief to share it all with Caleb. It's been buried down so deep.

I tell him how it felt to sit outside with Lynne. That the hug she greeted me with was warmer than any hug Mom's ever given me. How familiar and comfortable it felt to sit and talk to her after so many years. I tell him that I loved being with her, but that it made me sad too. That kind of relationship is something I'll never have with my mom. He holds my hand and listens, wiping away more tears as they fall. When I'm finally out of words, he holds me.

"Brooke," he says, pulling back to tuck a strand of hair

behind my ear. "You're the best thing for me. No one could be better. You're nothing like your mom. She doesn't hold a candle to you. You're the best wedding planner not because of her, but in spite of her. You're kind and generous. You care about the people around you. You make plans and lists and color-coded binders for them and your clients, all so they can be their best. You champion them. You support them. We'll celebrate the farm. But, Brooke, I need you to know how incredibly special you are. How perfect you are. How perfect you are for me. I'm not going to let something Judy did twenty years ago get in the way of the best thing that has ever happened to me."

Caleb's words have me crying all over again.

The office is empty when I arrive early on Tuesday morning. I know Mom won't be here—she likes to waltz in as close to the team meeting as possible and have a Miranda Priestly moment—but I'm still relieved when I see her office empty. I haven't spoken to her since my world shattered at the Foley's dining room table last week. It's been shattering, slowly, for as long as I can remember. I'd just gotten so good at pretending it wasn't.

I spend the morning getting organized for the week and weekend ahead. My checklist is three pages long, I have dozens of emails to send and several final planning meetings—all for the Quincy wedding. The most important wedding of my career. No pressure.

Mom arrives five minutes before the meeting. It's good she's instituted such strict boundaries around our work relationship. That's the only thing keeping me in my seat and not barreling into her office to have it out. I guess I wouldn't do that. I shouldn't do that despite the small part of me that so badly wants to.

During the thirty-minute consultation yesterday, the therapist Jordan recommended made it clear that I should not engage in any confrontational conversations with Mom right now. I need to get through wedding season so I can distance myself and get some clarity.

If I'm lucky, Mom will announce her retirement soon, and most of this can be swept into one big box to be forgotten about forever.

Dr. Drury wasn't too thrilled with that plan. But she was pretty impressed with the outline I emailed her ahead of my session. It included names and descriptions of family and friends who might come up in our sessions. As well as a list of the memories my mind refuses to tuck back away. It wasn't color-coded—I didn't want to scare her—but I was pretty chuffed with myself.

"Ladies." Judy claps her hands three times, and the room quiets instantly. "Let's get started. As you all know, we have the most important wedding of the season, of the year, of my career, this weekend. This wedding will be featured in the *Times* and all over social media. We've planned a full weekend of luxury events for the Quincy and Redbank families…"

"Using the word *we* pretty loosely there, Judy," Maddie whispers from her desk.

I'm too enraged to laugh. I shush Maddie quietly.

"Brooke, something you'd like to share?" Judy chides.

Shit.

"Yes. *We* have been working hard," I say, my tone coated with anger. I rise from my chair and look her square in the eyes. They go wide for a brief moment before she puts on her unaffected mask. She doesn't like my display of insolence, but I no longer care. I've never spoken to her with this much defiance before. I might not be ready to confront her narcissistic behavior right now, but I am ready to stand up and take claim to the events *I've* been planning.

"Before I get into the logistics for the weekend, I want to thank everyone for the hard work you've put in leading up to this wedding. This scope of work takes many hands, and every single piece is important. Now, on to the fun! Load-in begins this afternoon. Warehouse Rentals will have the tent up tomorrow morning. On Wednesday at four o'clock, we have the final walkthrough followed by an all-hands meeting with the Warehouse Rentals and Foley's teams."

Mom scoffs loudly at the mention of Foley's. I assume she's forgotten herself, but when we make eye contact, I know she meant for it to be heard by the entire room.

"Judy," I say, refusing to cower and holding her gaze, "Caleb and his team have been nothing but professional throughout this entire process. We'll show them the respect they've earned and work with them as partners like the professionals we are." When I look back to the staff, I'm met with wide eyes and dropped jaws. I may have avoided direct confrontation, but I've certainly made a scene.

"The assigned staff have received the timelines and remaining action items for the week…" I continue presenting to the staff. Eyes return to normal size and mouths close, but I must black out because the next thing I know, I'm back at my seat and the next planner is up.

As soon as the meeting ends and Judy is tucked back in her office with the door closed, I grab my phone and dart for the door as calmly as I can manage. I hear the click of Maddie's heels not far behind me.

"What the actual fuck was that, Brooke?" The door slams behind her and she runs down the stairs after me. "Because that made my fucking week. Did you see the look on her face? I thought she might slap you. Don't worry, I would have gotten up and slapped her right back."

I'm already halfway down the block from the office. "Maddie," I turn around, interrupting her. "I love you, but I need a minute."

"Got it!" She balls her hands into fists at her sides, as if that could contain her palpable energy.

I turn around and hands land on my shoulders, stopping me from bumping right into... "Jordan! What are you doing here?"

Her eyes move to Maddie. "This one texted me forty-five minutes ago." She looks at her phone and reads: "'SOS Brooke is having a nervous breakdown. Get downtown ASAP.' So here I am."

"Seriously?" I raise my brows at Maddie. "A nervous breakdown?"

"You basically gave Judy the professional equivalent of the middle finger in front of the entire staff. I think we're in nervous breakdown territory. Jordan, you should've seen her. Judy was all, 'blah blah blah, we hate Foley's...' and Brooke's like, 'um, don't you talk shit about my boyfriend,' and..."

"Maddie!" Jordan and I both shout in unison.

"That is *not* what happened," I tell Jordan.

"Don't worry." She shrugs. "I don't believe a word she says most of the time."

"Rude," Maddie says, frowning.

"Wait." I look at Maddie. "I thought you were mad at me about the whole Caleb thing."

She waves a finger at me. "First of all, I wasn't mad. I'm looking out for you. Second of all," she says, waving two fingers at me. "We now share a common enemy, so all is forgiven."

I can't hold in my laugh. "You're something else, Maddie."

We walk toward Old Post Coffee. Maddie tells Jordan the real story of what happened in the meeting, and I zone them both out.

I'm going to throw up. What the hell did I do in there? My

whole life I've stood by and done what Mom told me to do or what I thought she'd want me to do. I've always known she was a little harsh, that she parented me differently than my friends were parented. She's my mom so, until now, I've always defended her. But I didn't fully know who I was defending. Or I did and I didn't want to believe it. How the hell am I going to get through this week? She's forced herself into every part of this wedding. Into every part of my life.

I take a deep breath. In. Out. I can do this. I'll pretend things are fine. I'll pretend the glass hasn't been shattered. That the glitter isn't everywhere. And I'll deal with it after the Quincy wedding.

The Quincy property's been completely transformed by the time I arrive for the walkthrough, with the signature Sperry Tent flags waving against a bright blue sky. I refuse to look at the weather report until tomorrow, but that doesn't stop me from saying a silent prayer to Mother Nature for Saturday's weather to be even half as beautiful as it is right now. Friday and Sunday too, while I'm at it. The wall-to-wall flooring inside the tent has been installed. Forty tables and four hundred chairs are arranged around the black-and-white checkered dance floor. Between Warehouse Rentals, Foley's, and Spencer Soirees, there are about two dozen people completing various tasks.

This is the best part of it all. Seeing the pieces come together and fall right into place. The energy and excitement of all the hard work finally paying off. It's like the penultimate episode of an HBO Max series. This wedding is the season finale and everything feels a bit more relaxed. At least for us vendors.

I'd be enjoying this a lot more if I wasn't waiting for Mom's inevitable arrival. My eyes have been darting in all directions like a deranged owl for the last fifteen minutes. I've positioned myself on the far side of the tent by the water, giving me a view of the entire property.

I turn to the ocean to read an email on my phone. The glaring afternoon sun makes it difficult to see my screen. I feel a hand on the small of my back followed by a kiss on my bare shoulder.

"Caleb!" I turn from the water and swat his hand off my back. "There are people here! People with eyes!"

"Oh no, not eyes!" he jests.

"I mean it," I say with a laugh. But I don't. I wish we weren't hiding. If I'm still wishing and praying, I wish we could be back at my house, making an early dinner together. And by that, I mean Caleb cooking and me providing moral support. Drinking wine outside on the patio before heading into bed, or the couch, or the floor, or a surface we haven't tackled yet. It's going to be a long four days. We're both working around the clock until Monday—no time for ripping each other's clothes off. I hoped the morning we just spent together would make it easier to pretend all weekend. But looking at Caleb, I was so wrong about that. I'm so screwed once he puts on his chef coat.

"No one is paying attention to us." He grabs my hand, interlacing our fingers and turning us to face the water so no one can see the small public display of affection. I take back my earlier wish. I want a day at the beach with Caleb. The real beach. I'm a proud Nutmegger, but this part of the Sound leaves a lot to be desired. I want clear, blue waves and soft white sand. A cocktail in my hand. Caleb shirtless…

"Good afternoon, Caleb, Brooke." *Shit.* Mom's voice echoes behind me. Caleb drops my hand and quickly takes a step away from me. We both turn to face my mother.

"Hello, Judy," Caleb says, giving her a cold hug and an air kiss on each cheek. How does he pretend everything is fine?

"Good afternoon, Mom...I'm sorry, Judy," I say, tripping over my words like I've never addressed her by her given name before.

"You two seem to be getting along." She looks me square in the eyes and purses her lips. "Bring me up to speed."

"Of course, Judy." Caleb offers his elbow, and Mom puts her hand through it. "Let me show you where my team will be working and I can answer any concerns you have. I'm sure there won't be many, as Brooke has been meticulous in making sure we're doing everything up to Spencer Soirees' standards."

"I sure hope she has," she says.

Caleb turns his head and winks at me. Winks! I mouth *thank you* and watch him walk away in those goddamn ass-hugging jeans.

Judy's occupied with a few of the groomsmen who have arrived in town early for the festivities. Scouting them as potential partners for me, no doubt. They seem nice enough. Polite and well-mannered. Dressed well with jobs at hedge funds or tech startups. Carbon copies of Kent.

"Hey." Caleb comes up behind me. "Hannah and Preston want to introduce us to Kevin from the *Times* while Judy plays Mrs. Robinson."

"Gross, Caleb," I say. "That's my mom!"

He smirks, showing off that damn dimple. I so badly want to kiss him right here in front of everyone. I'm tired of worrying about the fallout that will inevitably follow with my mom.

I want to skip ahead. I've pictured what a life together

might look like a million different ways. Each scenario is different, but in all of them I'm happy.

Then I remember who my mother is and what she's done. What are we supposed to do? Sit down and enjoy Christmas dinner together? Is Mom going to walk me down the aisle with Lynne and Paul sitting in the first row? What if we have kids? Everything we do will be criticized. Oh god, she's going to ruin every birthday party. Either by making it completely over the top or making it all about her. Probably both.

"Brooke?" Caleb says in a tone that suggests it's not the first time he's saying my name. I get out of my own head and find we've made it to the front of the house where Hannah and Preston are waiting with Kevin.

"I'm sorry." I extend my hand to the well-dressed man in front of me. He's wearing bright blue dress shorts and a white long-sleeve dress shirt. His ivory tortoiseshell glasses pop against his warm brown skin. "It's nice to meet you, Kevin. I didn't realize you were stopping by today."

"Nice to meet you, too," he says with a smile. "My husband and I have a cottage in Litchfield. Thought I'd pop down to get the lay of the land and introduce myself before the day."

"That's great," Caleb says. "Anything we can show you or help with?"

"Preston showed me around a bit. On Saturday, I'll have a few questions for you both. Hannah's been singing your praises."

Hannah smiles at us. Kevin's phone buzzes. "Ah, that's my editor, great to meet you all. See you Saturday." He waves and walks to his car.

"He seems nice," I whisper to Caleb. "But it still makes me anxious."

"Okay, so," Hannah says to us with a sly smile. "I was thinking since you're both pretty much going to be here all day for the next few days, it makes no sense to be driving back and forth so much. There're still some renovations being done on the second floor of the carriage house, but the first floor is completely done, and I think you both should stay here tomorrow through Sunday. What do you think?"

What do I think? I think it'd be so nice to be on site twenty-four-seven. I think my favorite thing in the world is waking up next to Caleb. I think my mom can't show up out of the blue like she does at my house. I think Hannah is an angel sent from above to help me get through this weekend. But I don't say any of that because staying at my client's parents' carriage house with my boyfriend, who is also their caterer, must cross some kind of professional boundary.

"Hannah, it's important that we maintain a level of professionalism this weekend," I say, avoiding eye contact with Caleb. "Especially with the *Times* coming."

Hannah pouts. "Well, that's not fun."

"You two can christen the new mattress," Preston says with raised brows. *Oh my god.*

"Preston, please!" Hannah chides. "Technically the carriage house has three bedrooms. Only one on the first floor, though. But no one has to know that!"

"I'm with Hannah and Preston," Caleb deadpans, moving to stand next to them so they all face me. Partners in crime. Hannah smiles like she's already won.

I roll my eyes playfully at them. "Are you sure? We don't want to put you or your parents out on your wedding weekend. There's already so much going on."

"Are you kidding me, Brooke? Having my wedding planner here all weekend—"

"Her motives are entirely selfish," Preston adds.

Caleb looks at me expectantly.

"Okay, fine," I say with a shrug. "If you insist!"

"Oh, I do. I absolutely insist!" She smiles, victorious. "Oh, I just love love!"

Love.

This constant swelling in my chest.

These butterflies in my stomach.

The all-consuming pull to him.

I tried *so* hard to make these feelings materialize for Kent. They never did. The night I bumped into Caleb in June, they began to simmer. Now they're boiling over. We've moved so fast, and this wedding season has been so insanely busy that I haven't stopped to think about it.

I love Caleb Foley.

Chapter 34

Caleb

IF THERE'S ANYTHING SEXIER THAN BROOKE SPENCER RUNNING a wedding rehearsal, I've never seen it. This woman. She manages to make the officiant feel like he's in charge (he's not), chats with the bridesmaids like they're old friends, and keeps the groomsmen, who definitely hit a bar on their way here, in line. All with a beautiful smile on her face and clipboard in hand.

One groomsman, I'm going to guess the one who suggested the bar by the glossy look in his eyes, is giving her a tough time. He's the kind of guy everyone pictures when you say you're from here. They give you that raised brow, and you have to say *no, no, I'm not like that.* His story is exactly like the others, guys like Kent. Grew up with lots of money, prep school, then an Ivy League he got into by the skin of his teeth. All resulting in a job in finance and a superiority complex.

From where I stand, which is too damn far away, Brooke's holding her own. We're trying to keep up the professional appearance. I don't need to assist setting up the bar on the far edge of the lawn, but I can't take my eyes off of her. I nearly lost a finger while cutting limes, so unfortunately, I do have to look away every so often.

A chorus of *oohs* and laughs forces me to stop slicing and look toward the rehearsal. By the look of it, Brooke has put the troublesome groomsmen in his place, much to his chagrin, and he's not hiding it well. Brooke looks in my direction and I catch her proud smirk before she shifts her gaze behind me.

"Caleb," Judy says. I roll my eyes in Brooke's direction and then plaster on the fakest of smiles before turning around.

"Hello, Judy," I say, thankful that the bar back is between us and I don't have to engage in her ridiculous habit of air kisses.

"Shouldn't someone a bit more junior be doing that?" She gestures to the cutting board and limes beside me. "Or is your staff not ready? This event is crucial to set the tone for the weekend. I wouldn't want your lack of preparedness to make me look bad."

How did my parents ever work with her? In the stories about the early days, she sounded like a completely different woman. Almost. Her true nature was always lurking beneath the surface. I gently place my knife down and clench my fists at my sides.

"We've got plenty of staff to handle everything tonight," I say. "And tomorrow. And Sunday. I like to help out where I can. It shows the staff I'm not above any of the work we do."

"Ah, I see." She purses her lips and walks away to catch the end of the rehearsal. I don't know what reason Judy has for thinking she's above reproach, but she certainly thinks she is. It's going to be a long weekend.

The weather is damn near perfect tonight, warm with a comfortable breeze. I can't say the same for tomorrow. The last

Brooke updated me, tomorrow's forecast calls for torrential rain in the morning. There's a possible break midday, but a threat of thunderstorms at the exact time of the ceremony. She's keeping her composure on the outside, but I know Brooke. This, the one thing she cannot control, is killing her.

I head out of the carriage house where I changed from my prep clothes into my short-sleeve chef coat. Taking an extra minute to roll the sleeves the way Brooke likes. She mentioned it once, so I'll be sure to wear it this way for the rest of my days. The long-sleeve coat I brought will have to wait for cooler temps.

With the rehearsal over, more guests arrive for dinner. Plus-ones to the wedding party, extended family, and however else you get to a rehearsal dinner for this many people. It's more people than I'd even want at my own wedding.

Brooke and half her team are managing the rehearsal dinner logistics while the other half continue reception setup. The elevated family-style clam bake makes it fairly turnkey for my team, but Brooke's managing multiple vendors including a band, watercolor portrait artist, and cigar bar, as well as the timeline for toasts.

Guests happily mingle and enjoy cocktail hour in the side yard. Judy's among them, champagne glass in hand, with the woman I saw her with last week. It's gnawing at me that I still can't place her, but I don't have time to figure it out now.

The veranda is covered with long tables draped in navy blue gingham tablecloths. Each setting has a galvanized bucket with lobster-cracking tools, a custom embroidered lobster bib, and napkins. My waitstaff is lighting the tea lights under the butter warmers. I see Brooke check that task off her list as I approach her.

"How's it going?" I ask, fighting the instinct to place my hand on the small of her back.

"Perfect," she says, a little too brightly.

"Brooke." I study her face. "How's it *really* going?"

"It's fine." She sighs. "Except for Judy, but that's nothing new. And the weather. What did I do to piss off Mother Nature so badly? It's going to be total shit. Now the forecast is calling for torrential rain all day. So even if, by some miracle, it doesn't storm during the ceremony, the ground is going to be a disaster."

"You know you can't control the weather, and we've got a great rain plan in place. Baxter already said he has flooring ready for an aisle and a space for the bridal party to stand. He and Maddie have that covered when you make the call tomorrow morning."

"I just want it to be perfect for them," she says, looking across the yard where Hannah and Preston are standing together. "Look at how happy they are. They deserve a perfect day, like we planned."

"And they'll have it. Thanks to you. It might not all go to plan, but we're going to make their day as perfect as it can be. I promise," I say, trying to reassure her. "Looks like Judy's enjoying herself. Have you talked to her?"

"Only when she brings another eligible bachelor my way. So far, I've met James, an investment banker from Greenwich; Jared, an investment banker from Manhattan; and Westley, a real estate mogul from town. That was after that obnoxious groomsman, Gage, let me know he's got a great hotel room if I need a place close by to crash tonight." She rolls her eyes and puffs out a forced laugh.

I see red. "What?"

"Oh, don't worry. I get hit on at most weddings," she says, like it's not a big deal.

"You do?"

"Are you seriously shocked by that?"

"Yeah, I mean, not that someone finds you attractive…look

at you. But you're working and guys are hitting on you. What the fuck?"

"You sweet innocent man. All. The. Time. We all do." She gestures to her staff. "We're used to dealing with it. It's usually an over-served groomsman shooting his shot, but sometimes a creepy uncle. We all watch out for each other."

"That's pretty fucked up, Brooke," I say. I think back to all the women I've worked with and wonder if they've ever experienced this. Then I think about all the obnoxious men I've dealt with at weddings and I have my answer. *Christ.*

"It is," she says, like it's not a big deal, again. "C'mon, chef, time to transition to dinner." She walks backwards toward the patio, smirking. "Coat looks good, by the way."

Judy had better leave her alone for the rest of the night. And I'm going to keep an eye on that groomsman. I scan the crowd and find him at the bar. Of course.

It took much longer than I planned to clean up after the dinner and get the kitchen in shape for tomorrow. I would have left it to Joey and the rest of the crew, but that's not the kind of boss I want to be. I made sure my staff all got to their cars safely, grabbing one of the golf carts Brooke rented for the weekend and dropping everyone right at their car door.

Brooke finished earlier after I insisted she get some rest. She had that slightly dazed look in her eyes that means a migraine attack is coming. She tried to fight me on it, but—in a rare showing of solidarity—Maddie was Team Caleb and walked her back to the carriage house.

I open the door quietly. Part of me hopes Brooke is fast asleep. Tomorrow's going to be one of the longest workdays either of us has ever had. The other part of me hopes she's awake, because watching her shine at what she does all day is the biggest turn-on. It's been foreplay all damn day and I need a release. When I don't hear Brooke's voice greet me, I smile knowing she's getting the rest she needs. I head to the bathroom so I can handle my needs alone in the shower.

Light from the bedroom fills the hallway and I peek in, finding Brooke fast asleep on top of the bed sheets. Curled on her side, hands tucked under her chin, her beautiful brown waves cascading around her. Cascading over the familiar white coat she's wearing. One of my fucking chef coats. This shower cannot come fast enough. I take a few steps into the room to get a closer look at this perfect woman. I'm met with the sight of red lace underwear peeking from beneath the coat that barely covers the curve of her ass.

Well, fuck me, chef.

"Caleb," Brooke says, her voice gravely with sleep. "You're back."

"Hey, babe." I kneel next to the bed. "Whatcha got here?" I touch the collar of the coat. She smiles, eyes slowly blinking as they adjust to the light.

"Oh, this old thing." She shrugs and sits up, feet dangling over the side of the bed, giving me a sleepy smile. Fuck, it's not even buttoned. "Just threw it on."

"Is that so?" I rest my hands on her bare thighs. I'm in the perfect position to simply devour her. She nods, biting her lower lip. "How's your head?" I ask her.

"Fine, took my meds." She cups her hand on my cheek. "Thank you for asking."

"You know we have a long day tomorrow?" I place my hands on her bare waist, thumbs grazing her pebbled skin. "Like stupid-long day tomorrow." As much as I want this, always want this, it only ever matters if she wants it, too. We both could use some sleep. But she's sitting here on display for me in my fucking chef coat with *Foley* embroidered over her left breast.

"I know," she says, her lips curling into a devious smile. "What'd you say when you came in here?"

Did I say something? She leans closer to me, grazes my lips briefly and brings her mouth to my ear.

"Fuck me, chef," she whispers.

My hands are on her ass, pulling her to the edge of the mattress before I have time to contemplate if I'd actually said that out loud or if she's a mind reader. I don't care either way. She squeals and I pull her face to meet mine, claiming her mouth and coaxing it open with my tongue. The built-up tension of the day explodes with every brush of our tongues. She moans in my mouth as I toy with the band of the lace underwear.

She wants me to fuck her, and I will, but she's going to have to wait. The feeling building in my chest is making it hard to do that without saying one particular three-word sentence. Or even asking that four-word question. I see her wearing my name and I'm ready. All in.

Instead, I drag my mouth away sucking on her bottom lip. I look at my name on her chest again. "This looks so fucking good on you."

Before she can respond, I push open the coat to find her beautiful breasts taut, nipples hard. The coat falls off her shoulders, and I take her breasts in my hands, bringing my mouth to one nipple, making circles with my tongue, pinching the other between my fingers. She releases a gravely moan and my jeans get tighter.

"Caleb, I need you to touch me," she groans. "Please."

"I *am*, Brooke," I mumble, mouth still on her breast.

Pulling away, I brush my hands up her thighs until they meet the curve of her hips. Her breathing is already reduced to pants and we're only getting started.

"Ca...leb...please," she says with a needy sigh, opening her legs for me. Her underwear is glistening. I brush two fingers over the wet lace at her center as she arches her back, head dipping back at the teasing strokes. I palm her clit and move in slow circles.

"Fuck, I…need…more," she whimpers with need.

That's all it takes for me to put my mouth on her, lace between us making the friction that much sweeter for her. Her taste is heavenly and there's so much of it for me. Her quiet cries make my cock throb, but I'm taking my time. I pull away a moment. Brooke's chest heaves and her arms shake behind her as she holds herself up.

"Lie down, babe, I've got you." I pull off her soaked underwear and get back where I'm supposed to be, lightly stroking her clit with the tip of my tongue, even though I know she wants—*needs* more. She rests her legs on my shoulders, her heels grazing my back. I take two fingers and glide them between her before driving them deeper inside.

"I love your hands," she moans with relief.

Oh, don't I know it. I move in and out slowly with controlled pressure as I suck on her clit. Brooke runs her fingers through my hair and tugs me closer. *Fuck.* Her thighs tighten around me. She's so close. I've learned a lot from Brooke Spencer this summer—understanding her noises and tells has been the fucking highlight. She fists my hair with both hands and I keep the pace with my tongue, but my fingers that she loves so much, I leave them inside her and start to curl the tips, stroking her inner walls. She draws in a sharp breath and pulls my face closer into her, if that's even possible. God, I could die here with her writhing around me.

"Caleb, I…"

"I know, babe." Her muscles pulse around my fingers. She moans my name as she climaxes. I don't stop devouring her until she's finished riding the wave of her orgasm. She releases my hair from her grip and goes limp on the bed, fully spent.

"You are so fucking perfect," I tell her.

"I need you."

"I know you do." I smirk, bringing a hand to my back, pulling off my shirt. She sits up and starts to unbuckle my belt, unbuttons my jeans, her eyes focused on what's underneath. She sits back on the edge of the bed and looks up at me through heavy eyelashes. I won't last a minute with what she has in mind, but a second won't hurt.

I step out of my jeans and boxers, and she takes me in her mouth before I'm even standing upright. She takes me deep and pulls back, circling the tip of my cock with her tongue. Her nails dig into my ass, claiming me. *Fuck.* I fist her hair as she bobs in front of me. As good as this feels, I need her to stop. I step back and she pouts.

"Brooke." I lift her chin with my finger, so her eyes meet mine. "I refuse to come into that beautiful mouth when I know how badly you need me right now."

Chapter 35

Brooke

Caleb lifts me off the bed and I wrap my legs around him. His hands grip my ass, and he shifts me against his hard length. God, he feels so good. I need him inside me. Bare. We established a week or so ago that between birth control and clean bills of health, we can ditch the condoms. It's been a wonderful development.

I'm still wearing his chef coat, and if this is the reward I get for wearing it, I'll wear it every night. I hadn't meant to fall asleep, but I needed rest after taking my medications. I planned to be waiting in the kitchen for him, but this is working out nicely. I'm going to be so exhausted tomorrow, but it's worth it. So worth it.

"What do you want, Brooke?" he whispers in my ear, then nuzzles my neck.

"I told you," I smirk. "Fuck me, chef." I don't know who I've become since this began. With Caleb, I can say what I want, what I need. It makes me damn near feral for him.

He growls into my neck with a playful bite, laying me down slowly on the bed. Crawling above me, he rests his elbows on either side of my head and pins me down with his hips, his cock so close to where I need him. He's torturing me, hands playing with my hair like he's planning on keeping me waiting. His eyes, dark and wanting seconds ago, are lighter. They're still hungry, but there's a softness to them too.

"We'll get to that," he says and kisses me hard. "What do you want after…with me?"

I want it all. I don't know how we'll do it. Our schedules are insane. My mother's a big problem. He has this amazing dream he wants to work on. I don't know how to plan this out. How to make it happen. I don't say any of that now, but I still tell him the truth.

"Everything, Caleb. I want it all."

He rests his forehead on mine. "Everything," he says with a laugh. "I think I can do that."

He kisses me slowly, tenderly, then pulls away to grab a pillow and shifts it under my hips. I tremble with anticipation at the sudden heat in his stare as he spreads my legs apart. Warmth pools at my core and he drives into me, hard, exactly how I wanted it. My back arches as I take in every inch of him.

"Thank god." I'm full and aching all at once. Caleb starts thrusting steadily, hitting me so deep. My skin pebbles as delightful aches flood my body. It's pure bliss.

Placing a hand low on my stomach, he thrusts harder, deeper. Between the pressure he applies with his hand and how deep he is at this angle, I'm losing myself. Feeling him in places I didn't know were possible. Heat pulses through me.

"Don't…stop…Caleb," I say, my breath catching.

"Never," he groans, shifting his hand lower until his thumb reaches my clit, stroking me with perfect pressure. It might kill me, but I could do this forever.

I arch further into his touch as tension coils through my bones, bringing me closer and closer. I close my eyes, consumed by each sensation my body is feeling. Caleb rolls himself in and out of me in a delightfully hard rhythm. The noises out of my mouth pitch higher and higher until inaudible. God, he's good.

"Brooke," he says, his voice thick. "Look at me. Look at me while you come."

Fuck. I open my eyes. Caleb's dark brown eyes bore into mine. I shiver. I have no words, no noises, only tight, breathless pants. It's intimate and terrifying.

He palms my cheek and runs his thumb over my lips. "Come for me, Brooke."

I'm completely undone. Coasting through release without taking my eyes off of him. He smirks proudly and follows me there.

There's so much I want to say as Caleb holds me, our skin slick with sweat. As my heart rate slows, Caleb looks at me, opens his mouth, then closes it. He shakes his head so slightly I almost miss it.

"Everything, Brooke. I'm going to give you everything," he says, kissing me on the forehead.

This. Whatever comes next, however my mom reacts to my relationship with Caleb, will be worth it, because I'll get to have this. Love.

The sky is dark. Ominous clouds stretch across the Sound and sheets of rain pelt the water outside the window. Each weather app on my phone—I have five—has a different prediction for the day. What they all agree on is a shit ton of rain all morning. It's too early to tell what the afternoon will bring.

It's going to be an impossibly long day that'll require unhealthy amounts of caffeinated beverages.

I go through the checklist for the rain plan in my head while I shower and get ready. We'll need the portable flooring to cover the grass for the ceremony, and all the clear umbrellas from the office. We might be able to get away without siding on the tent. If we can, it'll be worth it. Nobody wants an enclosed tent when the humidity is this high. It's an unpleasant experience for everyone involved.

Dressed for the day, I sit on the bed and shoot Baxter and Maddie a text to confirm flooring and ask when I have to make the call on the tent sides. The more time I have, the better.

"Good morning, beautiful." Caleb places a hand on my waist and kisses the back of my neck. I have my hair slicked back in a high pony. Whatever the humidity has in store for my hair today is officially out of my control.

I turn to face him. "Good morning."

"What do I have to do to get you back in bed?" He smirks.

"Get Hannah and Preston to call off the wedding?"

"Done." He grabs my waist and pulls me on top of him. I give him a peck on the lips. Anything more than that and I'll miss the all-hands meeting with my team.

"I have to go, Caleb! I'm on a schedule," I say, picking up my clipboard from the nightstand. "And you have to get up and start cheffing." I force myself to pull away from him.

"Fine," he grumbles, getting out of bed. "But I plan to have you in this bed one more time before the weekend is over."

The property is calm and quiet this early, with only a few vendors already getting started. Soon enough, it will be another day of organized chaos that ends with a spectacular, albeit wet, event.

Inside the house, it's another story. When I enter the kitchen, I'm greeted with girlie pop music blaring. The bridesmaids sip mimosas, chatting in matching toile bathrobes.

Jordan's already here, snapping candids. I spot Hannah across the room and she gives me a warm smile.

She's sitting on a kitchen stool with large rollers in her hair and a champagne glass in her hand. At her feet is the flower girl, no more than three, coloring in her *I'm A Flower Girl* coloring book.

"So…how are you feeling?" I ask when I make my way over to her.

"Well…" she laughs. "Don't they say it's good luck to have rain on your wedding day?"

"Who's they?" the flower girl asks with an adorable lisp.

Hannah and I both laugh. "You know, sweetie," I say. "I've always wondered that. Who *is* they?" The flower girl goes back to her coloring, not at all amused.

I look at Hannah with soft eyes. The weather sucks, but it's literally the one thing out of my control. What I can control are the nerves telling me this is all going to be a disaster. It's not. No wedding of mine has ever been a disaster, and that includes a late-2020 wedding that started as an intimate gathering for fifty before growing to one hundred and fifty guests who didn't believe a global pandemic was something to worry about. I was convinced I'd end up on the news as the planner responsible for a superspreader event. Imagine how Judy would have handled that.

"Do you think we'll still be able to have the ceremony on the lawn?" Hannah asks with the smallest bit of worry on her face. "I've been envisioning the ceremony out there by the water. Even in the rain. Is that crazy? I know you'll make it amazing if we have to do it inside the tent, but I don't know. I'd like to try to keep it outside, if that's okay."

If that's okay? Does this bride not know how much of a dream she is? I've had clients yell at me because of the weather. *Why didn't you tell us it was going to rain?* I did. *Why didn't you know the time of the thunderstorm?* I'm not a meteorologist. *What do you mean forest fires in Canada are making it smell like smoke, can't you do something about it?* I think it's because of wind patterns, and no, I can't. *Why didn't you bring us coats if it was going to be this cold?* Uh, I don't have extra coats laying around.

"Hannah, I'm going to do everything in my power to keep your ceremony outside on the lawn. It's the perfect spot and it'd be a shame for something like a little rain to stop us." I wave my hand in the direction of the window, dismissing the downpour happening outside. "We're on it."

We're on it, yes, but it's a muddy, sludgy mess. The rain hasn't let up, and even though I promised Hannah her ceremony on the lawn, I'm worried we made the wrong call. I mentally prepare for comments from the guests. And my mother. But if this is what the bride wants, it's my job to get it done.

Maddie's by my side as I lead our all-hands meeting. My team includes two assistant leads, Maddie and Krista, and six assistants. Around us, the Foley's team handles place settings while the florist places the arrangements.

We review the timeline for the day, last-minute changes, and final prep. It's a long list that'd be manageable in any other circumstance, but the weather isn't on our side. I hand out assignments, including a very necessary fountain Diet Coke run. As we finish up, Judy and the woman she had in the office a few weeks ago make their way under the tent. I saw that woman last night, too. They stand talking a few yards from us, Mom pointing to various people on the team.

Krista takes the lead on the final reception details and Maddie takes the lead on the ceremony. When I see the look on her face as Baxter stands next to her, I'm tempted to swap them. They were fine yesterday.

"What's going on there?"

"What?" Maddie looks at me, confused. "Oh, him...we're just off again. He told me I was quote *too much*. Like I've never heard that before. He'll be groveling by the time we're done here." She winks, throwing on the hood of her raincoat and heading out to work with Baxter and his team on the flooring, leaving me with Judy and this mystery woman.

"Good morning, Judy." I smile and extend my hand to the tall blonde. "Hi, I'm Brooke."

"Brooke, this is my friend, Paige," Judy says. Friend. She's never been one to have friends. Acquaintances, sure. Colleagues, of course. Friends, actual friends, I don't think she's had one of those in a long time. Now I know why. The anger I've been holding on to for the last week slowly melts into pity. I can't imagine not having people like Maddie and Jordan in my life.

"Lovely to meet you, Brooke," Paige says.

"Paige wanted to see Spencer Soirees in action, so I thought I'd bring her along today."

I have so many questions, like who is this woman and why does she care about seeing us in action, but I'm interrupted by Krista calling me from across the tent for what I'm sure is the first of many fires I'll be putting out today.

"You'll have to excuse me," I say. "Lovely to meet you."

Paige looks so familiar, but I don't have time to figure out why, because it's raining sideways into the tent and the tables closest to the edge are about to be ruined. *Shit.*

"All hands!" The team hears my call and rushes over to the side of the tent that's currently getting drenched. Krista and I move the nearest table and chairs as close to the next table as possible. Without needing instructions, everyone knows exactly what to do. We make quick work of moving the tables along the edge as far in as we can. A few of the tables are soaked, but at least it stopped raining sideways, back to a regular old downpour now.

We strip the ruined tablecloths and I make a plan. Krista takes the linens into the house to throw in the dryer—we'll iron them later—while the assistants dry the silverware and plates. We'll put the tables back together in a few hours. I've already made the call not to put the tent sides on. I hope I don't regret it later.

"Impressive."

I peek out from under the hood of my raincoat. "Kevin, hi! Thank you."

"Is now a terrible time to ask you a few questions?"

I survey the room and find that everyone is on task. "No, not at all."

"Great," Kevin says, pulling a small notebook from his coat pocket. "I had the chance to speak with Judy earlier, sounds like there are exciting things to come for the agency."

"Oh." I feel myself stand taller as a smile creeps at the corners of my mouth. "Yes, yes, very exciting things."

"What are you looking forward to about the next chapter?" Next chapter. He's asking what I think he's asking, isn't he?

I clear my throat. "Spencer Soirees has been a cornerstone of the wedding industry in Charter Oaks for decades, and we're honored to work with so many esteemed vendors and lovely clients. Carrying on the legacy Judy built will be a huge honor."

Kevin looks up from his notebook and gives me a curious look.

"Yes, of course, love that," he says. "Tell me what it's been like working with Hannah and Preston." I tell him about how wonderful they are and answer his follow-up questions about their vision. The rest of the day goes by in a blur.

By the grace of Mother Nature or some karma I'm owed from a past life, the skies clear around five o'clock. Right in time for guest arrivals at 5:30. All my weather apps show mostly clear skies. The chance of intermittent thunderstorms for the remainder of the evening is down to twenty percent. That I can work with.

The grass is still a complete disaster, but the aisle Baxter put down will allow us to keep the ceremony outside under what is now a picture-perfect sky. Exactly what Hannah envisioned.

I check in with Maddie and Krista. Both are on top of their work, per usual. We all do our last checks to be sure we're good to go, assistants following each of them in case anything needs fixing. My phone buzzes in my belt bag.

> Jordan: SOS groomsmen need help with their boutonnieres.

The florist was supposed to use magnets. Or are they already so drunk they can't figure out magnets? I let Jordan know I'm on my way and head to the pool house.

The lovely aroma of stale beer and too much cologne hits me right in the face when I let myself in. This place needs fresh air, stat. Even if that air is hot and humid. I prop the door open with a rock.

"I'm all set with them," Jordan says by way of greeting. "They're all yours."

"Whoa, put that down before you crush it and stab your friend here." I rush over to a groomsman with his fist over the small floral arrangement, about to poke his fellow groomsmen right in the chest. I take everything away from him and get to work pinning boutonnieres to each of the groomsmen's lapels. I pick up the largest of the boutonnieres and head over to Preston, where he sips what is hopefully only his first glass of whiskey.

"How are you feeling?" I mumble, pinheads in between my teeth. He's either ready to run or enjoying a quiet moment alone.

"Um…good…I think," he says, looking for the right words.

"…just a little nervous, maybe. I don't usually get nervous. It's weird."

Oh, to be a wealthy white man. I hold the boutonniere to his lapel and push one pin up from the bottom. "It's a feeling I know well, Preston. And it's a completely normal one to be having right now. Anything I can do to help?"

"Have you seen Hannah?" he asks, bashfully.

"I have," I say, smiling as I push the second pin into the boutonniere from the top. It's always a treat to see the grooms like this. Anxious, excited, not trying to hide any emotion. "Tell your best man to be ready to catch you. She looks stunning."

"Thanks, Brooke." He smiles with a little more confidence. "I'm sure she does."

Heading out the door, I grab the best man. "Get that one some coffee, ASAP," I say, pointing to Gage, the groomsman who was a royal pain in my ass yesterday. "I can't have him stumbling up there during the ceremony. Make sure the two of you who are next to him keep him upright. I'll tell the bridesmaid paired with him for the recessional to do the same."

Chapter 36

Caleb

THE LAST-MINUTE AISLE WORKED OUT PERFECTLY, AND ONLY A few guests complained about mud on their shoes or their heels digging into the wet ground. Hannah and Preston exchanged meaningful vows they wrote themselves. And Gage stumbled only a little bit during the recessional.

"Looking good, man." Joey claps my back as I survey the patio. It's crowded with guests avoiding the damp grass, and the line at the bar is longer than I'd like.

"We're not out of the woods yet," I say. But we're close. So close.

"I think I like this better."

"Hmmm?" I turn to Joey.

"Working with Foley's, not being the one in charge…fuck, don't make me say it," he groans.

Oh, I'm so making him say it. "I'm not sure what you're talking about."

"Asshole. I'd rather be a sous. It's so much easier. Think Paul will have me back for good?"

Thank god, because having Joey back is part of my plan.

"Yeah, man, I think we'll be able to work something out. C'mon, we've got to plate salads."

I should get to work, but I can't move as I watch Brooke approach Judy and Kent fucking Chadwick. He hugs her and kisses her cheek. My stomach turns. I'd prefer he keep his hands and lips off her. Not that I'm at all worried about Kent, but that doesn't keep the jealousy and anger at bay.

"You coming?" Joey asks, but he follows my gaze and keeps walking to the catering tent alone.

I stride across the patio and make it to the trio as Kate, one of my waitstaff, holds a platter of hors d'oeuvres in front of them. Roasted tomato and goat cheese crostini.

"Brooke," Kent says. "You have to try these. They're delicious."

"Oh yes, dear, you must." Judy's eyes meet mine. "Not too bad for Foley's." She can't help herself, can she?

"No, thank you," Brooke says.

"Don't be silly," Kent says. "I'm sure your boss doesn't mind." He smiles at Judy who basks in the attention. Kate stands awkwardly holding the platter.

"She said *no, thank you*," I say, firmly. "Thank you, Kate, we're all set."

Kent scoffs. "I think Brooke can speak for herself."

Asshole.

"She can and she did. It seems you can't listen. Or remember that tomatoes give her migraines," I say, fisting my hands into my pockets. Either to keep them from grabbing Brooke's face and kissing her in front Judy and Kent, or to control the rage currently coursing through my veins. I turn to Brooke. "They need us in the tent."

"Excuse us," Brooke says politely, following me off the patio. I thought I kept my anger in check enough, but Brooke's silence as we walk is making me think otherwise. She stops once we round some trees between the patio and the tent. She fists my chef coat, smirk on her face.

"What is it?" I ask.

She casts her eyes down and shakes her head, ponytail waving behind her. Then reaches up on her toes, holds my face in her hands, and gives me a soft, sweet kiss.

"Let's light the votives in the tent in about ten minutes," she says. Back in planner mode. It's so fucking sexy how impressive she is when she's working. "And I gave you the list of tables with dietary restrictions?"

"You did. Twice."

"Okay, good." She looks around. "This is all going well, don't you think?"

"It's amazing, Brooke. You've done an incredible job."

"*We've* done an incredible job." She smiles up at me. "I think we make a good team. I'm sad it's all coming to an end."

My fingertips graze hers. "*We're* not coming to an end, Brooke." I'll miss this, though. Working on the same team. Having excuses to be together all the time. We're both going to be extremely busy once I start work at the farm and Judy retires.

"I know, it's just…I've enjoyed working with you this summer. And not only because of how well you wear a chef coat and…you know…the incredible sex."

"Brooke." I look at her, faux-scandalized. "There are people here. People with ears." Then, only because we're hidden by trees, I pull her in to give her a good and thorough kiss.

"Ugh, gross," Maddie says behind us. "Brooke, I do actually need you now."

Brooke pulls away and brushes her fingertips to her lips. "See you later, chef."

Two hours later, entrees are plated and I can finally breathe. The only glimpses I've managed to get of Brooke have been from afar as she darts around putting out the various fires of the night. But when she spots me, I'm met with a gorgeous smile. It makes the anger and frustration I was feeling toward Kent and Judy dissipate into thin air.

From here on out, it should be a breeze. Once Hannah and Preston cut the cake, we'll slice and serve it and start packing up for the night. The guests will continue to drink and dance, and in no time, I'll be back in the carriage house with Brooke.

I stand outside the tent and watch the last of the entrees being served to the tables in the back. We've got a great crew tonight, and I wish Dad were here to see it. He'd be proud of what we've accomplished.

"Well, Caleb, it seems you can handle this level of wedding, after all." Judy stands next to me, surveying the tent. Suddenly the anger is back, more intense than it was before.

"It seems I can," I bite.

"You may think proving your competence after all of these years will make you a match for my daughter, but you're mistaken."

"Excuse me?" I say, turning to her.

"You heard me," she says, giving me a cursory glance. "I had my suspicions, but your friend Jennnifer filled me in. You're simply a good-looking man who happens to be there. Brooke will realize you can't give her a life like this. Look around, Caleb. So many attractive young men with money, from the right families."

The right families. My nostrils flare as heat roars through my body. But instead of letting that rage take over, I remember Brooke's hands on my cheeks and the look she gave me a few hours ago at the end of cocktail hour.

Breathe in. Breath out.

"You're right, Judy," I say. "What I can offer Brooke is not the same as what some of these guys can. I understand that."

"Good," she says. "I'm glad we're in agreement."

"Agreement?"

"That you'll end things with Brooke. Just like you ended things with Jennifer when you realized you weren't good enough for this way of life." She gestures behind us to the Quincy mansion. "Everything I do for Brooke is in her best interest."

Anger pulses through my veins, self-doubt lingers at the edges of my mind.

Breathe in. Breathe out.

Once, this would have broken me. I scoff, looking down at her. For too long, I worried about what Judy would think about me and Brooke. I always have been and always will be good for Brooke. I don't need anyone else's approval for that. Only hers.

"You can keep telling yourself that, Judy," I say. "It might help you sleep at night. I've seen how you treat her and how you put yourself before her. But you're right, one day Brooke is going to have a realization. Only it won't be about me. It'll be about you, and it'll be too late."

She purses her lips. "Be careful, Caleb. There is a lot I can do to make things hard for you and your family." She's so confident it's almost funny.

"You've already tried that, Judy. You tried to ruin my parents' marriage and they survived it."

Her face falls, but she quickly adjusts into her signature resting face.

"Yes, I know the truth," I say. "And so does Brooke."

Shattering glass interrupts us. A lot of it. This late into the evening, there are plenty of women who have ditched their heels to dance barefoot. A recipe for disaster. Brooke's already on the dance floor blocking guests. I run to the catering tent to grab a broom.

When I get back, Brooke and Kate are both crouched on the floor picking up the larger pieces of broken flutes and tumblers. I work my way through the tables, moving the empty Chiavari chairs out of the way. A group of guests near the dance floor block my way, too drunk to care that I'm trying to keep them from injuring themselves.

Over their heads I see Gage stalking toward Brooke. He has that hazy look he's had all night, but all of his focus is on her. She stands and places another piece of glass on the tray.

Gage grabs her waist, pulling her close to him. *Fucking asshole.* The broom falls from my hands. Brooke's quick enough to put the arm holding her clipboard between them. He sways her back and forth, pressing his body against hers in a way that's entirely inappropriate.

I'm still blocked.

Fuck this.

I climb on a cushioned chair and onto the table, finally catching the attention of the guests who wouldn't move. When I jump off the table, Gage's hand is on Brooke's ass and she's trying to push him away. Kate is trying to help, but she's young and unsure what to do. We've always instructed our team not to make a scene when any issues arise. I'm about to change that policy to "punch anyone in the face who lays a hand on someone without their consent."

"Get your fucking hands off of her," I shout, grabbing his arm and pulling him away from Brooke. He stumbles back drunkenly when I let go.

"Caleb," Brooke says, face filled with relief. Until she notices I'm seething. I haven't had a chance to process my conversation with Judy. I'm riled the fuck up.

"It's okay. I'm fine," she says, her voice shaky. She brushes invisible dust off the front of her dress. She's clearly rattled and uncomfortable.

"Yeah, man," Gage slurs. "It's fine."

"No, it's not fine," I say, standing toe-to-toe with him. "Don't you fucking touch her again."

"Chill out, my guy. She's been flirting with me all weekend." He's the kind of asshole who thinks a woman politely doing her job is flirting with him. I feel terrible for any woman in customer service who's ever had to deal with him. Any woman who's ever had to deal with him, period. A crowd grows around us, but my eyes don't leave his face.

"Don't mistake my professionalism for flirting," Brooke says. "Go get some water and call it a night."

Brooke wraps her hand around my arm and pulls gently to lead me away from the confrontation. Gage looks between us and I see it register on his face.

"You're with this guy? The fucking caterer?" he chuckles. "It's your loss, stupid bitch."

Fuck. Him.

He can belittle me all he wants, but calling Brooke a bitch —that's the last straw.

Sensing what I'm about to do, Brooke takes her hand off my arm and steps back. I pull my arm back, channel all the anger I've felt today—Kent hugging Brooke, Judy patronizing me, Gage touching Brooke—and punch him in the goddamn face.

There's a collective gasp around us as Gage hits the ground, hand on his jaw. Behind him is the *Times* reporter with his camera.

"Oh my god," Brooke says.

Shit.

That felt really fucking good, but I've fucked up big time.

Across the dance floor, two other groomsmen walk toward us. I weigh the pros and cons of an all-out brawl erupting in the middle of this wedding.

Instead of coming for me, one groomsman helps Gage off

the floor and the other extends his hand to me. Reluctantly, I take it.

"Thanks, man," he says. "You won me five hundred bucks. I bet Preston that Gage would get punched at this wedding."

"You're...uh...welcome," I say skeptically.

He walks away and the small crowd around us starts to disperse. Some guests look at me and whisper to one another. Others go back to dancing like their friends get punched in the face at social gatherings all the time. It wouldn't surprise me.

Eventually, it's just me and Brooke, but Hannah and her parents are walking over.

Brooke takes my hand and rubs her thumb over the red knuckles. "Caleb, thank you for defending my honor and all that, but you need to go cool off, okay? I'll take care of this."

"I'm so sorry, Brooke," I say. I should stay and apologize to Hannah and Preston, to the Quincys, but Brooke's pleading eyes are enough to convince me it'll be better if I walk away.

Chapter 37

Brooke

I close the carriage house door behind me, lean back, close my eyes, and let out a long breath. I need a moment to myself before finishing up the night.

I couldn't have planned for the events of this weekend. Especially Caleb punching a guest in the face. I shouldn't have found it as wildly hot as I did, but I'm also furious with him right now. I handled damage control as best as I could. Preston thought the entire thing was hilarious. Hannah was concerned about the *Times* piece and word getting out on socials—Mr. Quincy's influence was enough for Kevin to delete his photos, but the internet is another story.

I push off the door and walk further into the house.

"Mom!" I jump at the sight of her and Paige in the kitchen. "What are you doing here?"

Mom clears her throat.

"I'm sorry," I say. "Judy."

Paige straightens a stack of papers on the kitchen island. Mom clicks the top of a pen.

"I'll leave you two to talk. Thank you, Judy," Paige says,

giving Mom a sidelong glance. She places the papers in her bag and moves toward the door. She turns the doorknob and looks back. "I'm looking forward to working with you, Brooke."

I'm sorry. What?

The door shuts behind her.

"I'm very disappointed, Brooke," Mom says.

"Mom…can I call you that now?" I say, my stomach flipping. "What's going on?"

She purses her lips. Whatever is going on, I'm not going to like it.

"I raised you better than this. I worked so hard to give you the things I didn't have. Made sacrifices you wouldn't begin to understand. Handed you a career on a silver platter. Hand-selected a man from a good family who could give us, you, everything you deserve. So you didn't love him, but that was no reason to give up a comfortable life. Not only for you. For me. How selfish of you to throw all of that away."

Give us. For me.

We've had this fight before—and so many others like it. But she's never spoken to me like this, with such blatant disdain. She's never admitted to being this self-serving. Unlike the fights before, I'm not backing down. I'm not apologizing. Whatever she's upset about is not my fault.

"How selfish of *me*? Kent and I weren't right for each other. I wasn't happy, Mom." My heart pounds. "Your version of a comfortable life and mine aren't the same. I don't need a big house and fancy things. I need someone who loves me, cares about me, believes in me. Someone who makes me happy."

"Someone who believes in you…makes you happy." She laughs. "Brooke, listen to yourself. It's ridiculous. Does Caleb believe in you? Does he make you happy?"

"Yes, he…"

That's what this is about.

"You weren't as discreet as you thought you were, dear. At first, I thought you were simply silly enough to have a little fling. Fine. I didn't think you'd actually be foolish enough to fall in love with him. That's what this is, isn't it? If the stolen glances all weekend weren't enough." She waves a hand toward the bedroom. "It's clear you're both staying here. Brooke, you should know, his family—"

"Don't you say one thing about his family," I say, fire coating each word. "They're wonderful people."

"Whatever they told you—"

"Enough!" I yell. "They told me everything, Mom. And I didn't have a moment of doubt when they did. For so long, I told myself you weren't what you so obviously are. That you were a strong single mother. That you had to be tough because you were forging a life for us on your own. That you had to be tough on me to prepare me for taking over the agency."

"Which you won't be anymore," she says, casually shaking her head.

"What? I know you might not be ready to retire but—"

"Paige Summers has bought Spencer Soirees," she says.

My vision blurs and I feel dizzy.

"We've signed the paperwork. I *am* ready to retire Brooke, but when I realized how foolish you've been with your life, I had to take matters into my own hands. If you weren't going to secure my future, I'd have to do it myself. I've taught you well, but you'll never be as good as I was leading a wedding agency. You don't have what it takes. Despite my best efforts, you have too much heart."

I need to sit down, but my legs won't budge.

"Too much heart," I laugh. "Is there such a thing?"

"You've always been this way." She says it like it's an ugly trait. Every time I cried at a wedding, she'd chastise me. Each time I supported my colleagues rather than critiqued them, she told me I wasn't tough enough. I've never been enough for her. I've been the burden she had to bear. She's never believed in me. There's a stinging behind my eyes, but I won't let her see me cry. She doesn't deserve to see a single one of my tears ever again.

"You were always going to sell the business," I say, grabbing a kitchen stool for support. "Even if Kent and I had worked out." It's not a question.

She avoids my eyes.

"You would've convinced me to stop working and push out a bunch of babies. Or kept me on but convinced me to let someone else take the lead. Wouldn't you?"

This is vicious, even for her. "Spencer Soirees was never going to be mine." My voice shakes. "This was always your plan."

She collects her purse from the island.

"You'll enjoy working for Paige. And if you're thinking about resigning," she threatens, "take a look at your employment contract."

When the door closes behind her, I sink to the floor.

It's two o'clock in the morning when I finally hear the door of the carriage house open. After Mom left, I texted Maddie to ask her to handle the event breakdown with the promise of a later start for the farewell brunch tomorrow. I told Caleb I was taking the early setup tomorrow and needed to get to bed. It wasn't a complete lie. I'm in bed, but I haven't slept at all. I've gone over the conversation with Mom a dozen times. I've combed through six years of memories, searching for the signs I missed. My head and eyes ache from crying for hours. Finally, there aren't any tears left.

Caleb tiptoes into the room.

"You're up," he says softly, finding me sitting on the bed, arms wrapped around my legs.

I lied. There are so many more tears. They pour out so quickly, I'm breathless.

"Brooke." Caleb's brows knit with concern. He rushes to the bed and throws his arms around me. "What's wrong?"

The tears fall so fast I can't speak, my nose is running, I'm an absolute mess. Full ugly crying in front of him. Again.

"Brooke," he says gently. "In and out, okay?"

After a few deep breaths, I try to speak. "Earlier…"

"I'm so sorry, Brooke," he says, wiping tears from my cheeks. "Actually, no. I'm not sorry I punched that asshole. He fucking deserved it. I'm sorry he touched you like that. That I wasn't there sooner."

"It's…not…that," I sob. "My mom…"

Caleb grabs the tissue box from the nightstand and hands me one. I attempt to gracefully blow my nose, but I sound like the foghorn on the Port Jefferson ferry. While I signal to nearby watercraft, Caleb sits across from me and rests his hands on my knees. I've changed out of my work dress, wearing cotton pajama shorts and one of Caleb's undershirts that I've taken to stealing.

"Look at me." He takes more deep breaths in and out. I mimic his breaths while wiping tears from my face and snot from my nose. We've come a long way from being stuck in the storage closet. "Talk to me," he says.

"My mom, she knows about us."

"Shit, Brooke. That's my fault. God, I really fucked up tonight. She confronted me and I didn't deny it. I know you wanted to wait, but the way she spoke to me…I couldn't hold it in anymore."

"She what? Actually, no, that's not surprising at all. I'm sorry, you didn't deserve that."

"I took my anger toward her out on Gage," he says, rubbing his right hand. "I messed up. I'm sorry."

"Don't be. That's the least of it." I take a steadying breath and tell him what happened with Mom tonight. There are more tears, but now I'm not alone.

Chapter 38

Caleb

BROOKE MAKES IT TO THE FAREWELL BRUNCH. BARELY. SHE insisted on being here despite me and Maddie both telling her to take the day off.

She stays on the periphery of the event, hiding her bloodshot eyes behind large sunglasses. It's a beautiful day, but not even that can lift her mood. She's still in shock. We were up until four this morning, me holding her while she cried herself to sleep. We just have to make it through a few more hours, then I can take her home.

Of all the weekend events, this is by far the most relaxed and casual. Though that doesn't mean much. It's about as casual as a royal wedding. Round tables on the patio are covered with simple light blue linens, yellow-striped napkins sitting on top of blue Mediterranean-patterned chargers. The centerpieces are a mix of blue and yellow. All a nod to the honeymoon Hannah and Preston are taking on the Amalfi Coast.

We've set up a big buffet with an omelet station and waffle bar. The line at the actual bar rivals last night. I don't know how everyone is drinking again already. Hair of the dog, I guess.

Each guest looks so effortlessly put together. Except Gage, who's sporting quite the bruise. It *almost* makes me feel guilty. He threatened to press charges. Preston and the guy who won five hundred dollars reminded him that Brooke could easily press charges, too. Part of me wants her to.

Hannah finds me at the omelet station, Preston by her side. I haven't had a chance to talk to them since last night. They give me their orders.

"I'm so sorry," I say, cracking eggs into the pan. "I was out of line."

"Don't worry about it," Preston says. "He's my cousin, but he's also a huge asshole."

Hannah laughs. "This isn't the first time Gage has gotten punched on the dance floor."

That doesn't surprise me. "Even so, I was way out of line."

"My dad took care of the photos Kevin got, and I haven't been tagged in anything yet, so I think we're okay," Hannah says nervously. With all the drama last night, I hadn't thought about my own reputation. Someone could easily identify me as the chef for Foley's. Dad may be proud of a lot of things I've done, but he won't be proud of this.

I serve up their finished omelets.

Hannah takes hers and heads to a table. Preston lingers. "So how was the carriage house?" He raises a brow. This guy.

"It's very nice," I say.

"Cool, cool. You two make a good team. For all of this and like, life and stuff. Brooke was telling me about your restaurant. Can't wait to check it out."

"Thanks, Preston."

He takes his omelet, and I'm that much closer to the end of this wedding weekend.

It's Tuesday and the only outreach Brooke's gotten from Judy was one text late last night: *See you tomorrow, dear.* Brooke isn't going into the office. How can she when she's barely gotten out of bed? If she never walks into that office again, I wouldn't blame her.

Once service for the farewell brunch was over, Joey and Maddie managed breakdown and cleanup while I grabbed our stuff from the carriage house, got Brooke into the Wrangler, and drove her home. She was silent for the fifteen-minute drive across town, curled against the door and staring out the window. I managed to put the doors and top back on before the terrible weather on Saturday.

When we got back, I wasn't sure how to take care of her. My always capable Brooke was a shell of her usual self.

As if Mother Nature knew what she needed, the beautiful morning turned into an overcast afternoon and the air turned cool. A small taste of autumn to come. Dad's words came to mind: *When they're having a bad day and need comfort, we help them.* Then Brooke's: *Soup is for warming up the soul.*

I asked Jordan if she could drop off the ingredients for the Market's lemon chicken orzo soup before she hunkered down to edit photos from the weekend.

"I'm going to run you a bath, okay?" I told Brooke while I waited for Jordan.

"Okay," she answered quietly.

When her bath, complete with bubbles and a bath pillow I found under the sink, was ready, I walked her into the bathroom. I was about to leave when she wrapped her arms around me and let her head fall against my chest. I pressed a kiss into her hair.

After holding her for a while, I unwrapped my arms and pulled her hair to the side, allowing me to reach the zipper of her dress. I unzipped and kneeled down to help her step out of the dress. She reached behind her back to unclasp her bra, then rested a hand on my shoulder while I slipped off her underwear. I took her hand and she stepped into the bath, sighing as the warm water touched her skin. I hated what she was going through, but I loved taking care of her.

"I'll come check on you in a little bit, okay?"

"Okay," she said.

Ingredients delivered, I worked on prepping and checked on her about twenty minutes later.

"I'm going to help you get out, okay?"

"Okay."

I got her out of the bath and wrapped a towel around her. She got dressed in sweats and took a nap. Hours later, I went into her room. I found her curled on her side, similar to the position I found her in the night of the meeting she missed. This time, though, she looked peaceful. I climbed into bed behind her and wrapped my arms around her. She stirred a little and turned to face me.

"I made you some soup. Come have some, okay?"

"Okay."

I could see her come back to life as we ate. Her soul warming up a little. I've never been prouder of what I'm able to do with food. It's so much more than ingredients and plating. It's the love that goes into it. The love that's helping Brooke heal.

That's how it's been for the last two days. She's slowly coming back to life, but she's not ready to face her mom. Not today. Maybe not ever.

Today, Judy is officially handing over the reins to Paige at the staff meeting. Paige Summers. Celebrity wedding planner from San Francisco. That's why she looked so familiar. I'd done all of two weddings with her team, but I should have been able to place her and save Brooke this heartache. I don't think I could have stopped Judy, but I could have prepared Brooke. Maybe it wouldn't have made a difference, but if there is anything I can ever do to make Brooke's life easier, I'm doing it.

Maddie got a copy of the employment agreement all Spencer Soirees staff sign, and it's absolute bullshit. A two-year noncompete clause for all full-time employees in the coverage area of Connecticut, New York, Massachusetts, and Rhode Island. Interns nearly sign their lives away so that they won't disclose trade secrets. It's one thing to make any random employee sign, but your own daughter?

Brooke signed it six years ago, when Judy promised to one day hand the agency over to her. I don't want to believe Judy had always planned to sell the business, but the contract makes me think that Brooke's right. Judy never planned to give it to her.

Mom stops by with Wendell and brings more food than this kitchen's ever seen, at least since Brooke's lived here. Has she completely forgotten that I cook for a living? I unpack the five Foley's bags on the counter.

"Seriously, Mom, three key lime pies?"

"It's her favorite, Caleb," she says, like she knows Brooke better than me.

"I know, but it's a little excessive, no?"

"Honey, there is no such thing as too much key lime pie. Put one in the freezer." She pats my shoulder. We bicker about how to fit everything in the small refrigerator until Brooke comes into the kitchen. She's in light blue sweats, her hair is piled on the top of her head in a messy bun, and her face is free of makeup, showing off all her beautiful freckles.

My heart does so many things when I look at her. It swells with love for her, aches for what she's going through, burns with anger. I'm furious that anyone would ever hurt her.

"Oh, honey." Mom spins to Brooke and opens her arms.

Brooke melts into Mom while Wendell dances at her feet. I've tried so many things to help her since we got home. The one thing I want to tell her the most has to wait. It's not the right time. Not when she's navigating all of this. The next best thing I can do is share the love I so easily receive from my parents. But especially, right now, from Mom. Nothing will ever fill the hole Judy's left in Brooke's heart, but between me and Mom, I think we can get pretty close. Brooke doesn't know it yet, but she's stuck with us.

Mom runs her hand over Brooke's hair in a soothing motion. She hugs her like a Disney cast member, not letting go until Brooke pulls away first.

"We're here, Brooke," she says. I walk over and wrap my arms around both of them. The two women I love more than anything else in this world.

We're interrupted by the whirling dervish that is Maddie. Per usual, we hear her before we see her.

"That bitch." She storms into the kitchen. "I swear to god I was about to punch the smug smile right off of her face today. She told the staff Brooke's been working with her to sell the business to Paige and can't wait to work with her. Said Brooke needed an extra day after the weekend. That's an awful lot of food. Perfect, I'm starving but I also need a drink. So listen, we're going to figure this out. I have a plan. Okay, I don't, but I'll figure one out. It's my turn to make the plan. You need a fucking break from figuring it all out."

Mom and I look at Maddie wide-eyed. "Take a breath, Maddie," Brooke says with a stuffy laugh.

"You must be Maddie," Mom says, extending her hand. "I've heard so much about you."

Creases form between Maddie's eyebrows as she looks toward me.

"All good things, I swear," I say, placing a hand over my heart.

"Better be! You and me," she says, pointing between us. "We're on the same team now."

It's only mid-afternoon, but Brooke skipped lunch, so I warm up an assortment of the prepared foods. Garlic and herb grilled chicken, roasted asparagus, couscous salad. Foley's Market favorites.

I pour glasses of wine for the four of us and we sit at Brooke's small kitchen table. While we eat, we talk about the weekend, filling Mom in on the highlights, the funny moments, and the drama. We avoid discussing the biggest drama of all. Mom already knows, and there's no reason to make Brooke relive it.

Mom scolds me for punching Gage, but she's not surprised that I did. I'm not sure if I should be flattered or offended. Brooke recalls the speech from Hannah's dad and starts to cry again. This time, thankfully, they're tears of happiness. This woman loves love, and I need her to know how much I love her. That I will help her through this and everything else that comes our way.

We never said it out loud, but Mom, Maddie and I made a silent agreement to wait until after Brooke eats a giant slice of key lime to talk about Judy. Mom cuts Brooke another piece and places it in front of her.

"All right, honey," Mom says. "I'm going to give you a little tough love, okay?"

Brooke scoffs. "I know all about that, Lynne. Judy's love has always been tough." She's been calling her Judy exclusively since Sunday.

"Oh, sweet girl. Everything you've been through with your mom has been tough, but I'm afraid it wasn't love. At least not the kind you deserve."

"I know," Brooke says, her eyes glistening. "It's…just…she's my mom, you know?"

"I'm positive that she loves you, Brooke. How could she

not? You're one of the most incredible young women I've had the pleasure of knowing."

"I second that!" Maddie mumbles, mouth full of pie, making Brooke laugh.

"Me too," I say, placing my hand over hers on the table.

"But your mom, she's...she's always going to be looking out for herself, which is no fault of yours. Until she realizes what a mess she's made of things and decides she wants to make a change. Maybe go to therapy or something."

Maddie guffaws, nearly spitting pie across the table. "I'd pay to see Judy in therapy."

I give Maddie a look that says *you're not helping*.

"Sorry."

Mom keeps her focus on Brooke. "From what Caleb's told me, you've always done what makes it easier for you two to maintain a relationship, right? It was easier to go along with things to keep her happy. When you didn't, things got tough, and she made you feel guilty for wanting something else or doing something against her wishes. None of us are going to tell you what to do Brooke, only that you need to do what's best for you. What's best for Brooke."

How am I so lucky to have two parents who love me unconditionally and Brooke got stuck with Judy? It's hardly fair.

Brooke sighs and looks at me. "What about the noncompete? I've made my life, my whole personality, weddings. I can't imagine not being able to do this work."

"I can't imagine you not doing it either," I tell her. "But I looked into it a little more. Connecticut law says a noncompete can only be enforced if it's reasonable—"

"It's pretty *fucking* unreasonable!"

"Maddie..."

"Sorry, Mrs. Foley." Maddie sinks in her chair. "It is though."

"Maddie," Brooke looks at her best friend. "What do you think?"

"This isn't about me, B." Maddie gives her a tentative smile. "You always thought Spencer Soirees was going to be yours. Do you still want to be a part of it when your name isn't on the door anymore?"

"I think...I...I need more time to think about it. And I need to talk to Paige first."

Chapter 39

Brooke

JUDY'S OFFICE—NO, IT'S PAIGE'S OFFICE NOW—IS ALREADY redecorated. The Spencer Soirees sign out front has been taken down, ready to be replaced. I sit in a new ivory arm chair across from Paige. The desk is the same, but a new iMac sits on top of it.

Paige tells me the other side of the story. She was told that not only was I aware of the sale, but I was looking forward to it. That I never wanted the pressure of owning the agency and was relieved that Judy found someone to buy it.

All of it bullshit, straight from Judy.

She asked to meet with me about the transition weeks ago, but Judy used the Quincy wedding as an excuse to keep me out of the loop. Paige had been looking to open an east coast branch for her San Francisco-based agency for a while. Judy heard through an industry friend and approached Paige last summer. *Last summer.*

The overwhelming hurt of Judy's actions hasn't subsided, but I'm relieved Paige isn't the villain I thought she was. Despite her somewhat cold exterior, she's kind. She speaks to me as an equal and compliments the execution of the wedding weekend.

I've all but made up my mind about what's best for me, but I need to have this conversation first. Since the business is now hers, it's up to her if she wants to enforce my noncompete, for me or anyone else who might leave because of this transition. I swore Maddie to secrecy about what Judy did. I care about my coworkers too much to put them in the position of choosing between their livelihood and what they might think is the right thing to do. As far as they need to know, Judy's lies are the truth.

"You were a huge part of the reason I wanted to buy this agency, Brooke," Paige says. "Your reputation is impeccable. You've got Manhattan planners keeping an eye on your work. A few of my friends felt pretty snubbed when you managed to get Hannah's wedding."

"I was just as surprised as they were."

It's still a shock to me that we landed it. That we were forced to work with Foley's, with Caleb. Nothing this summer went according to plan. When Judy stunned me by agreeing to work with Foley's, I prepared myself for some inevitable drama. Nothing could have prepared me for what unfolded.

"Not to mention all the wonderful things your mother told me about you."

I'm unable to hide my laughter. Paige looks at me quizzically. "I'm sorry…we have a complicated relationship."

"Mothers and daughters usually do," she says. She's not wrong, but I think we're on a different level. "But she spoke so highly of you and your work. Showed me reviews from your clients. She's proud of you, Brooke."

She's proud of how I reflect on her. My praise is her praise. But Judy only ever wants the good. Not the bad or the ugly. Not the mistakes. Not the struggles and hardships. She never once told me she was proud. And her actions never reflected it.

"Thank you," I say. What else can I say? I'm sure she's not interested in our dirty laundry. Mom's character doesn't matter anymore. The papers are signed. The wire transfers are complete. The new Summer Soirees sign is being installed. All Paige needs to know is Judy created a successful wedding planning agency that executed their biggest event with flying colors. The feature will be in the *Times* next Sunday.

"My hope was that you would run this office, Brooke. You're more than capable. I'll be back and forth between here and San Francisco. Here a bit more as we transition, but for all intents and purposes, this," she says, gesturing around the office space, "would be yours."

It's tempting. It's *so* tempting. Spencer Soirees has been my life for six years, and weddings for longer than that. I did learn a lot from Judy. All the wonderful things she passed along, but also the pain points of running this business. Paige and her team in San Francisco might handle a lot, but is the headache of being a business owner worth it if it's not truly mine?

This is what Caleb has been trying to explain to me. That making something out of nothing yourself can be so meaningful. I want to build something from scratch, but I don't want to do it on my own. I want to do it with him.

"I appreciate that, Paige. But Summer Soirees won't be the same as Spencer Soirees would have been. Taking it over was always my dream, but I have a new one now. One I didn't realize until recently. I'd like to stay on and finish out my weddings for the season, if that's okay. I hope it is. There are a lot of amazing planners here, but I don't want to bail on my couples."

"I understand," she says, clasping her hands together on the desk. "I wish this had worked out differently."

"Me too," I say, getting up to leave.

"Brooke," she says as I reach the door. "This new dream…

will it be an issue with the noncompete? I don't want to have to enforce it, but I have to look out for the business."

"No, I don't think so," I say. "It's going to take a little while to come together."

Being a wedding planner has taught me that you can plan and prepare as much as possible with dozens of backup plans, but something is always going to come up. With weddings, I've always managed to roll with it, figuring out how to fix the problem and putting the fire out. It's time for me to apply that to my own life. I need to learn to roll with it. I start by rolling myself right to therapy.

I had my first real appointment this morning.

"You're dealing with a textbook narcissist," Dr. Drury said. That's when the tears came again. Deep down, I knew it. My friends tiptoed around it to keep me safe, but it all blew up. "It'll take a lot to work through it," she told me. "The first step I'm going to recommend is a hard one: It might be best to go no contact with your mom for a little while."

Not so hard, Doc. Judy took care of that for me. I haven't heard from her. I'd gotten so used to her constant checking in and micromanaging about work that her silence is deafening.

Dr. Drury thinks Judy is distancing herself so she can manipulate the narrative. She can tell her lies. The people that matter to me know the truth. She also tells me to stop calling her Judy. She understands why I'm doing it, but I'll be able to work through this better if I acknowledge she's my mom and call her that.

I hate that she's probably right.

After the session, I'm not sure if I feel better or worse. But I'm meeting Caleb at the farm, so I let myself forget about all of it for a little while.

It's golden hour when I arrive, and it's breathtaking. The entire view is drenched in the soft glow of the sun. Some of the trees are beginning to turn stunning shades of red, yellow, and orange. Jordan's going to love this spot for photos if everything works out the way I hope it will.

Wendell comes barreling toward me on his little legs. I squat down when he reaches me and give him some love. Caleb's up at the main house with the inspector. I catch his attention and point to the old barn.

Wendell walks by my side. Even with his bounding energy, he's slow in the overgrown grass. I chuckle watching him barely manage through the path. He's *so* not a country dog, but he's a good boy who sits patiently while I survey the outside of the barn.

The list forms in my head. Repair and repaint the outside. Replace the old doors. Cut out a matching entry on the opposite side. Install a patio. Add windows for more light. Electric. Plumbing. This will take well over a year.

Wendell whines next to me. "Okay, buddy. We'll go inside."

Nothing's changed since the last time Caleb brought me here. Why would it? But it looks different. The possibilities I first saw are still here, but they aren't a far-off vision for someone else to bring to life. They're the possibilities for me to build, with Caleb. If he'll have me.

The list for inside is longer. Repair or renovate...pretty much everything. Add flooring. Storage will be necessary to keep a stock of linens and chairs. Good chairs that couples will want to use. No client of ours will have to rent chairs. Painting. Lighting.

Last week, Caleb and his parents finalized the details of expanding the Foley's brand to include the farmhouse property.

It's still in the family, but it's all Caleb's. His dream, his vision. One that I hope can include me.

After the inspection, Caleb will go into contract and work will begin. Joey's coming back to Foley's to manage the Market. Paul will head catering, but he'll also mentor staff to handle on-site operations for weddings. Paul and Lynne aren't quite as ready to step back as they thought they were.

Somehow, this summer felt like a million years and only a few seconds at the same time. We dove straight into a relationship with barely a conversation about what happens next. Declarations in the heat of the moment are wonderful, but what *does* happen next?

"Hey."

"Jesus Christ, Caleb." I smack his arm. "One of these days, I'm going to end up punching you in the face."

A smile tugs at the corner of his mouth. He grabs my waist with both hands, pulling me closer. I wrap my hands around his neck and play with the waves at the nape of his neck. We sway back and forth. As I look around, a thought pops into my head, and I must make a face.

He taps my temple. "What's going on in there?"

"Nothing," I say, shaking my head and burying that this is the exact spot I picture a dance floor.

"I think I have an idea," he smirks, showing off that dimple I love so much.

"How did the inspection go?" I ask, changing the subject.

"Good, there are a few things we need to ask the sellers about, but we should be good to close next month."

"Caleb," I grin at him. "You're doing it."

"I'm scared shitless."

"As you should be. If it wasn't scary, it wouldn't be worth doing. It's going to be incredible. I'm so proud of you."

He kisses my forehead.

"Brooke," he says, at the same time I say his name.

I need to get over my nerves. "Me first."

His arms relax around me. "You first."

I take a deep breath. In and out. "I keep thinking about what you asked me a few weeks ago…if working at the agency is what I wanted. I thought it was. I didn't know anything different. I keep trying to come up with something else, anything else, but I love weddings. I know you wanted to do this for yourself. Creating this beautiful place is that something that was missing for you, and I want to ask if I could help. I love working with you and god, this barn would make such a beautiful wedding venue. I know it's not part of the plan but—"

"Brooke," he says, cupping my cheek. "It's you. You're my something. You were what was missing. I can't wait to make this dream come true, but even if it all falls apart, it doesn't matter as long as you're standing next to me…rolling your eyes at me for fucking it all up."

I can't help but roll my eyes at that. There's no way he's fucking this up.

"Is this what you want?" He's smiling. "To turn this run-down barn into a venue?"

I nod. Besides him, it's what I want more than anything.

"Thank god," he says, dipping his head back in relief. "It wasn't in the original plan, but I've been thinking about it ever since I first brought you here. This only works if it's you and me. This plan, this dream, it's been something I've wanted to do for a long time. It wasn't until I saw you at Warehouse Party that I started to work on it. Ever since, whenever I imagine what this will look like, you're there. And you've always been here."

He takes one of my hands in his and holds it to his chest.

"I should have told you earlier this summer. Hell, I should have told you five years ago. You're everything to me, Brooke. And I want to give you everything. I can't get Spencer Soirees back for you, but this barn is yours, if that's what you want. Is it?"

"It is," I say.

"Good. Because I love you, Brooke, and that's what I want too."

I smile and he looks at me expectantly.

"I know you do, Caleb."

He laughs with his entire body. "That wasn't the response I was expecting."

"I knew you loved me when you offered to make a hundred gourmet cheeseburgers for my clients and only charged them the cost of Happy Meals. I knew you loved me when you took me to urgent care and spent the half hour I was with the doctor learning about migraines. When you punched a wedding guest in the face. When you cook for me. When you draw me a bath.

"I've been told *I love you* before, but it was always conditional. I don't know that I've been truly loved by some of the people who've said it. I love hearing you say it…please keep saying it, obviously, but you've shown me you love me all summer long. You've done it without conditions and without expecting anything in return. I love you too, Caleb."

The goofiest smile appears on his face. He leans down as I lift myself up on my tiptoes. His lips brush against mine gently, his tongue parting my lips slowly, and we take our time. It feels like we have all the time in the world.

Until Wendell whines at our feet and jumps, pawing Caleb for attention.

"You're sure you want to do this together?" We may love each other, but this is a big step. A giant one.

"There's no one else I'd trust it with. It won't be as exciting as a new venue each weekend—"

I smile. "It'll be better."

"You're sure about this? You could be a lady of leisure for

the next two years until the noncompete is up, but I know you, and you've already got a laundry list of ideas."

"Well...I *am* getting sick of all the schlepping," I say. "But it'll be worth it to get to work with you every day. Walk home with you every night?" I know exactly where I got the boldness to suggest our home would be the same place. Caleb. I can say exactly what I want, what I need with him.

"You want my home to be your home?"

"Is that okay?"

"Is that okay?" He scoffs. "Obviously, babe."

Epilogue

Caleb

From the kitchen, I watch the first diners arrive. I brush my sweaty palms on my chef coat and take a deep breath. In. Out. It's only friends and family. Most of them are service industry professionals, too. They'll either give me a break or be the harshest critics for tonight's soft opening.

Brooke welcomes each party with her warm, inviting smile. If we're lucky and timelines stay on track—they will under Brooke's careful watch—the barn will open next spring for its first season of weddings. Until then, Brooke will manage front of house at Foley's Farm to Table. It's a job she handles with an ease not even the most experienced general manager could muster.

We spent the last week refining dishes, printing menus, assembling furniture (if I never see an allen wrench again, it'll be too soon), and putting finishing touches on the space. We kept renovations as simple as possible, preserving the charm and original details. Corner built-ins hold cookbooks and knickknacks, and Joey tracked down historic pictures of the area that now hang on the walls. The oak tables are accompanied by navy Windsor chairs. The place settings are simple with bistro napkins and vintage bread plates. It's refined but relaxed. The kitchen is as state of the art as the budget would allow. I feel right at home.

We also spent the last week keeping a secret we plan to share with our friends and family tonight, hence the sweaty palms. Asking her didn't cause any anxiety. Sharing it is another story. All eyes on me is the last thing I want, but if they have any sense at all, they'll be looking at Brooke.

The Warehouse Party on Sunday was the last place I wanted to be when we had so much to accomplish before tonight. But Brooke loves a theme party, and I'll do anything to make her happy.

We went all out for the Old Hollywood theme. I rented a tux with a white dinner jacket and black bow tie, and even attempted to tame my hair, slicking it back as best as I could. And Brooke…she was radiant. She wore a short sleeve fitted black dress with a voluminous white skirt and a V-neck that made me want to take it off the second she put it on. She added a faux pearl necklace and white gloves that reached her elbows. Her hair was pulled back in some kind of updo that sounded like a French pastry. Absolutely dazzling.

"Do I look as beautiful as Grace Kelly?" she asked, twirling in the parking lot.

"I don't know who that is," I said, grabbing her hand and spinning her into my arms. "But I've never seen anyone as beautiful as you look tonight, babe"

The party roared inside. Pop music played until a cover band took the stage for a short set of hits from the '50s and '60s. I pulled Brooke onto the floor and we slow-danced.

I didn't have a plan, just a ring in my breast pocket. We swayed while the vocalists crooned "Can't Help Falling in Love" to the crowded dance floor. We weren't the only ones starving for a slow dance.

Dancing face to face, I got lost in her. I took her left hand and slowly removed the white glove.

"What are you doing?" she asked, brows knitted together. I placed her hand on my chest, over the spot where the ring lay loosely in the pocket. Moving her fingers until she felt it.

"Brooke," I smiled when her eyes grew wide. "Do you remember when we played wedding as kids?"

"I do," she smiled, eyes sparkling. Laughing nervously when she realized she said *I do*.

"I've been thinking, we should do that again. I've been in love with you for as long as I can remember. I want to have the ultimate adventure with you. To do this life together. The wedding, the marriage, and whatever's in store for us along the way. What do you say?"

"Is that the question you're going with?" she asked with a wide grin.

"Babe," I sighed. "I was provided with extremely specific instructions on how to handle most of this."

She laughed. "I want you to say it."

I discreetly took the ring out of my pocket, took a deep breath, and looked into her sparkling blue eyes. "Brooke, will you marry me?"

"Caleb, I would love to marry you," she said, and I slid the ring onto her finger. A simple gold band with a round diamond, exactly what she wanted. Brooke looked at the ring as a tear fell down her cheek. I lifted her chin and kissed my beautiful fiancée.

"No ick?" I asked, slipping her white glove back on.

"Never."

We continued to dance. The crowd around us none the wiser.

She's been wearing the ring all evening and no one's noticed. Not Jordan and her date from the city. Not Joey and his girlfriend Morgan. Not Hannah and Preston, who are expecting a baby before their first anniversary. Not my parents. And not Mr. Edwards. He's been helping me with the kitchen gardens.

Judy doesn't know and I doubt she ever will. The crack she left in Brooke's life has been mended together by the rest of us, the ones who love her unconditionally and always will.

I leave the kitchen and reach the hostess stand as group of redheads come through the door. Maddie and her younger sisters. "Oh my god, Brooke, I'm so sorry," she says in her usual rapid pace. "I was stuck at work. Paige is in town and we had a ton to catch up on. We have this one client who's…" She abruptly stops talking and her eyes go wide. Her sisters, Brooke, and I all stare at her like something's wrong.

"Holy shit," Maddie shouts. "Are you two fucking engaged?!"

Well, that takes care of that.

Brooke smiles and Maddie shrieks. Every head in the restaurant turns in our direction. A chorus of cheers and claps echoes around us.

We both prefer to be behind the scenes, but for a moment, we relish the attention. I hold Brooke close to my side. She's wearing the same navy blue gingham dress that she wore for our first real date, making me wish this service was over already, so I could close up and walk her over to the house. Our house.

For now, I'll settle for celebrating our love with the people we love and who love us.

Acknowledgments

The sheer number of people who have encouraged me and cheered me on through this journey is overwhelming. But YOU, reader, are who I'm most excited about being a part of my author era. Thank you for taking a chance on a new indie author and spending time with Brooke and Caleb. Oh, how I've waited for their story to be in your hands.

This book would not have been possible without my husband, Ben. My unpaid copy editor for almost twenty years and my biggest cheerleader. Thank you for supporting every side hustle and impulse I have and, more importantly, everything you do for our little family so that we each can follow our dreams. I kind of like you a lot, babe.

N & C, you are the best things that have ever been mine. I love you. Please don't ever read this and please stop telling your friends and teachers your mom wrote a book.

To my parents. Dad, when I was in high school, I gave you a list of books I wanted to read and you bought me ALL the titles the Barnes & Noble near your office had in stock. Mom, you forced me to walk into the Sparta Book Shop my junior year of high school to ask if they were hiring. It's one of the best jobs I ever had. Thank you both for fostering my love of reading.

I'm incredibly lucky to have had so much encouragement from (IRL and internet) friends over the last two years of working on this book. Thank you to every single one of you! From liking an Instagram post to telling me you couldn't wait to read my book, you've all kept me going along the way.

Special shout outs to the CORE4, Fairfield Spicy Ladies, MAWCT, and the Omaha Bookstagram community. (Especially Jenn for welcoming me with open arms!)

Abby! Thank you for listening to my voice memos, helping me name characters, and so much more! You're NATP's biggest hype girl and I'm so thankful to have you as the bonus little sister I never asked for.

My early readers, Abby, Summer, and Ashley: You read a mess of a draft and gave me the feedback I needed to make this love story shine. Thank you!

Thank you to the Westport Writers Workshop for offering wonderful classes that helped me with the craft and the beast that is indie publishing. Special shout out to Libby!

Amy, thank you for taking such care with a newbie author during the editing process.

Rebecca, thank you for bringing Brooke and Caleb to life with a cover that is more beautiful than anything I could have ever imagined!

Alli, thank you for taking the time to proofread and copy edit! I'll be saving the file forever because your comments had me LOLing.

Lastly, I want to acknowledge how incredibly privileged I am to be able to indie publish my debut novel. I chose this route to get Not According to Plan into this world because I'm impatient and delusional. But I had the means to do it partly because of my own hard work but also because of a great deal of privilege.

Until the next one!

xx, Meg

About the Author

Meg is a self-described 40-something teenager. She loves Taylor Swift, Diet Coke, and being chronically online. She lives in Omaha, Nebraska with her family, but is a New England girl at heart, having lived most of her life in Connecticut. Not According to Plan is her first novel.

www.megdoody.com

www.ingramcontent.com/pod-product-compliance
Lightning Source LLC
LaVergne TN
LVHW091711070526
838199LV00050B/2356